DON KEITH

THE
FOREVER
SEASON

A Wyatt Book for St. Martin's Press

New York

Library of Congress Cataloging-in-Publication Data

Keith, Don
    The forever season / Don Keith.
        p.   cm.
    ISBN 0-312-13497-5
    I. Title.
    PS3561.E37586F67   1995
    813'.54—dc20   95-21089
                                     CIP

First edition: September 1995

10 9 8 7 6 5 4 3 2 1

To my own scholar/athletes,

Andy, Gary and Erin,

and to Charlene,

the cheerleader I married.

THE
FOREVER
SEASON

O N E

I died exactly the way I lived. Death's sneaky that way, matching its style to your life. If you are weak, it lets you linger until almost everything is gone, then it claims you with an almost welcome touch and a whisper. Or it taps you quietly on the shoulder in the middle of a nondescript existence and leads you away in the middle of the night. But sometimes, death lets you thrive, get so teasingly near to all you want, then swoops down hawklike and snatches you away. That's the way it was with me. I was stretching for the goal line, for the things that mattered most to me, but there were too many others who wanted to knock me down. That's when sly death winged in from my blind side.

I was born straddling the fence. It was close to midnight and everybody was so busy trying to pull me out of my mother's guts that nobody knew for sure if it was on the 29th or 30th of September. Dr. Creedmore flipped a coin and it came up tails, the 30th.

My name's a story, too. Father was gone so much and Maw was depressed and quiet so much of the time she carried me that a handle for their kid never got decided. Finally, somebody from the health department stopped by the house insisting Maw come up with something for the birth certificate. She gave them one name and told them to talk to Father for the other one as soon as he came back from off the road.

Maw wanted something like Jason or Scott. She thought they sounded rich and important. Even though we lived in a trailer park in a pine grove off old Highway 78 in Tallapoosa, Georgia. Father, though, wanted something biblical since he was in one of his religious-nut phases then. Maw just opted to please him, as she always did, and picked what she thought he might like. He stuck to his New Testament.

Neither knew what the other had picked until the birth certificate with my little footprint and the seal of the state of Georgia showed up in the mailbox. I've heard Maw hooted when she saw it, slapped the thing on her thigh and laughed like a chicken cackling. A rare thing for her, indeed. You could count decades by the times my mother laughed.

Corinthians Phillipians McKay!

Maw called me "Corey Phillip." My friends named me "C.P." Father called me "Boy." Or "that goddamn boy." Or "that goddamn bastard boy." Depending on his mood and state of drunkenness.

Fletcher McKay did have his phases. His religious-nut phase gave me my name. I was almost too young to notice his white-lightning phase. His breath smelled like kerosene and his hands hurt as bad as sticks of stove wood when he hit me for practically nothing.

Then he was gone for a while. I don't know how long. But when he came back it was like he'd never left, except he had now gravitated to his football phase. He wore a Georgia sweatshirt every waking moment and slept in a Georgia nightshirt. He watched football on the television when it worked and when it didn't, he went to Crew's Saloon up on the main highway and watched it there until they ran him home. He bought tickets to games from scalpers when we didn't have bread or milk in the house or money to buy it with, and he drove to Athens or Atlanta or Birmingham with friends we never met. Then he started to bet on the games. Bet on teams he didn't even know existed until they appeared on a little mimeographed line sheet he brought home every Friday night.

It wasn't long before he disappeared again. Dark, moody men would come by looking for him. I hid behind Maw's dress, a delicious thumb in my baby mouth, while she stood at the door of the trailer and talked with them.

"He's on the road. Gone till God knows when."

"Woman, he's gotta be home sometime."

"I swear I don't know. He left and I ain't heard from him."

"Well, if you do . . ."

I remember feeling her trembling as I clung to her. And the men spitting tobacco juice against the side of the trailer like animals marking their territory.

A truck came one day and hitched up to the only home I knew and pulled it away, while Maw and I sat on the warm, fragrant straw under a nearby pine tree and watched. I cried. She didn't. She was probably dry.

I remember an endless train of faces and back rooms and pallets hastily thrown down on rough board floors. We would stay with some of her kin for a while, and then some of Father's folks, moving every week or two so as not to wear out our welcome.

She wouldn't let me cry when I was hungry or wet.

"Can't disturb folks who put up with white trash like us, Corey Phillip. Hush now. Hold it in. We'll get a bite directly when Mavis and them get done eating."

"Corey Phillip, you're gonna have to be better or we'll have to leave out into the cold again. Suck on this sugar-tit a spell and I'll change your diaper when everybody else is up and stirring around."

We were staying with one of Maw's sisters just over the Alabama line when Father sent for us. Aunt Cleo was glad to get shut of us, and she gave us money for bus fare. Her drunk husband took us down to catch the Greyhound in Anniston. The bus made so much noise when it whooshed to a stop and blew its big air horn that I squalled most of the way to Atlanta. Soldiers and the colored people on the bus looked at me angrily, but I couldn't help it. I had to cry enough for Maw and me both.

We found ourselves in the middle of Father's family-man phase. Maw says he was glad to see us and that he bounced me all around our new apartment on his shoulders and took me to my new room and put me in my new baby bed. The first one I had ever had. Just in time for me to have grown too big for one.

She said that he even fixed supper for us that night on the little two-eyed stove. I never knew him to cook a thing, but Maw never lied, so I'm sure he did.

The apartment was in a big, square two-story building with six other families. We were on the second floor and because Maw was afraid of heights, she always crept down the back steps hugging the wall, looking not down, but straight out, feeling nervously for each step with her foot. She said that anytime she was up high she had to fight an almost irresistible urge to jump. She didn't know why. It was just a feeling she had.

Father was driving a truck again, hauling sheet-metal kitchen cabinets up the East Coast. He was usually gone from Sunday night until Friday afternoon, and then he'd come in with a headache and in a bad humor. Maw took to leaving him a full meal on the table, and when he sat down to indulge, she'd take me by the hand, lead me down the big, high steps to the sidewalk and we'd leave the apartment for a few hours. We'd give him time to eat, for his truck-driver pills to wear off, for him to get sleepy and pass away on the feather bed in their bedroom.

Sometimes, she'd take me to the drugstore a couple of blocks up Ponce de Leon Avenue and buy me a soda. Or a root beer float. Then we'd stop by the little park up the street and around the corner from the store and I'd swing on the tire-swing or ride the spinning-thing-with-no-name until I vomited. That was Maw's signal that it was time to go home, I guess. When Corey Phil spewed, it was time to make our way back to the house.

Father would be snoring loudly from the bedroom, so we had to talk quietly while we ate, or keep the volume on the little round-screen television set down so low we could hardly hear the people inside there talking. He'd be in a better mood the next day. He always was. And the football on the television made him even happier.

He would set me on his knee and read the Bible while he watched the games and drank beer. And the more beer he drank, the more he would preach to me and to the players on the screen and to Chris Schenkel and Curt Gowdy as they announced the game. And toward the late afternoon, he would be too drunk to hold on to me any longer and I'd finally wiggle down and go hide in my closet. Finally, he'd go to the bathroom and pee for about an hour and then collapse on the bed, dead to the world.

Sunday morning, even though he had to have a hangover bigger than Stone Mountain, he'd drag us to the Precious Blood of Jesus Church in Decatur. Preaching lasted all day. At least it seemed to me it did. Then it'd be back home and time for him to leave again for the week. Why was I so sad about that? Why did I miss him so much when I'd look down on his old Ford pickup as it pulled away from the apartment? And dread so much hearing the whine of its brakes every Friday afternoon right in the middle of "Howdy Doody"?

5

One Friday, as he fumed and ate his supper, we made our usual trip, Maw and me. It was Grapico and Cracker Jack that I sprayed all over the playground gravel that particular day, I think. I must have been building up some kind of tolerance, though, because we were at the park for a long time before my guts erupted. And it was late in the fall, with the coolness and approaching darkness also urging us back toward the apartment.

We rounded the corner and, for the first time, noticed the ivy-covered cement walls across Ponce de Leon from the park were beaming with brilliant lights, and a roar like a raging stream spilled over and bounced off nearby houses and buildings. There was music, too, mostly thumping drums and almost drowned-out brass.

Maw held my hand tightly, hesitated, then led me around the walls, to an entrance where people lined up to go inside. We joined them, she paid a man behind bars money, and we walked into a dark cavern that smelled of popcorn and red-hots.

Then we stepped through another arch into sunlike brilliance, though I knew for certain that it was almost dark already. And a world of swirling color, swimming noise, drifting smells. Red, green, music, shouting, cigars, beer, mustard, onions. My senses almost shut down from the immensity of it all.

As far down as I could see, there was a carpet of hair amid smokey fog, and behind me, a mural of faces. Across the stadium's green expanse of playing surface, there was another wall of people screaming back at us. And uniformed players piled into each other between the two masses, with almost every movement causing a roar of delight from one side of the stadium and a groan of despair from the other. The sounds rocked back and forth, as if everyone was part of some giant symphony directed by an unseen conductor.

It was football! I thought it only existed on television in black and white with inch-high players and a crowd that could be shut down with the twist of a wrist when Father wanted to preach and cuss.

I looked up. Maw was making some kind of sound foreign to me. Laughter. Damn! The woman was laughing! I had never seen her eyes crinkle up like that. Didn't even know her lips bent that way. She tugged me to an empty sliver of bench and we sat, me stunned by the avalanche of senses, she giggling like a school girl.

"Look, Corey Phillip! Cheerleaders down yonder!"

She was pointing to a line of girls, treading the white stripe nearest us, arm in arm, kicking, skirts flapping, giant Ws on their chests bouncing.

"I can see their diapers," I think I remember mumbling.

Maw didn't hear me.

"I was one, you know." She was talking so quietly I could hardly hear her, but the look in her eye made me turn my face up to her, then stand, my cheek next to hers. It was wet when we brushed against each other. She was crying. She cried even less often than she laughed. And now she was doing both at the same time. It was a revelation to me.

My Maw had feelings!

"A cheerleader," she said, the words almost stolen by all the cheering and the *whoomp* of the tubas across the way. "Coweta County Consolidated High School. Got elected and went through the whole summer workouts before Daddy made me quit. Wasn't Christian, he said. Games and girls jumping around wasn't godlike."

Then, I could barely hear her humming some kind of song, its words slurred and repetitive, something about "two bits, a dollar." But there was too much going on for me to pay her any mind.

Down on the field, one of the players in a red uniform had broken loose from the pack and carried the ball to the goal line. I pulled away from Maw and stepped to the railing as the player danced at the end of the field below. Fireworks exploded over-

7

head. The band nearest us played fiercely and the girls on the side-line turned somersaults and danced with each other in a wild frenzy. Other players on our side of the field threw their hats into the air and hugged each other.

I don't remember much, but I'll never forget the way it felt and sounded and tasted and smelled. The aroma of fresh-cut grass. The steamy fog that rose above us and the noise that followed it. The raw, open emotions of the people who stood and cheered and sat and groaned in unison.

Maw laughing and crying at the same time.

I must have been four or five years old. I'd never seen more than a few people together at the same time except in church. And though they did their share of screaming and screeching at the Precious Blood of Jesus Church, it wasn't the same at all. They always seemed so unhappy in their joy. Know what I mean? Like it was fear or guilt that made them quake with happiness and squeal in ecstasy. But in the stadium that evening, it was sheer release. Unbridled delight. Primal bliss. And it ate me alive. Chewed me up and swallowed me whole.

Kid or not, I noticed the changes with Father. He began inter-rupting his preaching to the players on the television on Saturday to make quick phone calls. He spoke under his breath, consulted small-printed sheets of paper he kept in his shirt pocket, and then became enraged at the slightest turn of events in the game on the screen. So livid he'd sling me off his knee. Fling the Bible against the screen. Slap the knob until the set went dark. Storm into the bedroom and slam doors until he'd finally throw himself on the bed and give up the tantrum.

He began to skip church, too, sending Maw and me, then finally lost interest in whether we went or not. He would spend an hour over the breakfast scraps, studying more pages of words and fig-ures, poring over the Sunday paper's sports page as if he was looking for some ultimate truth to leap out of its dim print and gray photos.

Then he was on the telephone again in the kitchen, talking low, scribbling with a stub pencil in a tiny spiral-bound notebook. The television again, turned to a professional game. More cursing. More beer. By late Sunday, he could only stagger down the steps and swerve away into the darkness to his waiting truckload of East Coast–bound kitchen cabinets.

Soon, more men came asking for him. Hard, sullen men in shiny clothes with heavy watches on their wrists. Shifting from foot to foot as they stood on the little porch at the top of the back stairs, the dry wood squeaking as if in pain with their rocking weight. I was too big by then to hide behind Maw's skirts, so I cowered behind the flowered divan in the apartment's living room, too far away to feel her trembling, but plenty close enough to hear it in her voice when she told them she didn't know where Fletcher was. She'd tell him they were looking for him.

They spat tobacco juice against the side of the apartment building, just like the men back in Tallapoosa did. And as I looked out the window behind them, one stopped and blew his nose on the steps and wiped the snot off his fingers on the bannister.

"Them's rude men, Maw."

"I know, darling boy. There's no good to come of it all. I ought to go get Father's big blue pistol . . ."

She must have gotten him word somehow because he didn't come home again. One day a sheriff's deputy and two colored men came and set our belongings out on the curb on Ponce de Leon. I sat on the flowered divan and watched the traffic pass by while Maw gathered our clothes and stuffed them into a couple of pillow cases.

It got dark and cool and I went to sleep, using one of the cushions as cover. Sometime during the night, Aunt Cleo and her drunk husband came and they put the divan and a chair and the ironing board and the pillow cases filled with our clothes onto the back of his pickup. Then they crammed me in among it all and we drove and drove, with Cleo's husband swerving and weaving and stopping and starting. I dreamed I was on the spinning-thing-with-no-name and I woke up and vomited on the flowered divan cushion, then went back to sleep, rocked by the motion of the truck. When I woke up again, I was on a pallet on the rough wood floor at Aunt Cleo's and Maw was lying next to me, holding me down and telling me to "Hush" and "Lay still" until everybody else was "up and stirring around."

I can still hear the sound in my mother's voice when she talked to Father on the phone the next time. How it tinkled and rang when she spoke, just like the ice-cream truck that used to come past our apartment on Ponce de Leon in Atlanta.

He was in Chattanooga, she said. The city's funny name tickled me. I was so busy trying it out on my little-boy tongue that I almost missed the rest of what she was reporting.

"He's working at the Incline. Mechanic on that car that goes up and down the side of Lookout Mountain. He's coming to get us Saturday, Corey Phillip!"

I can still remember the smell of the sour permanent-wave chemicals she had put on her hair to get ready for him. Vapors so powerful that they made me dizzy and nauseous and gave me a headache when she lay next to me on the floor. The cologne in the big silver bottle she got at Ben Franklin's. A concoction that smelled just like the pink deodorizer chunk that hung on a wire hook on the rim of Aunt Cleo's toilet. Like the one I had eaten when we stayed with her before and I didn't know any better.

I was sitting under Aunt Cleo's porch pushing out roads in the flourlike dust when he drove up. He was in a shiny new Ford pickup with silvery spotlights mounted on each side of the fender, a black plastic wind deflector at the front of the hood, a row of yellow running lights across the top, and a picture of a woman in a bathing suit etched into the rear window. There was a Georgia Bulldogs tag on the front bumper. He hopped down from the running board, dressed in a black suit, red tie, and a tan straw hat with a green feather in the brim. My mouth fell wide open at the sight of him and his gaudy truck and a big old horsefly flew right in and down my windpipe. I had such a violent coughing fit that Father ran over to the edge of the porch, got down on his hands and knees in the dust and fished me out from under the house.

He was a strong man. He held me upside down and whacked me on the back so hard that the horsefly popped right out, leaving me wheezing and sniffling and sobbing.

"How the hell you doing, Bruiser? Man you done growed up on me! You gonna make a damn fine linebacker for the Bulldogs here directly!" He was still holding me upside down when Maw came at the sound of his voice. She didn't smile. Just stood at the half-open screen door waiting for him to drop me and come on up on the porch to her. He did, and hugged her stiffly.

"I missed y'all, Clara," he said, and kissed her. And looked around nervously. "Could we . . . ? Is Cleo and them . . . ?" She slapped away some of the powdery dust that my hands had left on his suit coat.

"They gone after groceries."

He eased her back inside the house, reached to latch the screen door behind them, and both disappeared into the shadows inside. I stood there in the little grassy yard, listening to a mockingbird laugh at me from a chinaberry tree across the dirt road and the truck pop and crack as its engine cooled. The dust he had raised as he drove up had just now caught up and it caused me to start hacking again. I got myself a drink of water from Aunt Cleo's terracotta birdbath and crawled back into the shade under the porch and continued building my imaginary city with its scooped-out highways and oatmeal-box buildings and crabgrass park and orange-crate football stadium.

I stood in the seat between them that evening as we drove over and caught U.S. 11, winding our way along in the imposing shadow of Lookout Mountain. Every so often, a barn roof or a billboard beside the highway would order us to SEE ROCK CITY or VISIT RUBY FALLS and Father would point and tell us that that's where we were going. Maw stared out the window at the cows in the pastures while the white lines in the middle of the highway were gobbled up by the hood ornament of the truck.

I got tired and sat down. Then I lay with my head in Maw's lap and my feet in Father's and watched as the bugs slammed into the windshield and painted it yellow and brown and red. The hum of the Ford's eight cylinders and the rush of the wind through the open windows finally knocked me out.

I woke up and didn't know where I was. It was semi-dark and cooler, we were still moving, but at some kind of strange angle. I knew then what woke me up. The pillow of Maw's leg had suddenly tensed rock-hard and it had begun to tremble. I looked up and her eyes in the dim light were closed tightly and she was gripping the window frame and the back of the seat as if she expected them to fly away from her.

Suddenly, Father grabbed the gearshift lever on the steering column and downshifted with a growl, and the truck slowed noticeably, its engine straining to keep us in motion. He kept checking the rearview mirror.

"Clara, I told you we should've left that damned old flowered divan. It's fixin' to slide out and roll all the way to the Tennessee River."

I sat up, stood, looked out the windshield at a winding stretch of blacktop that seemed to go straight up. There was nothing but red clay and kudzu out Father's side of the truck. But out Maw's window was blue air, a dark carpet, twinkling stars, not just above, but below us, too.

Jesus! We were looking down at the stars! I felt dizzy and disoriented and it wasn't Maw's permanent-wave vapors this time. The road dropped away to nothing three feet from where the truck's tires rolled, and the stars below us were the lights on buildings. If Father missed a turn, we'd be flying!

Maw was white as a ghost. Her lips had disappeared. Her jaw was clenched so tight I thought she would surely fracture some teeth.

Then the road turned away from the bluff and onto level ground and we quickly pulled to a stop in front of a small but neat house with green asbestos siding, a brown shingle roof, and a tire-swing dangling from a big water oak in the front yard.

"We are home," he said. "Welcome to Signal Mountain."

I had my own room with a little square window that looked out at sky and sunshine. Maw had four eyes on her stove. There was a ringer washing machine on the back porch and a swinging bench on the front. The water only came from the spigots in a trickle because of the altitude, but it was a house, attached to the ground, with a roof and everything. And it wasn't the pallet of some reluctant relative on a rough wood floor.

Father left home every morning at seven and was back by four-thirty. I didn't understand what he did exactly, even when he took us over to Lookout Mountain and showed us the cockeyed rail cars that crept up and down the face of the massive mountain on long, straight tracks. He had a toolbox with his name on it and a locker in a tiny room that smelled like oil and grease and hot metal.

I stood at a big window in the station at the foot of the mountain and watched colored maids and schoolkids and tourists climb into the car, and then it got smaller and higher, while another exact car fell down toward us, growing larger and closer. Giant cables spun overhead on huge wheels and then wiggled away up the incline as the tracks cut a scar through the trees.

Father strutted and talked loudly with the girl behind the ticket window and the men who helped the passengers aboard the cars. I noticed they responded reluctantly and made faces when he had moved on.

About then, Father entered his civic-club phase. He joined the Fraternal Order of the Eagles, bragging about all the good these men did for poor children and destitute people. But mostly it was a place he could go to after work and on Saturdays when the ball games were on, and on Sunday when the bars were closed and he wanted to drink and carry on. He came home late and angry, smelling of sour beer and cigarette smoke.

Maw would have supper ready but he'd be mad and fuss that it was not hot enough to suit him. Or disgusted that it was pork chops instead of meat loaf. Or just mad and disgusted, period.

Then, every couple of weeks, some kind of guilt would seem to take him over for a few days and it would bring him home early, and he'd give Maw some kind of trinket he had found in the souvenir shop at the Incline. Or he'd stop at Kresge's or somewhere and get her a bottle of loud toilet water. She'd hug him, thank him, maybe put on the plastic necklace with the genuine Indian arrowhead pendant or splash on a gurgle or two of the perfume. Never smiling, of course, as if she knew by the time the grin had wrinkled her face he could be in a foul mood again and might split her lip. She saved her happiness like she saved string, balls of tin foil, and odd buttons. No use wasting the smiles God had rationed her on his rare kindnesses, then run out of them if something came along she could really use them on.

When he was in a good mood, he would hop from the truck before it even stopped shuddering, skip over the little white fence that marked the end of our yard and the road right-of-way, and toss me some gift as I sat on the porch steps waiting for him. A yo-yo, a box of Cracker Jack, maybe just a jawbreaker or a Snickers bar. Then he would roughly muss my straw-blond hair with his knuckles, call me "Bruiser," tell me how "goddamn big you done got for your age," as if he had just noticed me, like a bald front tire or a piece of siding that needed fixing, and then he'd head on in to give Maw her gift.

I was in the front yard, riding my stick horse, the day he brought me the football and Hutch helmet. I wasn't allowed to go into the backyard because of the cliff that dropped off like the edge of our dining-room table. It was mid-fall, I guess, the year before I started school. Late October. A cold snap had dropped the temperature suddenly and sneakily and my faded denim jacket carried the aroma of moth balls and cedar chips. And it seemed like everybody in the valley below had built a fire in their fireplaces to ward off the early chill. The air was smokey-blue and crisp as daylight fled for someplace warmer.

I could hear the truck engine growling its way up the side of Signal Mountain, the tires complaining as he made the ninety-degree turn at the top of the grade. I hitched my stick horse to the front porch, ripped up a few blades of Johnson grass from the roadside for it to eat, and sat on the top step to wait for Father, to gauge if this was a guilt-driven good day or a raging-storm bad one.

He was early. That was a good sign. No time to get tanked with the rest of the Eagles.

I spotted his grin through the windshield and relief warmed me. He opened the door, stepped to the ground, and threw something big and oblong toward me hard. I instinctively caught it, but its sharp end punched me in the belly and stung like a wasp. But I caught it and held on. I fought tears. Father just laughed, slapped his leg, and came closer. He had something else in his hand and he threw it my way, too.

It was hard, plastic, red, with a *G* on its side. I caught it, too, when he threw it. But he quickly grabbed it back from me and shoved it painfully onto my head, almost ripping off my ears.

"Now you're set, Bruiser! A real, honest-to-God Georgia Bull-dawg!"

Then he slapped me so hard on the side of the plastic helmet that my head rang, but I didn't cry then, either. I was already working on being tough.

He was gone then, on into the house with some bauble for Maw. I sat on the steps in the coolness, felt the grain of the football, and picked at the laces with my fingernail.

OFFICIAL NCAA, it said. I loved the pebbled grip of it. The faint animal smell of the hide. Even the scrawled signature of somebody that was, of course, impossible for me to read. But I imagined it must be some great football player in a red uniform who played on a fragrant green grass field in front of screaming fans and bobbing cheerleaders.

I found friends then. Or maybe they found me. We would play and kick and run and squeal all over the front yard, once they found out I had a football. There were three boys, and they were all older and in school and the day dragged until the big yellow bus would growl up the side of the mountain and disgorge my buddies at three-thirty.

Tommy Stokes lived two houses up the road and he was the first to get back to my porch every afternoon. He must have been seven then. Benny Ballard and his brother, Billy, lived a half mile away, so they were later getting there. And they were older. Maybe eight or nine. They'd odd-man to see who had to have me on his side when we divided up to play. The loser was always mad about getting stuck with "the squirt," but it was my football.

Things were fine for over a year, but one day Benny suggested we play in my backyard. They had tried to get me to bring the football and helmet and come to their houses with their big yards and open fields, but I knew Maw wouldn't let me. She had to have me in sight. I could always see her behind the curtain, watching, hovering. I didn't even ask and knew better than to slip off to somewhere else. She'd tell Father and he'd use his belt on me.

"We ought to play in your backyard, C.P.," Benny said. "You got all that room and it's nearly level and they ain't near as many rocks back there."

"Uh uh," I answered, shaking my head, chewing my thumb. "There's the cliff and we might fall off."

"Hell, we won't be nowheres near the danged old cliff. Let's go!"

Maw had just been on the front porch, shaking out some clothes, and I knew she'd be ironing in the kitchen. Maybe she wouldn't notice we had moved the game to forbidden territory. And it was an hour, surely, before Father would be home, even if he didn't stop by the Eagles lodge. So I followed the older kids through the wired-shut gate and into the big expanse of brown grass that sloped gently back to a single row of cedar and pine. Beyond the trees, I knew the earth fell away to nothing. Maw had told me, and she never lied.

We had only been playing back there about five minutes when it happened. Billy and Benny were on the same side, as they usually seemed to be, but somehow Tommy and I had tackled them three straight times, each one short of the dandelion stalk that marked a first down, and they had to punt the ball. Benny was mad they had been stopped by a couple of "pussies." Instead of kicking the ball directly toward Tommy, who waited in the shadows of a chinaberry tree near the house, he turned and angrily punched it down the slight grade, toward the cedars and pines and the bluff.

17

"No! No, Benny! No!" I screamed as loud as I could, and streaked after the bounding ball as it seemed to fly toward the end of the world.

I bellowed and pleaded for the ball to stop, but it didn't obey me, disappearing into the brush and rocks. I didn't care and dove in blindly after it. Then it was gone, and so were my feet, sliding in loose gravel and leaves and pine straw. I was flat on my back, skidding down, grabbing for anything I could get hold of. A pine root, I guess, was what saved me. A rock had gouged a chunk of skin out of my left leg and I almost let go my grip to check on it, but realized if I did, I'd be gone. Gone but good!

Slowly, carefully, I rolled over on my stomach and found a good hold with my other hand, too. Then I glanced back and down.

Jesus God almighty!

There was nothing under me from the waist down. Except trees and houses and roads, and they were hundreds of feet below. A few drops of blood dripped from my ripped pants leg and fell into thin air, carried away by the breeze. My football, two feet away, rocked precariously on a narrow stone ledge, and just then a mean puff of cool air dislodged it, shoved it on over the edge, and it was gone.

A record-breaking punt for young Benny Ballard, I do believe, Chris. That boot is one for the books. At least eight hundred yards!

That should set this fine offense back on its heels, Bud. It'll be tough to mount any kind of attack from that hole.

It certainly will, Chris. And now this word from one of our sponsors. . . .

I didn't even have time to think about reaching for it. I just held on for all I was worth, or I knew I would quickly follow my football.

The other kids stood, a safe distance away, eyes wide, mouths open. Then they ran. I can still hear their feet pounding as they tore off up the little hill, through the gate in the chain-link fence next to the house, and were gone.

Feet make an odd sound on ground when they are running and you have your ear to the turf. Like when some shifty halfback put his best move on me and left me grabbing air and spitting grass blades while he's high-stepping on toward the end zone. A dull *thud, thud, thud.* Like you were pounding the earth with a fleshy club. I remember wondering, as I held on for dear life on the edge of Signal Mountain, what kind of thud my seven-year-old body would make when it landed in somebody's backyard down there below. Preceded by a football. Right in the middle of somebody's barbecue, maybe.

Some birds were singing a happy song from the limbs of the cedar trees that shadowed me. An old crow was hacking up a caw out over the valley behind me. And there was the woodsmoke smell. Wonder if it could possibly be thick enough for me to walk across? Or if the old crow might give me a lift by the seat of my britches and set me back up on the shoulder of the mountain?

A bell was ringing somewhere way below my butt, maybe a train crossing, and there was a steady drone of traffic, people going home to supper and TV and bed. And the unmistakable grumble of Father's pickup approaching the switchback at the top of the mountain.

I could only count to ten. I counted ten times to ten. Then started over. Ten more times. Then I heard his bellow.

"Boy! Boy-eee! Hey, boy-eeee!"

And Maw's shrill cry.

"Coreeeey Phillll!"

"Over here, y'all. I'm over here."

"Goddamn bastard boy!"

"Oh, dear Jesus!"

Maw just sat on the back porch steps and kept quiet. Father

dragged me to safety, took me inside, ripped off his belt with a flourish and brought blood blisters on my legs and ass. I didn't cry but I did set up an involuntary moaning whimper that might have convinced some that I was bawling. The old man just stood there over me, debating giving me another round. I should have let well enough alone.

"Father, my football. It fell . . ."

His face was a thundercloud and he warped me again, five, six, a dozen times. Then he knocked open the back screen door with his log of a forearm and began lashing Maw across the shoulders and back with the belt. She just hunched her shoulders and took it. Didn't say a word or let out a whimper. Even when he stood her up and slapped her twice, hard, across her face with the back of his hand.

He raked the supper off the table she had set for him, grabbed the folded ironing she had worked on all day from the couch and strewed it all over the living room. Then he stomped out the door to the truck and was gone.

I had learned my lesson. Next time, let go the damned root.

My friends didn't come back anytime soon, and kept their distance at school. Scared, I supposed. Maybe ashamed they didn't help me. Or maybe just because I didn't have a football anymore and the helmet got left outside and got broke some way. Benny Ballard was killed in Vietnam when he fell out of a helicopter. Tommy moved up north when he was in the fifth grade. Billy got sent to reform school for stealing bicycles and a football from some people.

It was about that time, too, that Maw told Father and me over supper one night that we would have a new addition soon, a brother or sister for me, another child for him. He grinned sort of sideways and kept cutting his meat, considering what his reaction should be to such news.

"Old McKay's still got lead in his pencil, ain't he?" he said finally, mouth full of biscuit and mashed potatoes.

Toting that young 'un in her belly seemed to make Maw reflective. She began talking to me more than she ever had. She seemed quieter around Father. Different, somehow, as if she had a secret inside her now that she wanted to share with me and keep from him.

"Ever wonder why God put us here, Corey Phil?"

"To keep him company?" I had an idea we were like God's goldfish or parakeets, and he kept us around until he got tired of us. Then he'd open the cage or flush us down the toilet.

"Naw, I mean is this all we were meant to do? You know, just get up and eat and work and live and go to sleep and die?"

That seemed sort of a morose outlook, I thought. Even a kid had greater expectations than that.

"No, ma'am. They are birds to listen to and flowers to smell and songs to sing like on the TV. And football."

We were sitting on the back porch steps in the same spot where she had taken the whipping from Father just a week or so before. It was chilly, getting dark, a few brave stars just beginning to break through the blanket of night over our heads.

"I wish I could fly just once."

"Maw, you're scared of high places."

"No, Corey Phil. I mean fly with the angels. Just run down and jump off the cliff out yonder into forever and be picked up by angels and took up to see God and Jesus and Moses and Joseph and Mary and everybody in the Bible."

If her words weren't giving me the willies, the look on her face in the dying light would have.

"What if the angels fumbled you?" Dropped you like a muffed punt, I was thinking. No fair catch allowed out over open space like that, I didn't imagine. Sun gets in the angels' eyes. Tricky, swirling winds along those cliff faces, too.

"Angels don't drop people, honey. We all got guardian angels, and it's their job to make sure they don't let nothing bad happen to you."

Where was hers when Father was whipping the living daylights out of her with the belt and the back of his hand?

"That'd be the best thing I could ever imagine. Riding on the backs of beautiful angels. Not worrying about falling at all. Knowing they wouldn't let nothing bad ever happen. Having all your trust and faith wrapped up in their wings. Letting them keep you warm and safe and well-fed. Protecting you. God almighty! That'd be wonderful!"

She stood so suddenly, it startled me. And for a minute, I thought she was going to trot right on down to the edge of the mountain where my football had gone over the edge, and where I had held on to the pine root, and just fling herself out into the blue-smoke air and wait for angels to jump up from supper up there in heaven and swoop down to save her like George Reeves as Superman. But then Maw looked over at me, put a hand on her belly, turned her gaze up toward the multiplying stars and just smiled. She had such a wild look in her eyes that something tickled my heart.

"Angels won't never let nothing hurt Father nor you nor me nor this little one growing here, Corey Phil. Angels will take you to heaven if it ever gets too bad. Don't you never worry about that!"

Then she went inside and started mixing up Father's cornbread batter.

T W O

It's true what they say about dying, you know. About your life passing before your eyes. When I was a sophomore in high school and got kicked in the head at practice that time, I passed all the way from infancy up to the sixth grade before one of the trainers waved the smelling salts under my nose and brought me back around. And the time Man-cow Malone crashed from defensive end and I did a freelance blitz from the weak side at the same time and that damn Georgia Tech quarterback ducked and we hit head-on, helmet to helmet. Practically every event in my life unspooled for me before I woke up at the hospital with a headache and amnesia and a love note from a nurse tucked into my jockstrap.

But nothing could match the time I actually died. It was like I was in front of a drive-in movie screen, with those 3-D glasses they give you, and C.P. McKay's life was right there in Technicolor and stereo sound, jumping off the screen at me. I even had instant replay. I could stop it at the good parts, send it back, watch it again. Slow motion. Reverse-angle view, too. But the part I had to watch several times didn't involve the great plays, the women—no, it was the worst thing I could ever remember. Worse in some ways than getting killed myself. But I guess it's like driving past a wreck. Slowing down, craning to see the carnage like some kind of blood-seeking geek. I'm doomed to relive it. Even when I'm dead.

It was the summer between first and second grade. I expected to hate school. Father told me how boring it would be. How we would have to sit and listen to dried-up old bitch-teachers droning on and on about crap nobody wanted to know about. Dust in a dress, he called the teachers. But for some reason, I loved it from the very beginning. I was ecstatic at the prospects of learning to read and write. I practiced my letters on the wide-ruled notebook paper every minute I could, and filled up within a week all the ones Maw had bought at Woolworth's. And I jumped ahead in the simple little readers we had, anxious to see what happened to Dick and Jane and their perfect parents and pretty pets. I couldn't wait around for the rest of the class to plod through their lessons.

The teacher told me to slow down, not to get so far ahead, or she'd make me stand with my nose in a circle drawn on the chalk-board. Maw told me to practice in the white spaces between the pictures in the Sears and Roebuck catalog, to save the notebooks, because they cost good money. Father rarely got home early enough to tell me anything but "Hush" or "Get me another Pabst from the icebox."

I don't remember how it happened that Father was home the day the salesman knocked on our door. Maybe it was Saturday. It had to be spring, or he would have been gone or watching football on the TV. But I remember he was sitting in the living room on the flowered divan. Maybe figuring his income tax or balancing his checkbook. I know he was red-faced and cursing a lot and I was staying out of the line of fire. I was always wary of being the light-ning rod for his random bolts of anger.

I heard the knock at the door but stayed put. Maw was hanging clothes on the line out back. There was nobody else. He went to the door and even from where I sat, behind the bed in my room, reading a story about Patti and Tim and their grandfather and his rooster who made a sound that was spelled "cock-a-doodle-doo," I could see the storm clouds crossing his face at the interruption.

"What the hell you want?"

"Sir, I was wonderin' if y'all would be interested . . ."

"Why don't you just go on and leave us working folks alone with your . . ."

He stopped for a moment. I was all set to dodge a lightning bolt of rage if one struck, to seek shelter from the tornado in my closet or somewhere.

"What's that there on the side of your sample case?"

"Uh. It's a Georgia sticker, sir. See, I . . ."

"You like the Dawgs?"

"Yessir. I went to school there till my momma got sick and passed away, but . . ."

"Look. You can come on in and have a glass of tea anyhow. It's mighty close out today, ain't it? Baby, get this man a glass of tea. Lemon?" The voices had brought her back inside and she jumped, relieved, to get the drinks.

My father had a knack for turning his moods on and off like a hot-water spigot, but this was a new about-face record. Before I knew it, the salesman and my father were sitting on the couch, talking about players and coaches and bowl games as if they were lodge brothers. I guess maybe they were in a way.

Somehow they got around to what the young man was peddling and his words perked up my attention.

"Encyclopedias."

I had heard Jiminy Cricket on "The Mickey Mouse Club" on TV just a day or so before, singing and spelling that very word. I stood up and sang it now for the salesman and Father.

"Fine-looking young man, there, Mr. McKay. How old are you, son?" the salesman asked.

"Seven. Eight this fall."

"My, my. He's a big boy for his age." I could tell he meant it. Everybody said the same thing. "He'll be playing for Georgia before long, I wager."

Father's chest puffed up.

"I wager he will!"

"What grade you in, son?"

"First."

"Well, Mr. McKay, I think I got just the thing here to make sure the youngster's grades are good enough to let him play ball for the Dawgs."

This fellow had a great future as a salesman. He had found Father's hot button right off. It was *The Book of Knowledge* that the man began pulling from his sample case with the growling Bulldog and the red capital *G* on its side. I immediately fell in love with the brown leather covers of the volumes. They reminded me of the hide of my lost football. And when the salesman opened the pages and thumbed through them, I could see pictures and color and line after line of writing and words. Small letters and big words, not the giant three- and four-letter block words in my Dick-and-Jane readers. The challenge of discovering what was written in all those big brown tomes had my heart racing and my mouth watering.

"Here, you can look at this one, whippersnapper."

He handed me volume ten, and I sat back and held it on my lap a moment. It smelled of leather and binding paste and slick paper and colored ink. I opened it reverently. Its spine snapped quietly and the fresh ink stuck slightly as the pages pulled apart. Most of the words were too big for me but I loved the way they filled the pages, the way the margins lined up evenly on each side, how the pictures flowed from swirls of pastel ink, how the heft of the book implied great import for its contents. I wanted to run with the book and hide in my closet and gobble up the print.

". . . normally two hundred forty-nine dollars . . ." he was saying. My stomach flip-flopped. That was the same as a million, right? Or damn close.

I was smart enough to keep quiet and not offer any opinion as to our need for the books. Father always did what he wanted anyway.

Maw now stood in the door to the kitchen with a stack of tea cakes on a plate. She, too, knew to keep silent, and offered the sweets to the two men without a word.

". . . but just five dollars a month gets the whole set and our annual edition every year, and that also comes in the rich leather . . ."

Maybe it was a guilt day. Maybe he had lapsed back into his family-man phase while I wasn't looking. Maybe, in his mind, getting the books got me a step closer to college football. I don't know. But a week later, the mailman brought three cardboard boxes full of books and a cheap mahogany bookcase to put them in. Father had to put it together and it set right next to the TV in the living room. I could barely count to twenty, but I learned so I could keep all twenty of the volumes in their correct order. I used furniture polish and an old rag to make sure the bookcase shone and smelled clean and fresh and like lemons.

Maw caught the brunt of it. I was constantly running to her with this or that volume, asking what a word was or why something was happening as it was in a picture. I made her read the nursery rhymes to me in her halting, labored way, then we moved on to the real poetry, and it was obvious she didn't understand much of what she was mouthing. But I was astounded with the way the words fit together so beautifully, the sound they made when they were slid up next to one another so skillfully, the pictures they painted of people and places and things I had no hope of ever knowing or seeing.

The Book of Knowledge. Even the name got to me. The book of knowledge. Like the key to life's mysteries. The answer to every question I could ever think to ask and then some. Just the word was magical. Knowledge. To know. To experience knowing. I wanted to experience it all. Suck in the words and keep them in my head until I could weave them all together into some kind of tapestry that made sense.

School was out for summer, and as much as I loved it, I was glad. It just gave me more time to devour the fragrant, fake-leather books, unfettered by all the other kids and the teachers who wanted to plod along at a snail's pace while there was so much to learn and read. By now, the encyclopedia had developed a slightly musty smell, and I loved it just as much as the imitation-leather aroma. Maw was getting bigger and bigger, and was sick most of the time, so she couldn't help me as much. Father wasn't around very much at all, either. I had to get the words and their meanings out of context or go look them up in the old dictionary Maw used as a doorstop for my bedroom door.

Maw went into labor one hot, late afternoon in July. I didn't know what to do, and Father was at the Eagles lodge, I guess, or drinking at a bar somewhere. She sent me next door to tell Mrs. Crandall and she came running behind me, faster than an old lady should have been able to go. By the time we got back, there was bloody fluid all over the floor under where she stood, shaking and grunting, holding on to the kitchen sink counter to keep from sprawling on the floor. A pile of peeled potatoes was on the counter, and the kitchen smelled of muffins and black pepper and something musky I couldn't identify.

For the first time since she had told Father and me about the baby coming, I was scared. Her color was bad. Her face was pasty, her eyes red and clouded.

"Jesus Lord, honey. We need an ambulance," Mrs. Crandall said, hands at her cheeks. "Lay down here on the couch. Where's your telephone?"

"Kitchen wall," Maw grunted. "Above the dishwasher."

Mrs. Crandall started that way.

"We don't have a telephone," I told her. "We don't have a dishwasher, either."

She left me bathing Maw's red-hot face with a washrag while she scurried back to her house to call for help. Now I was really scared. Maw talked out of her head, called for people I didn't know—cusswords I had never heard coming from her mouth—had seizures of intense pain, grabbed me so hard it felt like she would break my arm. Once she even did some kind of chant that almost sounded like some kind of a cheer. A cheerleader cheer.

I watched them load her on a stretcher and haul her away. The ambulance's red lights were blooming, its siren begging. Mrs. Crandall rode with her in the long black car. She sent me back across the field to her house to keep Mr. Crandall company and spend the night. I took volumes eleven and twelve of *The Book of Knowledge* with me because I knew Mr. Crandall didn't excel at conversation anymore.

Good thing, too. Mr. Crandall was old, couldn't hear it thunder, and was more than a little daft. He watched the flickering TV screen, laughed at things I didn't hear as funny at all, took his teeth out and looked at them every few minutes as if he wasn't at all sure what they were doing in his mouth. Then he'd just break down and cry for no good reason, rubbing his old, twisted hands together dryly. I sat on their cement front porch, rocking gently in the glider, until it was too dark to read, enjoying the fragrance of Mrs. Crandall's potted plants, the buzzing of thousands of honeybees, and the warm, summer air up on the mountaintop.

I must have dozed off, because the telephone rang a dozen times before I realized what it was. Mr. Crandall never got up to answer it. He just sat and rocked and laughed and cried and looked at his teeth and rubbed his hands together so briskly I thought they might catch fire.

I had never talked on a telephone, but I grabbed the receiver and held it to my ear the way people on TV did. The voice was tinny and distant, but I could tell it was Mrs. Crandall.

"Corey, is that you?"

"Yes ma'am."

"You got a little brother, sugar. He's not . . . well. Your momma is gonna be all right, though, we think. Your daddy come home yet?"

I glanced out the window toward my house. The pickup was not parked in front.

"No, ma'am."

"Well, if that don't . . ." I could hear her clucking. "You go on and get you some supper out of the icebox and get on the bed in the back room, sweetheart, and go to sleep. Mr. Crandall will go on to bed by himself directly if he ain't already."

I put the telephone back into its cradle, picked up my two books and walked back to my own house, to my own room and crawled into my own bed. I lay there and thought of the way Maw had been hurting. The agony in her face. I hated my new brother. I hated my father who had put the baby inside her to grow. I fell asleep, hating.

Ricky Joe McKay. That's what they named my brother. At least, that's what Maw named him. She only gave Father a week to come up with a name for his second boy. When he didn't, she told the health department to go ahead and put down Ricky Joe on the birth certificate. My folks apparently had not had a chance to discuss a name over the past nine months, I guess. It was years later that Maw told me the names were those of two of her brothers who had been killed in World War II. Two brothers she hardly knew except through brownish photographs tucked between the pages of her mother's family Bible.

Father was spending a lot of time away from home. Avoiding the crying, I guess. Ricky Joe cried a hell of a lot. I could tell he wasn't right, even though nobody said anything to me about it. It was a month or two after they brought him home that I first heard the word *mongoloid*. I thought that was some kind of mad dog. No. It was a baby that looked like a chubby Chinaman. A baby who cried all the time, even when he sucked at Maw's breast, whimpering pitifully between swallows of hot milk. Mrs. Crandall let it slip one time in front of me that he probably wouldn't live long. That Jesus would take him away before he grew up. I hoped he'd cheer up before he had to leave, though. Shame to be on the earth such a short time and not have anything to be happy about.

I got away and played football up the road at Tommy's every chance I got. He had a football now. And I had grown big enough that everybody picked me first on their team and we usually won our games. Won them as bad as Billy and Benny used to beat up on us before the valley swallowed my football.

Slowly and surely, Maw got my brother to quieten down by letting him sleep in the bed with her and by singing to him quietly. Anytime he would refuse to hush, she only needed to take him to her bed, lie beside him for five minutes, hum her odd little nonsense song, and he would be out, for at least a little while.

Maw seemed totally taken with my brother. If she wasn't carrying him or lying beside him, she was trotting off to check on him as he slept. Standing at the door of their bedroom, gazing at him hard to make sure he was still breathing. I guess she saw him as an underdog, just like her. Two folks trapped in some kind of position and not a thing they could do about their lot in life. She just seemed to want to smother him with whatever it took to ease the pain he seemed to feel.

"He ain't like us, Corey Phil," she would say. "He's special. He's gonna take a peck of love. His guardian angel will have to be on overtime, for sure."

Father was soon tired of her obsession with the baby. I know now he was probably jealous. That he resented his meals being late, his clothes not pressed to quite the razor's edge he expected. He took it out on me sometimes, being especially curt, whacking me hard if I committed the slightest transgression. He made it rough on Maw, too. I never saw it, but she suddenly developed black eyes or mysterious scrapes and scratches.

Once he even slapped Ricky Joe across the face when his crying got to him. I was using his big old flashlight that night and had crawled under the bed to finish an Edgar Allan Poe story in volume six. Ricky Joe's bawling started low, then grew, and I could hear Maw start her singing and humming to him. Next I knew, she would get out of the bed and take my brother to the wooden rocker on the front porch if it was warm enough, to the flowered divan in the living room if it wasn't, and sit as long as it took, rocking and chanting and serenading him until he gave up whatever ache or fear or demon it was that was pestering him, and finally slept again.

But she didn't have a chance that night. Before she could quietly gather the baby up and roll from the bed, carefully so as not to disturb Father, he thundered awake with a growl like a bear.

"Some of us here gotta get up and go to work tomorrow, don't get to lay around all day!"

I heard the sharp slap of hand against flesh and thought at first he had hit Maw. I switched off the light to make sure the violence didn't spill over into my room.

"Don't you ever hit this child, Fletcher McKay! Don't you ever!"

I hardly recognized her voice. It was deep and vicious and terrible, coming from somewhere inside my mother that was hidden, rarely tapped.

"What are you saying to me, woman?" His voice was husky, full of sleep and amazement.

"You heard me. I'm not gonna let nobody hurt this child. Not you. Not nobody."

I could hear her footsteps, and Ricky Joe's crying, as they passed my door and headed for the front porch.

"Baby's being watched over by angels," she was muttering now, more to herself than him. "Special darling watched over by the angels . . ."

He never said anything more that night. Just rolled over, I guess, and went back to sleep. I eased into my own bed, left volume six underneath till morning, and listened to the soft squeaking of the rocker and her eerie singing voice as it harmonized with the crickets, mouthing the same hypnotic phrase that I couldn't quite understand over and over.

Maybe it was the residue of the unfinished Poe story that stayed in my mind. Maybe it was just the strange song filtering back into the house from where she swayed on the front porch with my odd little brother in her lap. But something filled me with such a dread that I shivered like a chill had taken possession of my body. I had to curl up into a tight ball to ever get to sleep.

It was a week, maybe a month later. I don't know for sure. I was sitting in the tire-swing and reading volume sixteen the day a car pulled off the road into the muddy gravel parking spot in front of the house. I barely looked up, deep in some question-and-answer about static electricity. But when I heard four car doors slam, it ripped my attention away from the book.

Four hard men were glancing about nervously. Dressed in dark suits, dark ties, a couple with dark hats concealing dark features. One had on some kind of strange shirt with a turtleneck collar and a mass of gold chains and necklaces that hung on his chest like a dozen twisting, squirming yellow snakes, and a little fedora on his head.

They hardly glanced at me as they sauntered up the steps and banged loudly on the front screen door. Maw came in a second. Ricky Joe whimpered at her chest. She didn't open the screen, though she was normally much more polite than that. Just stood there and I imagined how she must be trembling behind the film of the door.

"Evenin' ma'am," the one with the serpentine chains said, removing his hat to show a shiny, shaved head. The others stood, looking off in opposite directions, rocking on one leg, then the other, hands in their pockets.

"Evenin'," she said, her voice so weak it hardly overrode Ricky Joe's whining.

"We need to see Fletcher McKay, if you please, honey."

She bounced, patted Ricky Joe's butt, trying to get him to hush, but I guess he sensed someway that she was getting upset, because his whine was growing to full cry. I knew he would be bellowing like an ambulance siren in thirty seconds.

"He ain't here."

"When you expecting him home? We need to discuss some very important business with him."

"Hard to tell. He works late some nights. All night sometimes and don't even come home." Maw never lied. I was stunned at her words. Father stayed out as late as it suited him, but he always came home eventually.

By that time, Ricky Joe was approaching full throttle, pushed on, I'm sure, by the agitation he could feel in his mother's grasp and voice. The man with the snake chains suddenly reached and opened the screen door, took his hand and tapped Ricky Joe on his quivering, screaming chin with the knuckles of his fingers. The move was so quick, Maw didn't even think to pull him away.

"Tell ol' Fletcher McKay that Cooter came looking for him." The man gave Ricky Joe a pinch on his cheek and that only made my brother wail louder. I'm sure any passing cars along the road in front of the house would have pulled over to give emergency vehicles the right-of-way. "And tell him one more thing."

He eased the screen door closed and raised his voice so Maw and even I, still dangling from the tire-swing, could hear his words clearly above the baby's squalling.

"If we don't come to some kind of understanding, this little loud tyke here could come to some kind of bad end. You tell him that now, Miz McKay. All right?"

With that threat left hanging in the air like smoke from a smoldering fire, he put his hat back on, slowly turned and started down the steps, his mass of chains clinking like choked windchimes. One of the other men, one of the ones in the dark hat that hid his eyes, let fly a thick splash of brown tobacco juice that splattered down the length of the porch and across her rocking chair as it trembled slightly in the mountain breeze.

Maw watched them get back in the car, slam the doors in unison, and sling gravel as they peeled back onto the road. Ricky Joe continued his bellowing, as if he understood the words the man had dropped on our porch. I just held on to the cold rubber tire for dear life, half wondering why Maw didn't go back to the bedroom and get Father's big blue pistol and come shoot these dangerous men.

Ricky Joe was still in full voice when Father came home an hour or so later. But tonight, for some reason, he seemed to be in a good mood. Almost chipper for him, in fact.

Maw held the baby close to her and got him quieted to just a continual moan as she put the bowls and dishes of food on the table as best she could with only one free hand. Father was soon shoveling it in, watching the television set through the door into the living room, laughing at something silly on the show that was winking back at him from in there.

"Fletcher?"

"Hmmmm?"

"A fellow named Cooter came looking for you today."

She just blurted out the information as if she couldn't hold it back a second longer. He stopped, fork loaded with fried okra halfway from plate to mouth. I was in my chair across the table and I could see him instantly go white as he dropped the fork, the blood fleeing his face.

"Cooter?"

"Bald-headed man with lots of gold chains around his neck. Said he had some business . . ."

He stood abruptly, and was suddenly, instantly, red-faced. Lightning seemed to flash from his eyes. He slapped the bottle of milk on the table clear across the kitchen. Slammed his fist down so hard on the tabletop that two plates danced off and shattered on the linoleum floor.

"Dammit, woman! Stay out of my business!" Then he slapped her so hard spit flew across the room and blood instantly sprang from the corner of her busted mouth.

Ricky Joe, still held against her breast, let out a banshee scream that pierced the little kitchen like an air-raid siren signaling imminent nuclear detonation. Before Maw could do anything, stunned as she was by his sudden vicious swat, Father ripped the baby from her arms and dropped him roughly on the table, amid the okra, sweet potatoes, sliced tomatoes.

I sat right where I had been, scared still and silent. He had his hands around the tiny throat of my brother now. Choking. Squeezing. The kid's cry had became just a gurgle now. Father was killing his own son. I couldn't move.

Then, Maw reacted. Instinctively, I suppose. She grabbed the closest heavy thing she could get. Volume eleven of *The Book of Knowledge*, which lay on the corner of the table where I had set it aside just long enough to eat my supper. She drew the book back as far as she could and in a long, imitation-leather-brown arc, pounded Father hard in the back of his head, driving him face-first into a big bowl of buttered mashed potatoes.

Dazed, he rolled over onto the floor, wiping the sticky, burning paste from his face, sputtering as much in surprise as pain. He didn't say a word, but just slowly stood, drew back his sledgehammer of a fist, and punched my mother square in the face. She staggered backward, through the back screen door, and sat down hard on the wooden floor of the porch. Blood gushed from each nostril as well as from an ugly slice on her lower lip that was already swollen and blue and purple.

I've replayed the next segment of my life-before-my-eyes movie over and over. Just to make sure it happened exactly the way I remembered it.

Without even realizing it, I must have jumped from my chair. Volume eleven lay on the floor where Maw had dropped it, its spine split from the impact against Father's head. I picked it up, held it in both hands, felt the weight of all the knowledge it held. Then I took three steps closer to my Father.

He still stood, seething, clenching and unclenching his fists, daring her to get up so he could knock her sprawling again. Just as I had seen Maw do a half minute before, I drew back my precious book and brought it up as hard as I could, driving the sharp edge of its broken back into the knot at the base of Father's skull. There was a crack as sharp as I had ever heard. At least, until I heard the sharp report of the gun that was aimed at me. And that was years later. A crack so keen it seemed to split the electric air in our kitchen like a stroke of ground lightning.

Father fell as if he had been cut down by a scythe. He hit the linoleum hard, chin catching first on the sink counter and snapping his head back as if a giant uppercut had caught him a direct blow. He was out cold on the floor, not moving at all, his head twisted at an odd angle.

Maw sat on the porch, watching us, bleeding, shaking. Ricky Joe was sputtering, but seemed to still be breathing. I stepped to check on him and he looked up at me. His slits of eyes widened when he saw my shadow, I guess. And I swear to God this is true. He smiled at me. Smiled a huge smile that crinkled up his chubby cheeks, almost as if he knew his mother and brother had saved him from his madman son of a bitch of a daddy. I was trying to decide what to do with him so Father couldn't get to him when he woke up. Or get to me, either, for that matter. Maybe take him out under one of the pine trees, or hide in my closet.

Then I heard it. So familiar. So eerie. Maw was singing one of the lullabies she always sang and it drifted in from the porch like honeysuckle fragrance. So sweet. So strange. Perfectly on-key. Otherworldly. As if it came from her soul and not her throat. The same slurred words that weren't quite words. So familiar but so hard to hear.

She had managed to stand and worked to keep her balance, the blood now covering her breasts and staining her grease-stained apron. Slowly, she opened the screen door and slid her feet along the floor as she came over to check on Ricky Joe. Gently, she caressed his cheek with the raw, red knuckles of her hand, then she lifted him and pulled him to her, tears mingling with the blood.

"Maw."

"Yes, Corey Phil?" She stopped her song long enough to look at me, to answer me. Her voice was quiet, relieved, deadly calm. Her eyes ice-cold.

"Reckon I better go get Mrs. Crandall to come help you and Father?"

She hummed a little more of the song, and Ricky Joe was quieted by the tune this time. She had a strange, distant look in her eye when she turned and gazed at me, paused in her song again, and spoke.

"Yes, honey. That's a fine idea. Father may need some nursing. Run along and be careful you don't fall down and skin your knee."

I didn't want to be in that house when he came to. And I was worried about all the blood that was spurting from Maw's lip and nose. She needed somebody to take care of her. Probably even some stitches. Her nose probably needed coaxing back into shape, too. And Ricky Joe could take some looking at. I could hear his wheezing as he breathed, a little rattle and a cough or two.

To hell with Father.

I ran all the way across the big yard that separated us from the Crandalls'. Mr. Crandall sat in a metal chair under a dogwood tree in the backyard. He was giggling at some memory only he could call while he zipped and unzipped his fly over and over. I called for Mrs. Crandall and she answered me from the kitchen window.

"We had a big ruckus at our house, ma'am. Could you come look at Maw and the baby?"

She said "Oh Lord" a few times, rounded it out with a "Merciful heaven," and even an "I'm not surprised a'tall." Then she said she'd be along as soon as she could set the supper off the stove and out of the oven. I spun, waved to Mr. Crandall, and started back toward the house, having gotten suddenly braver, having convinced myself as I ran over that I'd stand up to Father again if I had to. He'd not hurt Maw or Ricky Joe again so long as I could get in his way. And dammit! I was only a foot or so shorter than him now anyway.

The sun had set already and darkness was about to come down, but I could still clearly see my mother in the growing gloom. She clutched Ricky Joe in his blue flannel blanket close to her bloody breast as she walked slowly down the length of the yard from the back steps. She walked deliberately to where the cedars and pines and stubborn rocks held to the edge of Signal Mountain, defying gravity. I stopped still, and realization hit me in the pit of my stomach like a well-landed punch.

"Maw! No! Lord, Maw, no!"

She didn't seem to hear me. My feet were frozen in place. I struggled to put one foot in front of the other. To catch her before she got to where she was obviously going. And I tried to scream the right words to convince her. But there was only a choking, pleading sound. And the wind seemed to snatch even that and send it back to where I was coming from, not to where she now stood, perched on the edge of god-awful.

She didn't hesitate at all or stop to think about what she was doing. She just stepped to the one spot on the overlook that was not choked with bushes and vines, and peered off and down to the rooftops and trees and roads and normal folks hundreds of feet below. Then she took the blanket-covered bundle, reared it back like a big baby-blue football, and sent it spiraling, end over end, into space.

I stopped ten yards from her, too late.

I could hear her singing softly. Crying and singing the lullaby.

I sat down on the green carpet of grass. Numb all over. Afraid for a moment she was about to follow after the warm bundle. Afraid any movement toward her might send her on.

"Maw?"

She turned slowly, a smile on her bloody lips, eyes empty and veiled, then walked to where I sat.

"The angels took him away, Corey Phil. Little Ricky Joe's guardian angel was waiting out there to swoop down and take him away so nobody else could hurt him. He's with Jesus now and he's made him normal. Ain't nobody gonna hurt him again."

She ruffled my hair and smiled. Dried blood flaked from her lips.

"Come on, Corey Phil. Let's go finish supper. Father's gonna be mad as a hornet."

THREE

Some say football is better than sex. I'm not certain about that, but I do know that the first time that I pulled on the hand-me-down pads and the ratty, cracked helmet at Mountain View Junior High, I was in love. As much in love as a thirteen-year-old could be, anyway. I felt invincible, like I could run through walls and not get hurt. That I could take on an army and emerge unscathed. That this was what I had been born to do.

Our little practice field was more a gravel pit with crabgrass than anything else. The coach dipped snuff and used semi-swear-words like "gad-dump" and "flickin'" when he got mad at us, which was most of the time. We were a ragged bunch, I'm sure. None of us had played anything more than pickup games in our backyards. We didn't even know the rules, much less technique and assignments and organized plays.

I remember our first game. We dressed out in the damp, smelly little room behind the junior-high gym and then climbed on board the school bus. We all were so nervous and queasy we could hardly speak. With our ill-fitting pads strapped on, we couldn't bend enough to sit facing forward in the bench seats and had to turn and twist at odd angles, looking sideways. That made us get dizzy and nauseous from the awkward riding position. Halfway there, we realized someone had forgotten the sack of scuffed-up footballs and we had to turn around and go back and get them.

"Gad-dump flickin' kids!" Coach Fields spat.

He was the bus driver, too, and drove the same way he coached. Erratic, semi-profane, and lurching. His foot was constantly shoving hard then easing up on the accelerator. He took sharp curves much too fast, then stood on the brake as our helmets and the sack of footballs flew around the inside of the bus like unguided missiles. He kept spitting black tobacco juice into a Dixie cup as he weaved in and out of rush-hour traffic, but he missed the cup more than hit it. Burning blue smoke spilled up through rust holes in the bus floor. By the time we got to Fort Oglethorpe, a stream of vomit ran down the aisle, and most of us were purple and retching.

We completely forgot our intricate and well-practiced warm-up routine. Coach Fields preached that we had to look like a team to be one, so I guess we weren't much of a team. Our side-straddle hops looked like skinny elm trees in a windstorm, our stretch drills like a couple of rows of collapsing buildings. When the coach whistled us to break up into groups by position, we had some collisions so violent that two guys were out of the game before the kickoff.

I was having trouble keeping my pants up without a belt and my left cleat had already worn a blister on my foot. I finally borrowed a belt, a fancy dress number, from one of the guys who didn't stand a chance of playing, and stooped and stuffed a rag into my oversized shoe to keep it from rubbing more blisters.

We sleepwalked through the coin toss, but I noticed the official was as nervous as we were. His first game, too, I realized. And the captains for the other guys were scrawny and ill-padded and as knock-kneed as we were. I began to feel better. Except I really needed to go the bathroom and it was too late now.

Back on the sidelines, I was as excited as I had ever been in my life. God, there couldn't have been more than a hundred people dotting the one rusty bleacher that had been dragged to the edge of the grassless field. The lights were minimal, just barely passing semi-darkness. The field had been only partially lined off, and a crew of ten-year-olds carried the down marker and chain.

But it was football. There were lights and a crowd and uniforms and real officials in striped shirts. The Fort Oglethorpe team had four cheerleaders, two skinny, two fat, dancing in front of the bleacher.

There was Father, and Maw standing next to him, at the end of the bleacher. When he saw me look up toward them, he made as close to a thumbs-up as he could manage. Maw just stood there, jittery, wringing her hands. She had absolutely forbidden me to play, but I had ignored her.

"Okay, if you're gonna get your skull crushed like a eggshell and your leg broke in seven places, I'm at least gonna be there to tell you 'I told you so,'" she had said.

Mickey Witherspoon kicked off for us and the ball wobbled maybe thirty yards down the field. The home team, in their mismatched blue jerseys, seemed confused, hoping somebody else, not them, would have to pick up the ball and run with it. Finally, number 12 bent, grabbed the ball, and stood up, trying to look for the most direct path to the sideline.

I'll never forget the number 12. I still sometimes see it on that kid's chest. And I can still remember how that first impact felt when I dipped a shoulder and cut him in half. How it sounded when all the breath left his lungs so fast there was none left to escape when the second impact came, this time with the ground and with me on top of him.

I had hit people in practice, sure. Coach Fields had even told me to not hit so hard or I'd injure the only guys we had who could play "worth a shoop." But there was nothing like the sweet, numbing collision, a pure lick passed in combat against another player who was trying to beat me and my team.

I jumped up immediately, pumped my fist once in the air, then tried to remember where it was I was supposed to be on the first defensive play. But the ref was still blowing the whistle, waving wildly for someone from the bench to come on. They slowly moved the kid off the ball, sat him up, and then helped him to his feet. He was crying, stumbling, as two scrubs helped him off the field. Number 12 didn't come back that night.

I think the final score was six to nothing, our way. Neither team could hold on to the ball because a light rain started in the middle of the second quarter. It sent most of the crowd home early and had us sliding around in mud in no time. I was bleeding from a bunch of scratches, bruised all the way up one side. I had blisters on top of blisters, and a helmet-to-helmet collision had my head pounding and me seeing double.

I was in heaven!

We sang all the way back to the foot of Signal Mountain, and even Coach Fields lit up a victory cigar. Its smoke made us all sick again, but we didn't care. We had won.

By the time we had scraped the mud off the cleats, hung the pads up to dry, and I had hitched a ride home with Charlie Woninger, Maw had already put Father to bed. But I heard his coarse voice calling me when I limped through the door.

"Boy! Come'ere!"

I stood at the foot of his bed in the semi-dark room, my bundle of dirty, muddy, bloody jersey and pants dripping on the floor. The bare bulb hanging from the living-room ceiling shone through the bedroom door, throwing my shadow across his skinny form lying there under a homemade blanket.

"Damn, I was proud of you tonight," he said, the effort of the words leaving him out of breath.

"We should've beaten them worse."

"First game. Plenty more. Y'all will get better."

"Yeah, we'll have to. I hear South Pittsburgh's got five guys . . ."

He held up his hand, just enough to stop me, then let it drop wearily.

"But I was proud of you tonight."

I just stood there a minute and the words finally hit me like a cross-body block. He had never said anything like that to me before. He was proud of me, and I didn't know how to respond. How to take his words, acknowledge them, let him know what they meant to me.

Luckily I didn't have to say anything. He was snoring almost immediately and I turned, eased the door shut, and went to the kitchen to beg something to eat.

Maw anticipated my hunger. She was ladling up a big bowl of her homemade vegetable soup over a slab of hot cornbread.

"Father just said the strangest thing," I told her, between bites. "He told me he was proud of me tonight."

"He said the same thing to me on the way home. I guess he's got plenty of time to think about things now, Corey Phil. Maybe being flat on his back and a cripple's made him realize some things finally."

She saw me wince at the word *cripple*.

"Darling boy, you ain't still blaming yourself for what happened?"

"It was me that hit him."

"You was just tryin' to keep him off me and your baby brother. That's all. You didn't mean to hurt him so bad."

Either the blow to the back of my father's head with the heavy book or the uppercut by the kitchen counter had broken his neck. Cracked some bone and damaged nerves so that he had no use of his legs and very little of his arms and hands. He was in the wheel-chair from now on. He would have to work hard to even get to a telephone to place a bet on a football game, and I suppose my game that night was the first he had seen, in person or on TV, since that night Ricky Joe went to be with Jesus.

Maw seemed to be a different person now, too. They had taken her away for a while, first to jail then to a hospital of some kind. She and Father both missed Ricky Joe's funeral, of course. I stayed with a foster family up the road in Cleveland for a spell, then another one down near the river, and a third one who lived up on top of Lookout Mountain. But the doctors said she was cured, finally. That she would be normal so long as she took her medicine and came back every so often for little talks with the hospital staff. And I finally got to go back home.

They let Father come home then, too, from the hospital that had kept him all that time. They had tried to get him to have more use of his hands, to do the exercises and take the therapy, but he didn't seem to want to try, wasn't interested. The muscles slowly wasted away, and now his arms were bones and yellow skin and not much more.

We got checks each month from the government, and I remember boxes of cheese and rice and split peas passed to us from the back of a big truck. Maw cleaned houses for folks all along the mountaintop, too. We seemed to be doing okay, lacking for nothing.

And I had football and books. The games didn't diminish my love for reading. I had memorized all *The Book of Knowledge* and was working my way through the Mountain View library, such as it was. Teachers seemed to have mixed emotions about me. Some praised my thirst for learning. Others fussed and told me to calm down and stay with the class. I had my problems with math and Miss Gleason said she couldn't understand why I didn't put the effort into equations and variables that I did into poetry and prose.

I couldn't answer her because I loved what I loved.

Girls weren't a real factor yet. I felt funny around them. I was too big and awkward. But as the football season started and they heard I was a good player, they began to stand in little bunches and giggle as I walked by. Some sent me notes in class and asked who I was "going out" with. I tore them up and sent back the pieces. Girls seemed like such a waste of time. And Coach Fields told us, "Floozies and football don't mix, men. . . . Makes you weak and vulnerable. Keep your attention between the white lines and off them little fuzzy things."

In the spring of my eighth-grade year I was fourteen and almost six feet tall. My size, I guess, was handed down from some especially long-legged uncles on Maw's side of the family.

"They tell me Ricky and Joseph was real tall and broad-shouldered," she would say, every time she went to shop for me for some new clothes. "You're growing like a weed by the side of the road, Corey Phil. You are gonna be a much of a man. A much of a man."

I had made myself a set of barbells with a length of pipe and a couple of wheels from an old car wired to each end. Coach Parker at the high school had already asked me to come up and practice with the varsity team during spring training and I wanted to be as strong as I could get before then. I planned on going to work as soon as practice was over to make enough money to buy a real weight set I had my eye on in the Sears catalog.

It was a Saturday, a warm day for so early in the season. I was outside, under one of the pines in the backyard, throwing the wired-together weights around.

Maw called from the kitchen window.

"Corey Phil! Telephone for you!"

We had had the phone six months, so Maw's customers could

call for her to come clean their houses or to pick up their laundry or ironing. This was the first time anybody had ever called for me, though. Who could it be? Maybe one of the silly girls from history class. I almost didn't go answer it. But I did, finally.

"C.P.?" It was a low, sultry voice, driven deep by too much time in smokey places with shrill laughter and dark liquids. She pronounced my name "Say Pay."

"Uh, yes . . . yes ma'am?"

"This is Grace Crandall, honey. I need you, if you can spare a little while."

Mrs. Crandall's daughter, Grace. She had come up from Atlanta to live with her momma after poor old Mr. Crandall choked to death on his false teeth one night when he forgot to take them out and put them in the glass by the bed when he lay down.

"Yes, ma'am. I guess so."

Maw was waving 'bye to me as she left with a big bundle of laundry over her back. When she came home from the hospital, she had just suddenly, one day, taken up driving Father's truck. We had hoped she'd just suddenly, someday, go get herself a driver's license. She never did.

"This grass is just taking off like topsy, C.P.," Miss Crandall was saying, but she called it "grice." "I'd appreciate it if you could come trim it for me. I'd pay you ten dollars, if that's okay?"

Ten dollars! A third of what I needed for the weight set I coveted. I told her sure and replaced the phone in its cradle politely.

"Father, I'm . . ." I started, but he was asleep, chin on his chest, sitting on the front porch. That's where he liked to spend his days now that it was getting warm. He watched the cars pass and the occasional plane vector for a landing at the airport across town. I made sure the wheel on his chair was locked and trotted on across the big field that separated us from the Crandalls' house.

"Mower's out in the carport, C.P. Should be gas in it." She said, hiding behind the screen door. I had to think what "guy-ess" might be and finally understood. "Momma's gone to git her hair fixed. The noise of that mower gives her a migraine headache anyway, you know."

I untangled the mower from Mr. Crandall's fishing gear and power-tool cords and the spiderwebs. It cranked, but only after ten or twelve pulls on the cord. I could feel Grace watching me from the kitchen window as I tugged on the starter. I figured she wanted to make sure that I did a good job for the money, trimming right up next to the rose bushes and under the grape arbor. I hung my shirt on a sweet-shrub bush and went to work, the sun warm on my bare back, already counting my money in my mind.

The smell of fresh-cut grass, until that day, had always meant football games. Ever since the night Maw and I went to the stadium on Ponce de Leon Avenue in Atlanta. Even mixed with wild onions and gasoline and hot oil, the fragrance had me imagining the red- and green-uniformed teams crashing into each other. The yelling people. And if I tried hard, I could imagine how it would actually be to play on a high-school team under the bright lights in uniforms that fit, shoes that didn't hurt and in front of a frenzied crowd that was screaming my name.

I had made only a couple of revolutions of the big yard through the tough, early tangle of grass when I noticed Grace, halfway out the front door, waving at me. I choked down the engine and cupped a hand to my ear.

"It's hotter than forty hells out there, C.P. Come here and get a glass of ice-tea before you dehydrate." I stood dumbly.

"I haven't really worked up much of a sweat . . ."

"Come on, now. I'll not have your sweet momma mad at me for working you like a nigger." She motioned determinedly and I had no choice. I left the mower sitting at the end of a dark green track of chewed weeds and bermuda grass and headed for the house. I wanted, after all, to be a good employee.

It was cool and dark inside and smelled of lemon furniture polish and lady's bath powder.

"Sit down on the couch. I just made a fresh pitcher. You take it sweet, I guess."

"Yes ma'am. Sweet's fine."

"Lemon? A slice of orange. Some people like theirs a little tart."

"No, this will be fine."

Her nails were long and red and frightening as she handed me the sweating glass, ice cubes tinkling like little bells against its side. She was wearing a bathrobe and lots of makeup. A bathrobe at two on a Saturday afternoon? I couldn't imagine someone not dressed by this time of day. Her hair was long and black and in a million curls all over her head and looked still damp from a bath. The aroma of gardenia blossoms was suddenly close to overpowering. Or maybe it was just her nearness that made it so hard for me to breathe normally.

Maw had said Grace Crandall was a hard woman. Not in front of her mother, of course. She'd never hurt Mrs. Crandall's feelings. Maw said she worked at one of the honky-tonks up the highway toward Cleveland. She didn't seem that hard to me when her hand brushed mine on the exchange of the ice-tea glass. Instead, she was soft, smooth, warm, almost hot.

She sat demurely in the chair, two feet from the end of the couch where I had lighted gingerly, trying not to transfer any grass clippings or honest sweat to Mrs. Crandall's immaculate sofa.

"My, my, C.P., you do have yourself some muscles," she sighed more than spoke, then leaned slightly forward and touched my right forearm with one of her long, scarlet nails. The hairs on my arm stood straight up and, hot and sweaty or not, I shivered as if suddenly attacked by a sneaky chill. "I been watching you lift your weights down there under that tree. Watching the way you raise them up and down. Even from way over here, I can see the muscles all over your back movin'."

Was she not aware her bathrobe had slipped open and that, if I had dared, I could have seen most of her breast? I certainly couldn't tell her, so I just noisily gulped half the glass of tea in one quick swallow. Then I had to ignore the intense headache its coldness instantly sent blasting through my brain.

"I knew you were thirsty!" She slapped her knees. The unfettered breast jumped and bobbed with the motion. I tried to look elsewhere. Mr. and Mrs. Crandall's wedding picture on the mantel grinned at me. The Dutch-boy-and-girl quilt was draped over a rocking chair in the corner, the cut-out children in its pattern holding hands, watching us as they danced. The family Bible scolded me from its perch on an antique sewing machine against the far wall, shaming me for the thoughts I was allowing to appear in my brain.

"Oh! C.P." She licked her lips and took a breath. "Long as you're in here and all, could I get you to do me one little bitty favor?"

"Yes ma'am."

Jesus! Was that the sound of my voice coming out of me? My voice had changed when I was thirteen and, unlike most of my friends, it was under control most of the time. But my answer to Grace Crandall sounded like an elephant had belched.

"Darlin', don't call me ma'am. You make me out to be so old and everything."

She stood quickly and the robe drifted open all the way down, barely held by the frilly belt around her middle. She wore no underwear. That I could see with an involuntary glance. Her legs were long and white. She was barefoot. Gratefully, she turned and walked away, her motion sending a fragrant breeze my way. I stood, watched her swaying backside, then followed her into a bedroom. Feeling a little dizzy and a little like I was in a dream, I thought I might faint dead away in a second or two.

"I'm gonna go back to Atlanta for a spell and I need that suitcase off the top shelf of the closet. It's so damn heavy. Could you fetch it down for me?" She seemed short of breath, just from the walk from the living room. So did I. And I thought I was in good shape.

She slid a chair from under a dresser and over to the closet door, its legs squealing on the polished wood floor. Then she motioned for me to hop up on it, and then stood, waiting, smiling. I had developed a very personal distress that made it difficult for me to stand on the chair in front of her, but she motioned again, impatiently now. I had no choice. Grace was my boss. I her employee. I stepped up on the chair as ordered, shielded my crotch with my hands, tried to turn my back to her so she wouldn't see the effect her parted robe was having on me, and peered into the dark, musty closet for a suitcase, for some kind of deliverance. I saw the suitcase and reached for it.

"My, my, C.P. You do have big muscles."

But this time, when she touched me with her long, threatening nails, I didn't just shiver. I almost danced off the chair. No one had ever touched me there. No one.

I don't know how long the whole thing lasted. I just remember thinking, sometime along the way, that I hoped the sounds she was making weren't drifting out the open window, then riding on the wind over to where Father snored on the front porch. Or that the gossip at Mrs. Crandall's hair appointment wasn't especially sparse that day and she'd come busting through the front door and catch us in the act.

I just remember the creaking noise of the bed. A noise I had heard plenty of times from my parents' room in years past but had somehow never connected with this particular activity.

The striking of the grandfather clock in the living room made me raise my head, only to be roughly pulled back into a clinch that buried my face in the crook of her burning neck. The smell of the fresh-cut grass managed to override even Grace's gardenia-scented perfume as it found its way through the screen of the window.

And then it was over. I was lying there, feeling her heat next to me as I struggled for breath. I was having trouble handling all the sensations that had just blindsided me. There was that intense tingle. A voice that sounded like me croaking nonsensical stuff. Her screams and groans in my ear. Something long and red and wicked scratching my back. And then, there I was, looking at the ceiling, gasping like I had just done wind sprints or trotted a hundred yards for a score. And so was Grace Crandall, lying naked and steaming right there next to me.

"Jesus God almighty," she said at last, still short of breath. Then she rose to one elbow and a lone drop of sweat dripped off her nose onto my chest. Her face looked smeared as if someone had tried to erase her features with a number two pencil. Makeup was running everywhere. "You really are something special for somebody your age."

She rolled away to sit on the side of the bed, her naked back to me slick and wet with sweat. Smoke was rising from her head. Sleepily I thought, The woman's on fire. I set her on fire. Damn! But she was just lighting a cigarette.

"How old are you anyway, C.P.? Eighteen? Nineteen?"

Lying there, so relaxed, still trembling a little, I couldn't, for the life of me, remember. I had to think for a second. But it never occurred to me to lie.

"Uh, fourteen."

She was immediately stiff and coughed violently on her cigarette. Then she turned to me, eyes wide, covering her breasts with both arms.

"You got to be kidding. Please tell me you are kidding."

She bent and found her robe on the floor, wrapping it around her suddenly remembered nakedness with one swoop.

"Fourteen? Damn!"

She paced the bedroom floor, smoking, muttering to herself about children and the law and prison. It finally occurred to me that I was totally exposed to her gaze and I quickly scrambled for my own clothes and pulled them on self-consciously.

But when I stood, my knees were weak and my legs almost buckled. God help me! Coach Fields was right. Sex did make you weak and crippled!

"Look," Grace was saying as she fumbled in a huge purse for something. "You done a real good job on the grass. Here's twenty dollars. Keep it, and don't mention to Momma . . ."

"But, Miss Crandall, I didn't finish the job. . . ."

"Oh, darlin', you finished the job, all right. You done a real fine job. Just don't ever say a word about this to nobody or I'll holler rape, sure as shootin'. You understand?"

No, I didn't. I wasn't sure what "ripe" was. But I didn't say anything to anybody, either.

She went on back to Atlanta that day or the next, I guess, and I didn't see her again for four years. Mrs. Crandall mentioned a time or two that Grace didn't seem to want to come home anymore and I always felt guilty, as if what had happened that stifling afternoon had been the reason she abandoned her mother. Then, when Mrs. Crandall died in her sleep one night, Grace had to come back and see to the funeral and the closing of the house.

I couldn't believe how old and hard she looked, standing by the casket in the front of the church as people filed past her. More like somebody's matron aunt than an object of wild teenage lust. In my fantasies, ever since that Saturday afternoon when I had mowed her grass, she had become more beautiful and splendid and glorious. She rivaled anything that unfolded from a *Playboy*. But now, I saw her in a far different light. In the mottled sunshine that forced its way through the stained-glass church windows, she was pudgy, her complexion pasty, black hair spiced with generous amounts of ash-gray, and ugly black circles ringed her eyes. She wore no makeup and her skin was pitted and uneven, her legs and ankles thick and mapped with blue varicose veins.

Maw and I had gone to the funeral together. After the graveside service, Maw visited with some of her customers in front of the church. I stood back, watching the people. That's when I noticed Grace lingering by the fresh grave after everyone else had wandered back in little groups to the church parking lot. She was salvaging gardenias from a big arrangement at the side of the freshly scarred earth. Someone had recently clipped the grass between the neat geometric rows of graves. I stood quietly, breathing in the aroma of the gardenias mingled with that of the green grass. She finally turned, started back to her car, and had to stop to keep from bumping into me.

"Remember me, Miss Crandall?"

She stopped a minute and looked at me from behind her sunglasses. In my dreams, she had been twenty, twenty-five at the most. She was at least fifty, now, so she had been in her mid-forties on that day.

"No, I'm sorry, I . . ."

"C.P. McKay. Your momma's next-door neighbor."

She paused a minute. Then a tiny smile broke her thin, unpainted lips. She lifted her sunglasses and looked me up and down, then square in the eye, without a trace of shame.

"You still got good muscles."

And she walked on across the cemetery, away from me, choosing her steps carefully so as not to tread on the graves.

I don't know why it was so important that she remembered me. But a lot of things had changed that day for me. I had experienced something real. Something that wasn't discussed in *The Book of Knowledge*. I had found something that ranked right up there with books and football. What Samuel Taylor Coleridge meant when he said, "For he on honeydew hath fed, and drunk the milk of Paradise."

And from that day on, no matter how big the game, how much I tried to keep my mind on beating the other team's brains out, I would always have that momentary distraction. I had to think at least a few seconds about Grace Crandall. Her hot breath. Her gardenia scent. Those shocking scarlet nails. Every time when I ran onto the football field and smelled the fresh-mown grass.

And, for some reason, I never played quite as well on artificial turf.

FOUR

I had lightning-quick reactions back when I was alive. Oh, God, I was quick! Coach Tack Rankin told us it was my quickness on the grainy eight-millimeter game film that first caught his attention. And it was there in spades when he watched me play. It was not only my upper-body strength or range of motion or hitting ability. That was all exceptional, all right. But he was recruiting pure quickness in those days. That was the way to beat Alabama and Tennessee and Georgia, he said.

It all meant a lot, the things Coach Tack Rankin said to me and Father and Maw that night, as he sat on the flowered divan in our living room. He had already bragged on Maw's meat loaf, and ate four helpings to prove it wasn't all a sham.

"Miz McKay," he growled, in that same voice I knew so well from his Sunday-night TV show with the replay of the previous day's win. "I know y'all been gettin' lots of other coaches in here and a peck of schools that are competin' for C.P. to come play for them. But they ain't a one of 'em that can make your boy a better home than Sparta University. We fit like a glove. A situation tailor-made for your son."

I had gotten my first letter from a college the summer before my junior year. I'd made pre-season all-state in several magazines but I was working hard at the sawmill from sunup until nearly dark, then going off to lift weights and to run wind sprints to get in shape for the season. I had no time or opportunity to read my own publicity. Father clipped them, every one, though, and worked for tedious hours carefully Scotch-taping them into a scrapbook he was building.

Father was still up that night, sitting on the porch in the quiet, humid air when I staggered in from the pickup, legs aching, back almost broke, hot, thirsty, dirty and tired.

"Son, I got some mail here for you," he said, and wiggled an envelope in his lap with his better hand. I dropped my work gloves, weight belt, running cleats, and sopping-wet sweat suit on the porch and sank down wearily on the step.

"You ought to be in bed, Father," I said. "It's got to be nine-thirty."

"I know it. But I wanted to give you this myself."

I could barely read the return address on the envelope in the yellow glow of light that filtered out the screen door from the living-room lamp. Georgia Presbyterian College. Valdosta.

"Read it to me. My eyes ain't so good no more." I knew his withered arms wouldn't allow him to hold the letter up close enough to see it.

"They just say 'Congratulations on being named all-state' and 'We will be following your junior year with great interest' and 'A school catalog will follow in the near future.' It doesn't really say much. Signed by their head coach."

"Aw, that's the first of many, boy. Pretty soon, you gone have to beat off them recruiters like they was buzzards circling a prime piece of roadkill."

That particular analogy would prove especially apt.

"Well, I've never heard of that college. Division three, I guess. They probably sent out a hundred letters just like this one."

"Just the first of many, boy. Now, can you help me in to bed?"

And I stuck the envelope and its letter safely in the middle of volume one of *The Book of Knowledge,* just as I would over a hundred others that drifted in over the next year and a half. It didn't take long before the letters swelled the books so big they would no longer fit into the cheap bookcase, so I took to stacking them on top. I hoped interspersing the compliments and flattery among the great poems and scientific discoveries and accumulated learning of mankind in the encyclopedia would help me keep it all in perspective and keep me from getting fat-headed.

We had a good year when I was a junior. Made it to the third round of the state playoffs before a school from Nashville nipped us on a bad call by a referee. We had two or three guys who were major college material, and when the coaches came to visit them, they always looked me up after the game, too. Winked at me. Some even shook my hand and told me they'd be back next year, even though even that limited contact was illegal. But, God knows, that was the least of it before it was all over.

My senior year was even better. Undefeated. Best defense in the state by far. If we had had any kind of offense at all, we would have won the state championship, but Coach Fields had no idea what he was doing and we lost the big game by a touchdown. I scored more points by myself than the offense did, with an interception for a touchdown and a quarterback sack for a safety.

An assistant coach from Georgia Tech led the parade and spent an hour eating Maw's pork chops and talking about Atlanta. Bear Bryant from Alabama came by and ate fried chicken. So did the coach from Tennessee, but he was in a hurry and didn't have time for more than just a piece of pie, but he bragged on it after every bite. Sometimes we had three coaches a night, all lined up on schedule as if we had arranged it that way, but I guess they had some kind of pipeline that helped them follow proper recruiting etiquette and not all show up at the same time. Those who didn't come by, called, every time it was legal, and again, the calls never seemed to come when one of their colleagues was wolfing down turnip greens or barbecue out in our cramped little kitchen.

I hate to think what happened to our grocery bill during those months. But Maw seemed happy to be having such seemingly illustrious company, even if she had no idea who most of these beefy, deep-talking men in their nice suits were. She just knew they appeared to love her cooking. Father and I had taken it for granted all our lives. And they all made a big fuss over her boy and seemed to sincerely want him to come study at their university. That really made her proud.

Father was beside himself. He would lift his palsied right hand, shake with each coach, and try to speak while each of them strained politely to try to understand what he was saying. Often he would quickly give out completely and just sit back in the wheelchair and listen and smile his crooked smile and beam. Many of these men were the same ones he had watched pace the sidelines on the television or saw live when he would pay scalpers' prices to go watch the games. Some of them had won him big sums of money by their expertise and correct assessments of game situations. Some had cost him much more than he could afford to lose, making choices that didn't work, or sitting on the ball to keep from running up the score on weaklings, no matter the point spread. They had no idea the names he had cussed them with. The vicious way he had questioned their heritage, mental capability, the marital status of their parents. All was forgotten now, though.

I took several trips, climbing from a warm bed early Saturday morning, still aching and sore and fuzzy-headed from the game the night before. I'd take a couple of biscuits and cold sausage with me and drive the pickup to the orange-splattered campus up in

Knoxville or over to Nashville where the preppies ate Brie and drank wine from foreign-car tailgates before Vanderbilt kicked it off.

I took so many tours of campuses and weight rooms and stadia and classrooms, that they all ran together in a montage of columns and brick and barbells and grass with permanently painted yard-line numbers. The lovely hostesses all smiled seductively. The players promised through clenched teeth that their school would be the best place in the world to play ball. The defensive coaches told me with straight faces exactly where I would fit into their scheme, assured me I had an excellent chance to start some games my freshman year, and showed me a jersey with my name on the back. In most cases, my high school number, 55, was on it. A couple even pointed out mocked-up news clippings on the bulletin board with blaring headlines: "McKay Seals Victory for Tech," or "C.P.'s Dee-fense Clinches Tigers' SEC Championship." I carried them home and showed them to Maw, who couldn't believe such a thing was possible. Father kept them in his bathrobe pocket, pulling them out to read over and over until they simply crumbled and then he filed the fragments and dust in his scrapbook.

Maw stood at the gate at the airport and wrung her hands and prayed to my guardian angel as I caught my first airplane for a visit to Notre Dame. They had the biggest party of anybody, but I caught a bad cold, and mostly just remember a dreary fog, leafless trees, and lots of people with sharp, abrupt accents. I was glad again for the warmth and evergreen pines and syrupy-sweet voices of my own kind when I got back to Chattanooga.

There were hints sometimes from the coaches, that even I was not too naive to catch. "We have special transportation accommodations at State, C.P. We don't want our best athletes to waste their strength walking to class." "And let me mention, we do have available some special monetary stipends to handle your incidentals not covered by the usual grant-in-aid, C.P. We have some very generous alumni who like to make certain you don't have to worry about needing anything, if you know what I mean." "Don't worry about money, either, McKay. We have some friends of the university who offer our athletes summer jobs that pay pretty darn good. You can do inventory on a car lot for a few thousand dollars, can't you C.P.?"

And there would be a wink and a nudge and a click of the tongue and I would always feel oily and shaky. Then, a few weeks before signing day, the other phone calls began.

"Hello?"

"This C.P. McKay?"

"Yes it is."

"Well, I just wanted you to know how important it is that you sign with Tennessee, buddy," a low voice might say. Or the low, whispering words might be, "I'm a good friend, Mr. McKay, and I'm just calling to tell you that if you don't decide on Tech, it could be a really big mistake."

"I'm certainly considering that school. Yessir."

"Naw, son, not 'considering.' You are going to sign with us. If you ever want a job in this state the rest of your life, you'll wear the right jersey. If you don't want some real unpleasant things to happen to your folks. Tell you what, if you don't sign with us, you better go all the way to California or somewhere where you ain't ever gonna play against us or somebody with a squirrel gun might just make sure you ain't able to play again. You understand me, Mr. Football Hero?"

Maw understood those calls were just well-intentioned supporters with best wishes for us all. That's what I told her, anyway. She never suspected they were only wound-too-tight rednecks who probably couldn't find the library at their favorite school unless it was next door to the stadium. Cases of arrested development who lived their lives vicariously through teenaged football players on Saturday afternoons. I simply ignored them. They'd move on to some other kid after signing day was come and gone.

Yeah, the money was tempting. I worried about how I would have money to buy clothes as nice as the other students would have. I had saved as much as I could, but there was no way I could dress as they did. I had no car. It would be tough for me to afford a movie or dinner for a date. But it wasn't totally honesty on my part that made me ignore the veiled offers. I just had a horror of getting caught, losing eligibility, getting kicked out of school. And as important as football was to me, it was school I was after and ball was just a means to that end.

It was Tack Rankin who did his homework the best and recognized that fact.

"Miz McKay, I can promise you your boy will be taken care of up in Sparta. We're a small town, not like Nashville or Atlanta where there's lots of . . . mmmm . . . distractions. We encourage very strongly that our boys get up and go to church Sunday mornings, no matter how bad they got beat up in the game the day before. We want our athletes to have a strong relationship with Jesus, ma'am. Our Fellowship of Christian Athletes chapter is the largest in the Southeastern Conference. We got a team doctor that lives in the athletic dorm. They get three home-cooked meals a day. Not quite as good as yours, but close, if you don't mind me saying so. You give me the recipe for this wonderful meat loaf and I'll make sure C.P. gets it once a week like clockwork. We wash the boys' sheets twice a week. And they have their own laundry service at no charge. Ma'am, we keep 'em well, clean, full, and spiritual and try to take care of 'em as close to the way you would as we can. We ain't their mommas but we sure try."

We had not been to church in ten years, but I saw he had reached Maw because she smiled one of her rare smiles then dried her eyes on her apron and went out to slice up some cherry pie. Tack Rankin next turned to Father, who sat in a corner of the living room in his wheelchair, still stunned that this legendary coach was in his house, eating supper and telling football stories.

"Mr. McKay, I got somethin' here for you," Rankin said, his drawl now even deeper, and pulled a sheet of folded paper from his suit coat pocket. "This is a letter from our director of stadium operations to you. It guarantees that you have a space on the press-box level at Spartan Stadium for every home game. A space for your wheelchair and for Miz McKay to set with you and watch your boy play. You also got a parkin' spot right there at the press-box elevator. They gon' come by and leave copies of the official stats ever' quarter and you can hear the radio broadcast on head-phones we'll give you. Or watch the TV with the instant replay right there above you."

Father took the offered piece of paper, held it as best he could, and pretended to read it. Tears rolled down each cheek. How did Rankin know this man, who had scraped and scrapped for tickets even if his family went lacking, had always dreamed of watching games from somewhere other than the bottom seats in end zones or behind support columns that blocked half the field?

"If y'all don't mind, I'd like to talk with your boy out on the front porch just a minute, then I'm gon' leave y'all be, so's y'all can go on to bed before it gets too much later," he droned on, his voice like honey. "But I do believe I'll take this pie and glass of sweet milk out there with me."

The air was cool, threatening to go chill by morning. Our breath was visible in the little light that escaped the house. He sat slowly in the old creaking rocker, swayed gently as he sampled the pie and washed it down with cold milk. I swung slightly in the porch swing, not sure if I was supposed to speak or if it was his call.

"Your maw is something special, son."

"I know, sir."

"It's been rough on her, I guess. Your father's paralysis and all. My own father spent the last ten years of his life in a wheelchair after he had a stroke. He was a mechanic, just like your father.

Worked with his hands all his life and then lost it. It's a tribute to your maw and to you, too, that you've held the family together. That you have excelled in your athletics and schoolwork through it all, too." The drawl had almost disappeared. His words were clear, distinct.

"Well, thank you . . ."

"Congratulations on your SATs."

No one else had even mentioned my entrance-test scores. They were high. Damned high.

"Just lucky, I guess."

"I don't think so. That's how I know you are the type we are looking for at Sparta University. You have the grades and test scores to get an academic scholarship for a free ride at most schools. You don't need all the work and hurt of playing football. You have to love the game as much as I do to make the sacrifice. What do you want to study, C.P.?"

Most everyone else had failed to ask that question, too. They just emphasized the tutoring program, the special schedules and classes for athletes, how understanding the faculty was of "the time constraints on football players," and that they would work around our schedules.

"Frankly, I would like to write. To study poetry, the great authors. Do scholarly research on the Victorian and Romantic period of literature."

God, why was I rambling on so? Being so goddamned honest. Couldn't I just say, "I'm not sure," and let it go? This man was a football coach, for heaven's sake. He didn't know Shelley from Shinola! He leaned forward in the chair and tapped my knee.

"I'm partial to Hardy and Tennyson myself. 'To strive, to seek, to conquer, but never to yield,' from 'Ulysses.' That whole passage is framed on my office wall. It's been my motto for years. My degree is in English. Specialized in the Romantic writers."

He paused to take another bite of the cherry pie and a noisy gulp of milk, and to give me time to close my mouth.

"C.P., you may not know this, but we have two Pulitzer Prize winners on our English Department faculty. One of them heads up our creative-writing program. I've got a letter here for you from him."

He reached back into the coat pocket, fished out the paper and left it lying on the porch bannister for me to pick up after he left. A Pulitzer Prize winner's letter? For me?

"And we have had two Rhodes Scholars at Sparta University. We think you are Rhodes Scholar material yourself. That you have a real chance to be our next one."

I had once or twice allowed the thought to enter my mind. But never spoke it aloud to anyone. How did Tack Rankin know?

He leaned back now in the rocker and listened to the crickets and a far-off dog barking at the grinning sliver of moon that rose slowly overhead.

"Son, we've won the Southeastern Conference championship three of the last five years. We had six young men drafted in the first five rounds of the NFL draft last year. Three of them were all-Americans. One was third in the Heisman voting. We were on regional TV four times and national TV three this year, including the bowl game. We've been to a bowl every year since 1965."

He turned to me and stopped rocking. I couldn't see but I could feel his eyes glowing as he talked.

"But don't come to Sparta University for any of those reasons. Come to learn. Yes, to learn more about football. But about metaphor and simile. Imagery and foreshadowing. People. Living. Learn how to live the rest of your life to the fullest. How to suck the marrow from the bone of life. I envy you, C.P. You are not only a talented athlete but have an excellent mind, too. I would be thrilled to help make it possible for you to expand your intellect. I would be honored to be your football coach."

He stood quickly and I could just make out his offered hand in the dim darkness.

"Tell your maw and your father I said good night."

And he was gone. I would have signed right then and there if I could have.

Sure, I saw a few other coaches, and made another recruiting trip or two, but they were almost ludicrous after Tack Rankin's performance. The other guys couldn't have sold ice water in hell.

The newspaper and two of the television stations came down to the high-school gym when I signed the grant-in-aid. Father was rolled in and Maw had on her new pink-flowered J.C. Penney dress. They both seemed frightened by all the lights and screaming people.

Tack Rankin rolled in just in time to make a few remarks about me over the screechy public-address system, and talked about the Spartans and the national championship I'd help them win. He shook my hand, gave me his pen to sign with and pointed to the dotted line just like a salesman closing the deal. I felt dizzy when I scripted out my name. The crowd in the gym erupted with cheers, but I suddenly felt like an alien. Just like that, I wasn't one of them anymore.

Coach Rankin immediately bolted to his waiting car. He had a half dozen more ceremonies to appear at before the day was done. I still held his pen. I took it over and gave it to Father, while the flashbulbs popped and the television camera lights followed me. He reached for it as best he could, and then his shoulders shook with sobs. The cheers went on and on.

The scrapbook and the pen and the clippings are in a trunk somewhere, I guess. Probably molded over and dry-rotted.

The rest of the year swung past like an out-of-control carousel. I guess I graduated. The diploma is in that dusty trunk, too, I suppose. Everybody else was wrapped up in graduation plans, going on to school, getting jobs, dodging the draft, trying to avoid Vietnam, trying to get laid, staying stoned or drunk. I spent every spare minute running or reading. Running seemed to sweat out the anxieties I was feeling. I knew I could play football. I was strong, quick, smart, and loved to hit. But somehow, there was doubt about going on to the next level. If I was in the best possible shape, if I could coax another tenth of a second from my legs in the forty, if I could just manage five more reps when I maxed out on the weights, it might be the difference in making it or washing out completely. And washing out was not an option. I had to make it. Had to make it with flair. Or I was nothing but another losing chunk of trailer-park white trash.

Dammit, I know guys going into accounting school wonder if they can hack the big numbers. Would-be biologists question their ability to remember every single phylum and species. But they aren't on national television or in front of eighty thousand screaming people who demand perfection. And nobody who weighs three hundred pounds is trying to knock them sprawling or crush their pelvis, either.

Reading took me away. You know how it is when you can climb into somebody's prose and hide. Ride on their images and become their characters and if it gets to be too rough, just close the book. Open another one or skip to another passage and ride off again in the flow of the words. I found Kerouac and Hemingway, Faulkner and Steinbeck. They became my only friends.

My teammates seemed so shallow suddenly. Only interested in skirts and dope. In my mind, I was a college student already. On my few off-days, I tried to dress the way I figured college guys did and I hung around the bookstore near the University of Tennessee–Chattanooga, leafing through the English and Literature class texts for hours. The manager finally gave me a stool and told me to sit in a corner and stay out of the aisle, please. And to have a good year at Sparta. And to kick some ass while I was up there.

Just as summer began to drag, it came time to quit the sawmill job, throw my worn-out work gloves away, hopefully for good, and pack up for school. Maw climbed up into the truck cab with me after I had put the two cardboard suitcases in the back. Father rolled to the edge of the porch and feebly waved to us. The neighbor lady staying with him kept trying to roll him back, but he insisted.

". . . proud of you, boy . . ." I could hear him growling as I cranked up and pulled away. He had begged to go with us, but we all knew he was not up to the trip.

Maw still closed her eyes and gripped anything she could find with white knuckles as we made the trip down the side of the mountain. Then again as we climbed the Cumberland plateau and wound along the twisting, twirling backroads to Sparta in middle Tennessee.

I had seen the athletic dorm before, during my official visit, but that summer day, shimmering in the August heat, it looked from a distance for all the world like the Taj Mahal. Maw caught her breath at the first sight of the place, half hidden by a grove of cool cedar.

"Corey Phil, it looks like a magic castle," she gushed. "Like some kind of fairy-tale place."

"It's just home for me for a while," I said, but I was awestruck, too.

My room was almost half the size of our whole house on Signal Mountain. Private bath. Bookcases. Study desk. I watched out the window as Maw drove away. She had been muttering again about my angel. My angel would take care of me. For some stupid reason, I felt like crying, but I didn't.

My roommate wouldn't be in until two days later because of his state high-school all-star game. He'd miss our first workout the next day. I only knew he was an offensive lineman and another freshman. Someone in the same boat as me, anyway. I'd be an old-timer by the time he showed up.

Supper was amazing. A choice like the biggest buffet I had ever seen. Only freshmen were in the dorm so far, and we all seemed skittish of each other. As if it was a sign of weakness to acknowledge the existence of one another. The competition had begun already. I tried to pick out the other linebackers between bites of roast beef and mashed potatoes.

I jogged for an hour, circling the campus three times, cutting across the huge tree-shaded quadrangle and breathing in the fresh-cut-grass smell. When I finally stopped to rest, it was on the library steps, which seemed to stretch from where I sat all the way to heaven. Sweaty or not, I had to go inside to breathe the bookish air.

The coolness of dry air-conditioning made me shiver. There weren't many books on shelves, though. I finally determined that I had to search through card catalogs and present my needs to bored work-study students behind the big desks, and they would retrieve the books for me. I tried out my new student ID card. It worked. I had *One Flew Over the Cuckoo's Nest* under my arm as I jogged back to Champions' Hall in the cooling, deepening darkness.

We were herded to cursory physicals the next morning at seven A.M., just after an obscenely big breakfast. Our first workout was at high noon. Freshmen dressed in a separate locker room from the varsity, and it reminded me of the word *spartan* in another context. Upperclassmen had carpet on the floor, track lighting, curtained personal lockers, their names painted on the shelves above where their bright new practice sweats hung already, waiting for the arrival of the athletic bodies to go in them in a week. We had only bare wooden cages, names inked on impermanent adhesive tape with a laundry marker, a dusty cement floor, and intense fluorescent lights overhead.

I knew it was big-time anyway. The sweats fit. They glowed bright red, first in the lights, then in the intense August sun outside. The cleats smelled new and custom-made and were snug on my feet. My helmet had 55 on each side in big Day-Glow gold letters. Big enough to see easily from the back row of the stands or on national TV.

There was Coach Tack Rankin just across the brilliant green, perfectly manicured practice field. He was chatting and laughing with a group of assistant coaches, each dressed identically in red shorts and gold Spartan T-shirts. I trotted over to where they stood, feeling the blood rushing through my legs as I pumped, the wind blowing through the ear holes in my new helmet with the speed as I accelerated. Pride and joy made me grin behind the grid of my face mask. God, it felt good!

"Hi, Coach Rankin. Sure is great to finally be here."

I don't know what made me run right up to the coaches and speak to the man, except maybe just the exhilaration of trotting onto that field for the first time. Sacred ground where so many great football players had sweated and bled, being a part of the tradition of the Spartans. The last time Coach Rankin and I had really spoken with each other had been months before, the chilly night on my front porch. And I would have jumped off the mountain for him that night.

He was saying something to one of the other men and stopped in mid-sentence when I spoke. Slowly he turned and gave me a dark look while the assistants studied the toes of their cleats.

"Son, which group are you supposed to be in right now?"

"Linebackers."

"You get your ass over to the linebacker group as fast as you can run, then."

His eyes shot lightning bolts, his face in a snarl. I raised dust on the grass field as I scooted the fifty yards to where the guys with jersey numbers in the 40s and 50s were stretching and running in place. They seemed to be staying away from me for some reason.

My position coach, Max Milligan, trotted up a few minutes later and stood for a moment, just watching me stretch. Then, he reached down, grabbed me by my face mask and pulled me roughly up and out of earshot of the others. He was nose-to-nose with me, teeth clenched, spit flying as he talked.

"Rookie, don't you ever approach Coach Rankin again unless he tells you to approach him. Don't ever talk to him unless he asks you a question first. If you meet him on campus, you nod and say good morning and keep on going. If you see him lying on a sidewalk having a goddamn heart attack and foaming at the mouth, you nod and say good morning and keep on going. He's too busy for the likes of you. Now, crab-walk the length of this field six times and practice keeping your mouth shut. Develop some discipline, son, or we'll be sending you right back to Mayberry where they give a damn 'cause if you think you're something special up here, we don't need your ass."

The bloom was off my collegiate athletic rose in one big hurry. By the time I had finished my third trip up the field, I was hurting too much to feel any shame for my friendly, spontaneous actions. It would be three months before Coach Rankin and I had anything approaching another conversation. And he did most of the talking that time, too.

Peyton Marshall arrived mid-morning the next day. I was just finishing the Kesey book, lying on my bed, aching so much from the workouts and the crab-walking that I was having a hell of a time concentrating on the words swimming in front of my eyes. I was on the verge of giving up and drifting into sleep. The door opened suddenly and without a knock, and the largest, whitest thing I had ever seen tromped into the room and dropped three stuffed duffel bags in the middle of the room. The man looked like an albino with a thatch of fine corn-silk hair, no eyebrows, odd yellow eyes, and acres of white skin. He didn't seem to notice me at all, just went about unstuffing the bags and depositing their contents in the chest and closet on that side of the room.

"Well, hello," I finally said.

He stopped his frenzied unpacking as if he had just noticed there was someone else in the world besides himself. Then he slowly sidled over closer, avoided looking me in the eye altogether, and reluctantly offered a hand the size of a small ham. But his grasp was shockingly weak and fleeting.

"Peyton Marshall. Pleased to meet you."

I almost laughed out loud. The voice that came from the massive, muscled person was so meek and feminine and high-pitched. Such a tiny voice from such a mountain of a man!

Then with his back to me he was once again stuffing clothes into drawers. I watched. When he finished, he kicked the duffel bags underneath his bed, fell on it like a massive oak blown over by a sneaky windstorm, and was snoring loudly within ten seconds. I had just found a position that didn't ache quite so badly and was absorbed in the book again when he suddenly snorted, rolled to his back, and sat straight up.

"What time zone are we in?" he squeaked.

I had to stop and think a moment.

"Central."

He checked his wrist, the size of a fire log, and I marveled that they would make a watch band that big.

"Two hours until lunch, then," he peeped with a noticeable lisp.

Then he tumbled back over and was instantly making the sound of a two-stroke engine in need of oil.

We finally talked a little over lunch. At least, he answered my questions. He had a real talent for eating, taking a massive chunk of roast or half a pile of mashed potatoes and swallowing it all without even bothering chewing. He could down a full glass of milk with one gulp. And he managed to give cryptic answers to my questions while he put away a stunning mound of groceries.

Peyton was from some tiny town in the middle of North Carolina. He was an all-state offensive tackle who tended to not be so offensive sometimes. He got the job done, but didn't seem to have the killer instinct his high-school coach craved. Size and quickness had won him a full ride to Sparta University, though. Peyton had permanently injured at least three kids he had faced his last season. But only when each of them made fun of him for the way his voice sounded when his team broke the huddle or when he called the coin toss as captain.

"Break!" He yelled the word as a demonstration, right there in the middle of the dining hall, and heads popped up from plates all around. They wanted to see what girl had infiltrated our sanctuary and was yelling "Rape." I hid behind a pile of biscuits. I threw one at him when it looked like he was going to scream "Heads!"

I didn't see him at the workout that afternoon until near the end. The freshman linemen were practicing at the far end of the field. It was not hard to miss Peyton's huge whiteness as I ran my final wind sprints. He apparently had become the object of several offensive coaches' wrathful attention. They had him crab-walking, doing grass drills, and lugging through forty-yard sprints. The last I saw of him, he was losing most of the groceries he had put away at lunch. He was gasping for air between retches, pounding the ground with his helmet. A lonely, pathetic, mammoth figure. The sun was setting behind him, his shadow stretching almost to midfield. I started to go over to reassure him it would get better, but I didn't because I wasn't at all sure it would. And I was afraid whatever he had done to anger the coaches might rub off on me like some horrid contagious disease.

He wasn't at supper. I already knew him well enough to know that was a bad sign. I took the Kesey book back to the library and got two more. When I returned to the room, Peyton was sprawled on his bed, facedown, apparently dead. But I could hear him breathing noisily, gurgling as if he was under water.

"You okay, man?"

"Yeah," the high-pitched word almost lost in the pillow.

"What did you do to piss them off at you like that?"

"Always happens with new coaches. I'm so lardy and light-complected and my voice is so funny-sounding that coaches think I'm queer or something."

"Are you?"

"Naw. It'll be this way until we put on pads and start hitting and they'll see what I can do. Then I'll show them I can play and they'll finally ease up on me. I'll be glad when the season's over, C.P."

He sounded so pitiful I wanted to say something.

"Not me, Peyton. I love it all. I want it to go on forever."

"More power to you. I'll be glad when I can turn my stuff in and rest awhile."

"Why do you play, then?"

"Look at me. Everybody from my dad to my preacher wouldn't leave me alone if I didn't. And besides, do you think any girl is gonna want me unless I'm some kind of football hero? Forget college without the scholarship, too. My dad's a tobacco farmer, for God sakes. We're poor as dirt."

"Oh."

"That's what attracted Coach Rankin to me in the first place."

"What's that?"

"His daddy was a tobacco farmer, too, right up until the day he died. Coach Rankin said he went to Jesus right there in the curing shed after working all day in the field."

"Oh, really?" Was that the same father who had a stroke and was in a wheelchair the last ten years of his life? "Did Coach Rankin ask you what you were going to study?"

"Uh huh. That's another thing. I told him I wanted to be a civil engineer. He said his degree was in engineering. That he still kept his slide rule in his middle desk drawer. Said he sometimes pulls it out and calculates a little just for drill."

"Yeah, he's a special man, all right."

I rolled away then, not wanting to look at that snowy, innocent face anymore. I tried to read for a while until I couldn't keep my eyes open any longer. Peyton was snoring, a little more softly now than before. The lights out, the room relatively quiet, I lay on my back a minute, as I always did, letting the day's events trickle out of my brain like a draining bathtub so I could find some peace in sleep. Drowsiness was taking me away finally when I heard that squeaky little-boy voice.

"C.P.?"

"Yes, Peyton?"

"Do you know Jesus as your personal savior?"

FIVE

Peyton Marshall was soon gone. He had so few possessions in our room anyway that I didn't even notice them missing. He simply didn't come back after the last day of two-a-day practices. Then I found several religious tracts he had left, and a note with some scriptures scribbled on them for me to check out. The room felt like an auditorium suddenly without his bulk in it. I relaxed. I had never shared such close space with anyone before anyhow, with no brothers and sisters. At breakfast the next morning, another of the freshman offensive linemen told me Peyton had gone back home.

"Said he was going to try to go to a junior college if his daddy didn't kill him first."

"But why?" I couldn't imagine someone passing up a chance to play big-time ball. To go to such a great school.

"The coaches stayed on him all the time, man. Not about his playing or anything. He was good. It was the way he looked. His voice. Called him a fag and everything. He just couldn't take it."

"It's just hazing. They're testing us. Trying to make us mentally tough. Couldn't he see that?"

"Guess he just got tired of it. I don't think he belonged here. You know what I mean?" And the guy had the look in his eye that told me he might not be long for Sparta University, either.

My privacy was short-lived. I got my new roommate that night. There I was, flat on my back, legs up in the air, trying to let the ache seep out someway, struggling to keep my attention on a Steinbeck book I had stuck in my face. I didn't even hear the door open.

"What's happenin', dude?"

I must have jumped a foot off the mattress and couldn't help the cry of pain that escaped.

"I'm not trying to spook you, man. Be cool. Be cool."

Elgie Munford was a black defensive back. A junior. And rooming with me was punishment. He was exiled to a freshman's room, on the same side of the building with the track men and basketball players and other lepers. And they didn't usually put the black and white players in the same room, either. I wondered what I had done. Elgie quickly told me it was him, not me.

"Me and the Tack-man had this little tiff, see? He told me to shave off my mustache. Said there was a team rule against facial hair. I told him he had more hair on his ass than I did on my upper lip. That all proud black men had mustaches or beards. That's the way we are. He said, 'Uh Uh . . . not on no team of mine.' So we had this stalemate, you know? This agreement to disagree."

He dropped his duffel bag and grinned defiantly, pointing to show me that the wiry whiskers under his nose still remained. As quiet and reverent as Peyton had been, that's how loud and obscene Elgie Munford was. Try as I might to get back into Steinbeck, his nonstop voice continued to rattle constantly on and on as he unpacked his stuff, made the bed to suit himself, sang off-key to some unheard tune, danced around the room, and shadow-boxed with Tack Rankin's ghost.

"One day, I'm gonna take that old milk-faced puke and give him a lick or two to his fat jaws, make him wish he never seen the Elgie Machine. Whack him once or twice upside his head, whup his ass up one side of that stadium and down the other before he even knows . . ."

"How do you know this place is not bugged?"

He stopped dancing and punching, thought a second or two, then grinned.

"Hell! Don't matter. Ol' Tack-less knows how I feel about his sorry butt already. That's why I ain't gettin' half the PT I got last year."

"PT?"

"Playing time, my man. They're going to a whole new scheme in the defensive backfield. Three backs instead of four. Me the only brother that started back there last year, guess who the nigger in the woodpile is? Third and long is gonna be the only time I get my butt off the bench after the national anthem gets sung. I'll be lucky to letter this year. Hell, I'll be lucky if they don't make me buy a ticket to the game, man."

I didn't tell him that the defensive change meant one more starting linebacker. And that I hoped to be that man.

I got to know my new roomie very quickly. He apparently never had a thought he didn't feel the need to verbalize. No matter how rough practice had been, how hot and dehydrated we were, he still managed to have the energy to dance and talk. Dance and talk until I'd finally heave a pillow at him, scream good-naturedly for him to shut up, and bury myself under the covers. He'd fall back on the bed, get silent for thirty seconds, then, as if he simply could not control himself, launch into some new tale.

He was from Atlanta. Raised by a grandmother. Family of nine kids. It was the third or fourth night we roomed together before he got on the subject of his recruitment.

"They was several that offered old Elgie bunches of money, C.P. We talking major dollars, man. One dude even drove my brand new car right up to the door and tossed me the keys while I was settin' there on the front porch. Big old shiny black Pontiac. I was all-state running back in Georgia, you know. *Parade* magazine all-American. But I buggered up my knee first game of my senior year. Money offers quit like they be chopped off with a hatchet. Couldn't make my cuts no more when I run like I use to. Damn leg just buckle up under me sometime. I looked like somebody done sawed down a oak tree, I swear. But old Tack, he saw I could backpedal like a son of a bitch. Run to a spot. Read a quarterback's eyes. And I always could throw a lick. Love to knock the slobber out of a dude, man. Help him up and then knock the slobber out of him again next play."

He laughed, a nervous bleat that sounded more like a choking goat. I was at my desk, trying to plan my class schedule but he wouldn't let me. He just kept talking.

"So ol' Rank-as-they-come hit me with both barrels. 'Come on up to Sparta and play defensive back for me,' he says. 'You be all-American before you a junior.' I like what I'm hearing, but Bear Bryant is saying the same thing, and the dude at Clemson is showing me the playbook with my name already wrote in and everything."

The class descriptions and credit hours and course prerequisites were swimming before me and I couldn't even remember what I had just read on the previous page. I was determined not to follow the crib schedule the athletic academic counselor had laid out for me, but Elgie was making my head spin like a spiked football.

"Then old tick-tock-Tack says the magic words. We're sitting out there on my Meemaw's front porch, just me and him, and he leans over and taps me on the leg and looks me right in the eye. 'Elgie, my best friend when I was growing up was a black boy,' he says. 'We're like brothers, me and him.' Shows me his two fingers all twisted together like this."

Elgie had Tack Rankin's delivery down pat, his voice jumping from his own high nasal pitch to a fair impression of Rankin's smooth, low growl.

" 'But when we get ready for scholarships to play ball in college, we gotta split up,' he tells me. 'Segregation still the law of the land and all. My blood brother, he ends up at Grambling, down in Louisiana. Has a great career. Wins a peck of games. We lose touch. Then, I get word that he has come down with the sickle cell and when I hear, I go down and see him. He's dying and all, but he gives me his National Black Football Championship ring, Elgie.' "

I was listening. You had to listen to Elgie. He was on his back on the bed, stark naked, hands behind his head, yakking to the ceiling, body English matched to the rhythm of his story.

" 'He give me his championship ring, Elgie.' I was fixin' to bust out cryin' by that time, C.P. I had me a favorite uncle that had the sickle cell. He was a damn fine football player, too, and wanted to go to Grambling all his life. 'And I still got that ring in the middle desk drawer in my office,' old Tack says. 'It means so much to me I take it out every single day and look at it and think of my lost friend, Whitney Jefferson.' Had me goin', young C.P. This ol' whitey having been such a good friend to a black man, he's gonna make a fine coach for me. So, I sign. And you know what?"

Time for my input, though I knew he would tell me anyway.

"No, what?"

"I got a woman friend that goes to Grambling and she does work-study in the registrar's office. Last year, I ask her to check. Ain't never been no Whitney Jefferson play at Grambling College. Ain't even been nobody by that name ever went to school there that she could find. Snookered! Elgie has done been snookered by the Rank-man!" He laughed so hard I thought he would roll off the bed.

I just smiled, nodded, wrote a note to myself about some class or other. Elgie's story didn't surprise me at all. I had been on campus two weeks and I had Tack Rankin pegged pretty well, I figured.

Two-a-days were hell. We were rousted from our beds at six and herded to a light breakfast. Light so we wouldn't have to take time to vomit our guts out and miss drills and conditioning. Then we would report for practice at eight, work for three or four hours, straggle to the training room to fix everything we tore apart in the workout, limp to lunch, then try to rest a few minutes. Afternoon practice started promptly at three and lasted until dark. Then it was the training room again, maybe whirlpool or heat therapy if we were lucky, an Ace bandage and some heat balm if we weren't. And we freshmen had to wait until the others finished to get patched up ourselves. Supper was cold every night by the time we got there. I lost ten pounds from the heat and work and got screamed at by the head trainer. He put me on protein supplements and potassium and sodium pills and they kept my stomach cramping and churning all night and made me light-headed and woozy during practice.

And we were just fodder for the varsity. We were opening in two weeks against a small school from Louisiana. One of the "directional" schools: Northwest . . . Southeast . . . East Central Louisiana . . . one of those. A sure-fire win for the mighty Spartans. But we were really spending most of our practice time getting ready for Ole Miss, our Southeastern Conference opener the week after that. On national television.

My job during scrimmage was to play the opponent's outside linebacker. I wore his jersey and helmet. I even had his name on my back. I watched film and tried to mimic his movements and reads and style so convincingly that Skip Gross, our starting quarterback, would feel right at home when he faced the guy for real.

But when the coaches screamed at the offense for not blocking me, for letting me get to the running backs or knock down a pass, my teammates just got meaner and nastier toward me. If they didn't get me taken out of the play legally, they would trip me, clip me, try to take my legs out from under me while they were sprawled on the ground with the wild swing of a leg. Then, they tried to get fingers into my eyes in the pile-ups, or to pull the hairs on my legs, or to spit in my face if they could muster enough saliva in the dry, dusty heat.

"Goddamn rookie. Get back to high school."

"Quit showboatin'. Take a fall, man. Lay down and we can quit sooner."

"One more cheap shot like that and you'll leave on a crutch, Mr. High School Hero."

If I didn't make the play, though, it was the coaches who were screaming at me, slapping the side of my helmet and kicking dust while they cussed and ranted.

"GodDAMN! We ain't got you out there to wave at the fuckin' play, son!"

"Give us a good look or we gonna be out here till game day, boy!"

"At least try to stand up and quit trippin' over the grass blades! Get in their damn way sometimes and slow 'em down a little!"

"Work hard! Help make us better!"

"Shorty? Did we screw up and give a girl a scholarship? Is that number fifty-five a goddamn girl? He ain't hit nobody since he got on campus."

Two things kept me going. Game day with its chance for me to at last play. And school starting soon. I was realistic but I thought I had shown I could play at this level. And I spent hours going over the schedule of classes I had registered for, reading and rereading the windy, convoluted course descriptions.

It was game week before I realized I wasn't part of the plan for the opener. I was still running scout team, imitating the Old Miss middle 'backer, and a guy from Nashville who had been red-shirted the previous year was running first unit in my position. A slow-footed senior who worked extra hard to avoid contact ran behind him on the second unit. I had not spent fifteen minutes running drills or working on the game plan with the defense yet, and heavy prep work was about over. Assistant Coach Max Milligan just laughed when I asked him about it.

"Damn, sonny-boy! Every swingin' dick out here feels like he oughta be startin' the game. I can't put seventy-six of you on first unit. You show us something in practice and we'll give you a look."

"Coach, I'm making the plays. I can do better . . ."

"You just be thankful we let you eat at the same table as these athletes, boy. Don't come whinin' to me about ridin' the bench. You make your own breaks in this man's game. Show us something besides bitchin' and moanin', then you'll play."

He walked away before I could say anything else, shaking his head, mumbling under his breath, something about "freshmen . . . gotta be some way we can avoid 'em . . . gotta be," as if he was cursing some dumb animal who didn't know any better.

Friday night before the opening game, I called home for the first time since Maw had dropped me off at the steps to Champions Hall. I had written several times and got back one brief letter, painfully scrawled in her spidery handwriting on wide-ruled notebook paper. No news, really. Just "Be careful" and "Eat right." No "We love you," exactly. Just a "Love . . . Maw" scribbled as an afterthought at the end.

"Maw?"

"That you, Corey Phil? Fletcher, it's Corey Phil!"

I could hear him, hoarse and far away, asking her something.

"Wait a minute. Let me talk to him first and then you can ask him."

"How is everything, Maw? How's Father?"

"Seems to be some better. Just talks about you and the football game all the time but it keeps his mind occupied and I expect that's helping him some. You taking care? Ain't got hurt or anything, have you?"

"Nah. Doing fine. School starts Monday and I . . ."

"Okay! Okay! Your father's driving me crazy. He wants to talk to you."

He dropped the phone and it clattered noisily on the hard kitchen floor. I could hear Maw fussing as she picked it up and handed it to him again.

"Boy!"

"How's it going, Father?"

"What position they got you playing? Inside or outside?"

"Scout team outside linebacker."

"Scout team?" He was instantly furious. "What the hell's wrong with them dumb bastards up there?"

"That's why I called, Father. There's no use in you and Maw trying to come up for the game tomorrow."

"What you mean?"

"Looks like I'm headed for red-shirting this season." Coach Milligan had called me aside that afternoon and told me to stop by his office after practice. I'd dress for games, just in case of a tragedy, but the plan was to hold me out a year, he had said. "Let you get stronger. Work on your speed some. Learn the system." I'd started to argue that I was signed to a scholarship because of my speed and knew the system better than most of the seniors, but he had begun fiddling with papers on his desk, obviously ready for me to leave his office. So I did.

"Damn, boy! I ought to come up there and clear me off a place and hold a prayer meetin' with them bastards! A real come-to-Jesus meetin'."

"Calm down, Father. Sell the tickets to somebody and just listen on the radio. It's for the best, I'm sure. It's going to be a rebuilding year, anyway. I don't think we will be as strong as last . . ."

"Little wonder! They got the best linebacker in the country and they gonna keep him on the goddamn bench!"

I didn't push the point. Shoot, I agreed with him.

"Tough break, my man," Elgie Munford sympathized when I told him. "That's what Rankin does, though. He manages to get the best athletes signed up so they can't go nowhere else, gets 'em up here to the prison, then messes with their minds. Makes 'em act like zombies like in that movie I saw the other day. Hell, we sleepwalk through the schedule, man. We're like robots. Follow the system. Do what he tells us even if it means jumping off a cliff. It works. Damn sure works. 'Shave them whiskers off, Elgie!' 'Don't take that Afro-history class, Elgie! You know you're too dumb to pass a course we don't set you up for.' 'Don't be bouncin' on that girl, Elgie. She's not good enough for you, a fine Spartan athlete.' "

He was punching holes in the air in our room already, dancing like a prizefighter. We were packing our bags after practice, ready to go check into a hotel for the night, go for a team movie, then make our eleven o'clock curfew.

"But Elgie, I can play. I know the scheme and game plan better than anybody on the depth chart."

"You're damn good, C.P. McKay. You gonna be a star up here. But they got to break you. I got good ears from my momma's side of the family. I hear 'em talking. Milligan and them. Talking about you reading too much all the time and worrying about your classes and bucking them on what classes they want you to be taking. They figure you gonna flunk out and then they lose their investment in you. Naw, they gotta break you. Bring you around to their way of doing things. Red-shirtin' you is just one more way to do it. Give 'em one more year to carve you out like a statue."

We were lucky to win the game the next day. Thirty-six-point favorites and we won by fourteen on a couple of late touchdowns.

The linebackers playing my position were okay, but the defense let the other team hold on to the ball way too long so our offense didn't have much chance to score. And when we did have the ball, the quarterback had trouble hitting wide-open receivers until he made a couple of long ones in the fourth quarter. It almost looked as if we were asleep, then woke up just in time to win the game if not beat the point spread.

Still, I got off on the atmosphere of it all. Dulled as my enthusiasm was by the recent disappointment in my athletic career, my spirit was set free by the color, the noise, the thud of impact and collision on the field. I enjoyed just being a part of it all. Small part or not.

The bright new game uniform on my back, the press of photographers and television cameramen, the roar of the crowd chanting cheers was a Technicolor swirl all around me and I admit I was caught up in the noisy whirlwind of it all. The screaming fans at the entrance to the field, calling my name as if they knew who I was, and then, after the game, the kids along the fence begging for my chin strap or for me to stop for an autograph. They didn't care if I had played or not. I was a Spartan hero. Only experiencing it all from out on the field in front of seventy thousand roaring people, plowing into the enemy players and doing my part to win the game would have been better. I hated my clean uniform, the lack of meaningful sweat, no blood.

After the game, Coach Rankin pitched a fit, slapped people brutally on the sides of their helmets, grabbed others roughly by face masks or shoulder pads, cursed us until the air turned blue and spat denouncements like a rabid wildcat. Then suddenly he quieted, as if suddenly exorcised of some kind of demon, kneeled and led us in a long, fevered prayer before going out to meet the media. Reporters flooded the dressing room, crowded around the key players, and got in the way of those of us who just wanted to get dressed and outside to air that didn't reek of liniment, sweat, and cigar smoke.

The phone was already ringing when I walked into my dorm room.

"Boy! I done it!"

"Father, that you?" His voice was startling in its happy strength. I had not heard him so up since . . .

"I knew if they was too stupid to play you they was too damn dumb to beat them boys by thirty-six points."

"Don't tell me you bet . . ."

"I put down five hundred dollars!"

"Father, you don't have five hundred dollars."

"I do now! Galls me to bet against the Spartans, but I sure will if it makes me money."

"You can't be betting on my team. You can't . . ."

"Easy money, boy! Easy money," he growled, his excitement making him short of breath and his voice raspy as he laughed. "They ain't gonna play you against Ole Miss, are they?"

"No sir. I don't think so."

"Early betting line is eight points y'all's way. It'll be up to ten by Saturday by the time all the amateurs load up on it. I believe I'll take me a big chunk of that action."

"Father . . ."

"Lemme know if you hear something, though. About anybody being hurt at Ole Miss or anything."

It all flashed in front of me then like an out-of-control movie and I felt my stomach fall as if I were riding a runaway incline down the side of Lookout Mountain. Pallets on cruel, hard floors, our little pile of furniture stacked beside Ponce de Leon, Maw answering every telephone call with hope on her face, dark figures on our porch with their sharp knocks and shifting eyes.

School started with my first three classes meeting on Monday.

History of Western Civilization was first. The auditorium filled with several hundred bored, sleepy students forced to take this course because it was required for practically everything, and an ancient professor who might just possibly have lived most of what he would be teaching. The squealing public-address system failed halfway through the first lecture and he shushed us on out with an order to read the first six chapters of the textbook by Wednesday. Beginning of mankind all the way to the Crusades in two days.

English 101. Freshman Composition. A carpeted, tiered lecture hall with bench seats and rows of tables. My professor turned out to be a fat, balding graduate student who spoke in a soft monotone that had most of the hundred bright young faces nodding off in fifteen minutes. Read the first hundred pages of the text by Wednesday and write a critique of each piece as we went.

Creative Writing. Finally! I had only enough time to stop by Champions' Hall and grab a roast beef sandwich before trotting across the quad to the beautiful, gothic Language Arts building. I had already walked the steps to all my classes a half dozen times in the last few days, so I went directly to the correct door in the hallway maze. Once inside, I was thrilled at how it looked. This, at last, was what I thought college classrooms were supposed to be! The floors were dark wood, fragrant with oil, not covered with pastel carpet. The student desks were old-style, with heavy wooden armrests, not made from cheap plastic and sheet-metal. A well-used blackboard instead of a screen for some fancy overhead projector covered the front wall. With its architecture, its furnishings, this all could have been lifted directly from Harvard or Oxford or the Sorbonne. And there were only about ten other students in the classroom. They all appeared to be older, much more serious than the other students I had encountered. Several of the men wore full beards. The women were in jeans and T-shirts, apparently without bras, the men in faded jeans and fringe vests instead of the latest fashion-driven sorority and fraternity button-down uniforms. Some even wore black armbands, signifying their open opposition to the Vietnam war.

I took a back desk and listened to the chatter among the students who obviously knew each other as I breathed in the dust and book-smell that signified a place of real learning. I tried not to stare at the girl to my left who seemed, as I did, not to be a part of the clique. She was blonde. Her eyeglasses made her look bookwormish, but in an attractive kind of way. Not as hippie in dress as everyone else, but certainly not standard Greek organization, either. I vowed to start working on my nerve right away and maybe I'd be willing to say something to her by midterm.

Professor Langston Wheeler, Pulitzer Prize winner and my teacher, was late. He finally entered in a rush, as if driven by a need to get the teaching going before the vast knowledge he had to impart grew stale and out of date. He was younger than I expected, hairline receding, slightly hunchbacked by the weight of all he had learned. He looked exactly like I would expect a Pulitzer Prize winner to look. Despite the temperature outside, in the high eighties, he wore gray wool slacks, a brown sweater and a tweed jacket. His shirt was plaid and buttoned at the neck for a green, mismatched bow tie. And damn! There were leather patches on his jacket elbows! I fully expected him to pull out a pipe and light it up.

Instead, he dropped his load of books on the rickety table and fell heavily into the chair as if almost exhausted just from thinking about teaching us, and he still avoided looking at us. He studied paperwork in front of him for two minutes while the room remained completely quiet. Next to me I could hear the girl's watch ticking like a bomb in the hot stillness. She had soft blonde down and a constellation of freckles on her arm and her perfume smelled wonderful.

"Mr. McKay." His first words were my name, and they sounded like a clap of thunder as they echoed in the room.

"Present." My voice felt thick and cracked slightly.

"I don't call roll, Mr. McKay. A simple yes will do. I need to see you after class, please."

My face bloomed crimson. I had needed permission from the instructor to take this class. The one class I most craved. I had left the request at the English Department office a week ago and had heard nothing from anyone, so I assumed I was in. Now, as Wheeler stood, paced, detailed exactly what he expected from each of us, I could only worry about why he wanted to see me. Why I was singled out. Apprehension blotted out most of the important stuff he was telling us.

When I finally stood across the table from him, he ignored me and continued to study the paperwork on the desk before him. He tiredly massaged his temples. It seemed the hour's lecturing had taken a lot out of him.

I didn't know whether to speak or not. Surely, he could see a 230-pound linebacker casting a shadow over him. Finally, he stood, looked me up and down as if he was sizing me up, as if he could tell from looking at me if I was worthy of his time and effort. He stopped at the eyes and stayed there as he spoke, slowly, evenly, a lawyer on cross-examination.

"Mr. McKay, you are a freshman, then?"

"Yes." Maw would have fussed, but it sounded so immature to say "yessir."

"You participate in football, too, I am given to understand."

"Yes, I do."

"I've never allowed a freshman to take this course, Mr. McKay. Most of the students are in their fifth semester here at the university, at least. And, if I may speak frankly, I don't particularly enjoy having jocks in my classes." He said "jocks" as he might have said "ax-murderers." "There is no way you can successfully complete the requirements of this course, Mr. McKay, so why don't you save yourself and me considerable angst and go register for something that requires muscle from somewhere else besides your cranium."

His eyes were black, piercing. My first reaction was hurt. But I had just been challenged, as surely as if by a blocking back from an opposing team. I refused to go down without at least a forearm shiver.

"I assume you have seen my verbals on the SAT, Dr. Wheeler? And read my admittance essay? Looked at my request for permission to be in your class?"

He winced ever so slightly, as if he was not accustomed to being warded off by defenseless students. But his voice was still filled with authority when he finally spoke.

"That's the only reason I gave you the courtesy of telling you face-to-face that I intended to deny your request to matriculate."

He sounded final. But the whistle had not blown yet. The play was not over.

"Then I can only assume that you are turning me down based on your preconceived prejudices against my class standing and athletic pursuits. If you tell me you don't think I have the talent or ability to benefit from and contribute to this class, then I will honor your decision. But if you intend to deny me simply because I'm young and play football, then I respectfully submit that you, sir, are full of bullshit."

God, where did that come from? I could only stand a little straighter, keep my gaze leveled with his, and hope he didn't throw me out the door. Toss a penalty flag and kick me completely out of the game. But there it was. Just a hint of a look on his face. A look I had seen many times before, just as I stuck the forehead of my helmet into the breastbone of someone not quite prepared to take it.

Professor Wheeler paused and dropped his eyes from mine in what I hoped was surrender. He waited thirty seconds to reply to my outburst.

"Mr. McKay," he said, finally, his voice now defeated. "If you feel so strongly, I'll allow you to continue to sit in this classroom. I'm sure you are aware that you have two weeks to drop this class and choose another that might better suit you. Time to pick up another course so you won't lose your precious athletic eligibility."

Now his eyes were back, meeting mine head-on, and force returned to his words.

"If you show as much fire in your work as you did here today, Mr. McKay, you may have an infinitesimal chance of passing this course, but it's rare that I am proven wrong about people like you. And I despise being proven wrong. Expect me to be twice as hard on you as anyone else. Your A is my D. Your perfection is my drivel. Your best work is my toilet paper."

He grinned a grin so vicious that I took a step back but never lost eye contact.

"Fair enough, Dr. Wheeler. Fair enough."

I didn't breathe until I was down the steps and onto the quad. Practice was fifteen minutes away and there was little time to even think about the showdown with the professor. But that night, as Elgie preached on and on in stunning detail about all the women he had conquered, the differences between the black ones and the white ones, the relative merits of oral versus regular sex, I lay on my bed and thought of the irony of it all. Just three weeks on campus, and I had totally screwed up with the two most important figures in my self-created world: the most famous football coach in America and a Pulitzer Prize winner, each of whom held my future in his hands. Both had benched me, one literally, the other figuratively. And I would have to work harder than I had ever imagined to try to please them.

Then, to top off my week, we lost to Ole Miss. Right there in our home stadium, in front of a packed house, and on national television, the Spartans lost a home conference opener for the first time in sixteen years. The defense got dragged up and down the field while the offense seemed dazed and confused. Skip Gross seemed to be off just a hair on every pass as they sailed an inch over the outstretched hands of our wide receivers. Just like the week before, he seemed to find the range late in the game, but it was not so easy to come back on a good team. And every time the coaches made an adjustment, it seemed the Rebels knew what was coming and threw exactly the right play or set against us.

Elgie had a great game, though. He intercepted three passes and brought one back for our only score, even though he played sparingly. I had to grin at the way he danced in the end zone, just the way he always did around our dorm room. But when he trotted off the field and tried to high-five Coach Rankin, the old man just turned his back and studied the clipboard and jawed with someone on the other end of his sideline headset.

I dreaded the locker room afterward. But mostly I dreaded the practice field on Monday. Rankin and the others would be devils, extracting revenge for our pitiful performance. And I didn't even play a down, of course.

Trotting off the field, the crowd that gathered above the archway to the locker room looked for all the world like a threatening, stormy thundercloud. Our fans rained drinks on us and thundered curses.

But just before I ducked under the cover of the cement wall, I thought I caught a glimpse of a frightening, familiar figure standing calmly on a bench in the middle of the roiling mob. Chestful of snakelike chains and necklaces reflecting the setting sun's rays like bolts of lightning. Shiny shaved head barely covered by a fedora.

But God, no! It couldn't have been. And that slight wave of a diamond-bedecked hand, a gesture that looked like a thumbs-up of approval? It wasn't for me, was it? No. No way. I had done nothing that would have gotten his approval. And if the man had been who I thought it was, how would he even know who I was? It had been years.

Skip Gross, our quarterback, trotted next to me, and I glanced his way to see if he had noticed the only figure in the crowd who wasn't cursing and spitting at us. I was afraid he might think the approving gesture was for me. But he had already ducked his head against the fans' deluge and clacked on up the concrete floor to the locker room. All our cleats sounded like machine-gun rounds echoing in the cavern under the stadium.

Several seniors threw their helmets angrily against the wall. A couple of fights almost broke out as some blamed others for the loss, for dropping the ball or missing a tackle that might have swung the game our way. But everyone instantly went quiet when the coaches stomped in and slammed the door behind them with a force so loud and final it sucked the air out of the humid room. They each glared at their own little covey of players, snarling like mad dogs, eyes mean-red.

Coach Rankin was eerily silent, seething, standing before us clenching and unclenching his fists.

"I . . . despise . . . losing. I won't tolerate anyone who can stomach losing. Players, from starters to scout team. Coaching staff. Trainers. I don't give a good goddamn who you are. I'll run off anybody connected with this program who is not sick to his stomach right now."

His words were even, clipped. "When the damn newspaper vultures get in here, you talk about how good Ole Miss was. How prepared they were for this game. How we are going to go back and get better and fight harder against Kentucky next week. Show a hell of a lot more class than you did out on that field today. Practice at six Monday morning. If you need to get taped, be there at four-thirty. Helmets and shorts. We are going to run until we learn the meaning of hustle and sacrifice. Or until some of you pansy-asses decide to go back home to your momma's tit."

Then he dropped to his knee, and we all followed, praying deeply, earnestly.

Elgie came by my locker on the way to the shower.

"They're movin' me out of your room, C.P.," he whispered, quietly, like he was at a funeral. "Looks like I'm back to the good side of the tracks for a while. Been cool rooming with you, man. You're gonna get your chance if you keep workin' hard. And especially if we keep stinkin' up the place like we did today. Don't know what's wrong with us. Just something missing, though."

He was shaking his head, but I could see he was fighting the urge to sing and dance his way toward the showers. After all, he'd had a great game. The rest of the locker room was so quiet I could hear the murmur of the newsmen as they questioned Skip and the others who had played. Several asked where Elgie had gotten off to. I pointed to the misty showers where the only sound was the hot water splashing on cement.

I stopped by the supply store on the way back to the dorm to get more materials for my writing assignments. I had to admit, I would miss Elgie. At least, though, with all the things I had due for class the next week, it would be good to have the room to myself the rest of the weekend. Surely, they wouldn't move anybody else in before Monday.

But when I got to the top of the stairs, I heard loud, fuzzy music that seemed to come from behind my closed door. And when I opened the door to my room, I smelled sweet smoke. My new roommate sat in the middle of his bed, legs crossed, smoking pot and drinking a beer, while Jimi Hendrix poured from a set of stereo speakers the size of small refrigerators.

SIX

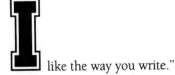like the way you write."

It was the first time she had spoken to me. We had been seat-mates for two weeks, sitting three feet from each other, and I had bitten my tongue many times to keep from saying something trite and silly. Built up a determination to at least say good afternoon to her but then let it fizzle in bashfulness. Now, she was talking to me.

"You did a good job in your essay of showing the feelings you have when you play football. Even though I don't care much for sports."

"Thank you. Thank you very much." Wheeler was late, as usual, and the rest of the class buzzed about rallies on the Union steps and a teach-in at the Arts and Sciences building. Maggie Vinyard was talking to me. She had said she liked my writing.

"I knew you looked like an athlete, and most athletes I've known were zeroes. But you let me see a side of it all I had never thought about before."

I had read my essay to the class at the last meeting. It was the first time I had read aloud anything so personal. And it felt exactly as I might have imagined it to feel if I had run naked across the quad at high noon. Nude, exposed, ten cynical students and one tough-nut teacher ready to pick at every scab and pimple and imperfection.

It had occurred to me that it was a mistake to pick football as the subject for my first effort. Maybe it was only a subconscious effort to rub Wheeler's nose in it. But it was, after all, what I knew best. That had been Langston Wheeler's dictum.

"Write of what you know. Your own life must be your research for this piece. Impress me with the way you have observed that which is most familiar and convey that observation to the reader. But attack it anew, from a viewpoint outside the box."

I chose the time my beloved football fell off Signal Mountain as a starting point. Then used it as a metaphor for seeking perfection in games that are won by preparation and lost through inattention to detail and planning. I brought in Houseman's "To an Athlete Dying Young," and a little Frost and Sandburg. It was all gobbledygook, of course. The kind of convoluted thinking I thought might impress Wheeler. I never dreamed Maggie would like it.

"Wheeler didn't seem to care much for it," I said, not totally in modesty. "I got a D."

"You really expected him to be thrilled with our first assignment? He ripped us all, didn't he? Except Clifford," and she nodded toward a tall, bespectacled senior in the front row. "And we all know why."

I didn't, but I let it pass.

"I do appreciate your compliments, Maggie."

"Have you written anything else? I'd like . . ."

But the door opened and in rushed our professor, abruptly ending the most meaningful exchange I had had with a woman since I got to Sparta.

She tapped me on the shoulder later as we left the classroom.

"Look. Let's grab a bite and talk sometime," she said. Her gaze was direct. No girl had ever been so bold with me. "Maybe you can help me open up in my writing the way you did in your essay."

"Sure. That'd be great." I tried not to sound as eager as I felt.

"How about Friday night? At the Pizza Palace?"

"Well, sure. . . ." Something ominous was in my way. There was something that made me hesitate. But it wasn't her brazenness in asking me out or the way her blonde hair looked as it swept across her glasses or the totally open way she looked into my face with her wonderful green eyes. "God! I forgot! We leave for Baton Rouge Friday afternoon. LSU. For Saturday's game."

"Oh. Well. Maybe some other time, then. See you, Mr. McKay."

And she peeled off and was gone between rows of shrubbery and amid a blizzard of falling yellow leaves. The breath was all drained out of me as I watched the place where she had been.

I had just enough time to run by the athletic dorm and get into shorts and T-shirt before practice. Dexter Flynt was sprawled across his bed and, as usual, half stoned. The room was overcast with cigarette smoke.

"Beer, C.P.?" he asked, and, as always, laughed uproariously when I simply ignored him. Dexter was a track man, a triple jumper, at Sparta on a full scholarship to just skip and hop two months out of the year. He rarely went to class. Never worked out, that I saw. He seemed to spend all his time getting high and listening to music. He had ended up in my room when his former roomie, a huge basketball player, beat the crap out of him and left him bleeding on the dorm steps. My sympathies lay with the basketball player.

"Got some killer weed. Want a toke before practice?"

"No thanks, Dexter. Maybe later."

"Skip practice, man. You're not gonna play this year anyway. Tell 'em you got strep throat. Anything contagious and they'll run you off from practice to keep the studs from getting it. There's a great party at the Delta Chi house tonight we gotta make."

"You see this?" I rattled my loose-leaf assignment book at him. "Two papers due this week and a major exam in Western Civ tomorrow. And we'll practice until it's too dark to see and then they'll turn on the lights and we'll practice some more."

"Good. I saw part of the Kentucky game. Y'all need all the practice you can get. You were lucky to win."

We had been. Skip Gross hit a long pass in the fourth quarter to save the day and emerge the hero, even though he had looked pathetic until then. Elgie intercepted a desperation pass in the end zone at the end. The point spread had been ten. We won by seven.

Father was ecstatic at the outcome of the game. The Spartans had won, but so had he. Five hundred dollars.

"Y'all don't win, all the big supporters will quit contributing money," Dexter was saying. "We may not be able to afford steak in the dining hall. I got to have steak when I get the munchies, C.P. Y'all better win." He laughed and cranked the volume up higher on the stereo. Bob Dylan was whining some slow, loud dirge.

I held my breath and ducked out of the smokey room, sniffed at my T-shirt, and almost gagged on the smell. I hoped the coaches wouldn't notice. Smokers got rehabs. Wind sprints and grass drills until they puked. My lungs already burned from just staying in the same room with Dexter.

Football practice had become routine. Conditioning on Monday and meetings to set the game plan for the next week. Pads on Tuesday with full-speed scrimmage, and me playing the part of the opposition's best linebacker. There was some satisfaction in that, at least. Wednesday, more game rehearsal in helmets and sweats. Thursday and Friday, walk-throughs in shorts. With the meetings and watching film and the conditioning drills and all the time actually on the field, football was taking six hours a day. There was little time for sleep. I had practically given it up until the season was over.

I confess, though, that on that Wednesday afternoon I was half sleeping while the offensive coaches went over and over the assignments the first team was to run at us. I stood there in the middle of the practice field, letting the cool breeze sweep through my face mask between plays, drying the sweat from my face. Coach Milligan almost knocked me over when he sneaked up and swatted me on the shoulder.

"McKay! You're looking good. Speed's better. Foot quickness showing improvement."

"Thanks, Coach." He usually was across the field with the defensive starters, working on their game plan. I rarely saw him.

"Tell you what." He turned and called another freshman's name. "Glenn! Get away from that damn water bucket and get your ass in here for McKay! Try to do half the job he's been doing and we might let you stay on this team."

Milligan motioned for me to follow him to where the defense was taking a break. I saw Frank Short, the starting linebacker, flat on his back, foot propped on a helmet while a trainer wrapped his ankle with a long snake of gauze.

"Short boogered up his ankle a while ago in a drill. Looks like he'll be okay and able to go Saturday, but we need to get you ready just in case. Franklin here has been piss-poor all week. We don't know if he can do the job or not. Sure as hell don't look like it to me."

Jesse Franklin, the second-teamer, was well within earshot. He dropped his head and tensed his fists at Milligan's lack of confidence in his abilities.

For a minute, I felt ashamed that I was so happy about Short's injury and Franklin's blessing-out. But there I was, wearing the red pullover jersey of the first unit, swapping in and out with Franklin. I tried so hard I kept getting in the way of everybody else during the quarter-speed run-throughs.

"Damn, McKay! Slow it down. You gonna step on somebody's

toe and put 'em out for the rest of the goddamn season!" Coach Milligan yelled as the other coaches giggled. A couple of older men in suits who were watching practice laughed along.

But I couldn't help it. I was working for a chance to finally play in my first college game! Suddenly, it was all worth it. The rest of the practice was a blur. I showered, got half-dressed, couldn't remember if I had showered or not and went back and took another one.

The walk from the practice field to Champions' Hall was about a mile. Most of the players had cars or hitched rides with someone who did, but I actually enjoyed the walk. It gave me a chance to cool down from a rough practice, or jog and get loose after the easy ones. And I liked to use the time to organize my thoughts. I could plan the night's study time, outline essays, and write papers in my head.

It was dusky-dark as I made my way, slower than usual, along the sidewalks, between dorms and administrative buildings and classrooms, through the cedar-wooded, parklike buffer that separated the athletic dorm from the real world. My mind was tripping, reeling with the emotion of getting bumped up on the depth chart, even if it was third unit. There was no thought of that night's studying. And I was so far away, picturing myself in that first play from scrimmage on the floor of the LSU stadium, that I didn't even notice when someone caught up and then matched strides with me. It was just a shadow on the edge of my thoughts until he spoke.

"Fine practice today, young man."

It was one of the men who had been watching the team. One of the gray-haired men in a business suit.

"Well, thank you. Thank you very much."

"You don't know me, do you?"

His face was familiar. From a picture. A picture I had seen somewhere. But I couldn't place it.

"I'm Grover Claxton, president of the university."

Thank God the darkness under the trees was enough to hide my crimson embarrassment.

"I'm sorry, sir. I didn't . . ." I had stopped, just standing there, almost forgetting to take his outstretched hand.

"Never mind, son. No problem," and he chuckled. "We did a survey last year and eighty-three percent of the students couldn't pick me out of a group of photos. Keeps me humble. Every single one of them got Coach Rankin on the first try."

He had turned and was walking again. I stepped quickly to stay beside him.

"You are C.P. McKay. Is that right?"

"Yessir." My ego got its third big boost of the day. Maggie Vinyard had asked me out, Max Milligan had promoted me to the starting defense, and now the president of a major American university knew my name when I didn't even know him from Adam.

"I was quite excited when you decided to attend Sparta, Mr. McKay."

He was? I kept quiet. I doubted I had the breath to speak anyway.

"I believe you embody the very essence of the student-athlete. You are a fine example for others who are so one-dimensional in their pursuits in life. A true renaissance man."

I had no idea where this was heading, but I slurped it all up and breathed it all in like Dexter Flynt did his cold beers and pot.

"Chauncey Forrest and I were just talking about that while we watched practice today. How important it is to aspire to excellence on all levels of one's education."

He was quiet then, for a full minute as we approached the edge of the park, almost to the parking lot at Champions' Hall. He stopped.

"I'll tell you what. Why don't you join Mrs. Claxton and me for supper one night next week after practice? When you don't have too much work to do. I'll send around a note with directions and a time. If you can't make it, just buzz my secretary and let me know."

Without waiting for confirmation, he turned and started off toward the beautiful antebellum president's mansion that was a campus landmark. Then he stopped and tossed one more comment my way.

"It will be my honor to visit with you, young man."

Only finding Dexter gone would have made the day any better but no such luck. He was so stoned he slurred his usual greeting.

"Howsh it hangin', She-Pee?"

"Just right, Dexter. Just right."

He was too far gone to notice what a great mood I was in. It wasn't his music or his loud snore when he finally passed out that distracted me from my work that night. It was the memory of Maggie's wispy blonde hair and lilac perfume, the feel of a sweaty red first-defense pullover jersey, and the cultured voice of a gray-headed man in a blue suit echoing in my head. That's what kept getting in my mind's way.

Neither Maw nor Father were as happy as I thought they would be when I called and told them the news about the LSU game.

"Lord, Corey Phil! I just know you are going to get hurt. Get your back broke and be flat on your back the rest of your days and me not able to take care of your father, much less yourself. Lord, Lord!"

"Damn! That really tears it! The line is six points, LSU's way. I can't decide which way to go anyway and now if you're gonna play, that makes it about even for me. Damn!"

"Well, I'm not sure I'll even get into the game. Frank just has . . ."

"Damn! That really tears it! On a red-hot roll and I'm probably gone have to set this one out! Damn!"

Then, in Friday's writing class, only three of us showed up.

Maggie wasn't there. A campus-wide antiwar rally had been called for the day and I assumed that's where everyone had gone. Wheeler seemed personally offended by the absenteeism but he took it out on those of us who had turned our backs on fashionable protest and had shown up.

"I suppose they are all taking part in the big march to end war for all mankind. With their black armbands and their wide-eyed innocence, I'm sure the establishment will crumble before their righteousness." He was actually sneering, angry.

"Well, the tide of academia cannot be set back. Mr. McKay, please read aloud the first passage from Thoreau and analyze it for the class. Such as it is. What is Henry telling us here, Mr. McKay? What does it mean, Mr. McKay? What the fuck does it mean?" He was screaming the words by the time he finished. I just hoped his anger wasn't directed solely at me. The other students squirmed uncomfortably but I began to read and stammer through some kind of answer to his shrill questions.

Halfway through, he waved at me to stop. Waved disgustedly and slammed his fist down on the table. Two books bounced off with the force of the blow.

"Not even on the same planet with Thoreau and his ideas, Mr. McKay. Not even in the same universe." God. He seemed to have tears in his eyes and his hand holding the textbook trembled. "Clifford had the correct take on Thoreau. Clifford understood what he was trying to tell us. Ecology be damned! Clifford understood there was so much more in Thoreau's words."

He dropped the book loudly. Dust scattered at its impact. He removed his glasses. Took a neatly folded handkerchief from his tweed jacket pocket and wiped his eyes. The room was so silent it seemed his last words still echoed. But then his voice was so soft, we could hardly hear it over the quietness.

"But Clifford is not here."

Frat guys played Frisbee on the quad on the other side of the room's windows. Scarlet and gold and chocolate leaves filtered down in the hazy autumn sunshine. Girls in hippie uniforms tacked antiwar posters to light poles. A boy and girl necked enthusiastically under a big oak. From far off, we could just hear the thumping of a public-address system as someone railed against the war to a crowd that cheered at all the appropriate places.

Professor Wheeler slowly gathered his books and papers, stuffed them into his leather briefcase with the broken handle and then walked, defeated, from the classroom. The three of us looked quickly at each other. Then, when we knew enough time had passed for him to be gone, we bolted from the room.

I am sometimes amazed at my own naïveté. I was bright. I had the SATs to prove it. But why didn't I see all that was brewing about me? Was I so modest that I assumed that someone like me could have such little impact? That the forces that were gathering over my head like a tornadic thunderstorm were intended for someone else altogether? Not for someone so insignificant as I, surely. Hindsight is always twenty-twenty.

I never suspected a thing or saw any of it coming. SATs don't measure awareness. Book smarts don't prepare you for blindside catastrophe.

We lost to LSU by eight points, and I didn't play a down. I stood as close to Milligan as I dared just in case the mood struck him and he could get me in before he thought better of it. But he just stared at the field while Frank Short hobbled on his bum ankle, seconds slow to every play. Then Jesse Franklin went in and looked as if he was at the wrong game. Play goes to the left, he was stumbling to the right. Pass play, he was crashing to the wrong side, all by himself, a mile from the quarterback or the offensive receiver he was supposed to be shadowing.

Tack Rankin glared at Max Milligan. Max deflected the look and sent Frank Short back in after new tape had been wound around his swelled ankle. Milligan wouldn't even look at me. I had no idea what was going on.

Father was on the phone before I had dropped my duffel bag back at the dorm. He was crowing, voice stronger than I had heard it in years.

"Hoo boy! They was awful, boy! I knowed I should of took the Tigers. Knowed it. But I figured they was gonna put you in and that would'a cooked my goose. So I laid off. Didn't put nothin' down. That's as good as winnin' five hundred, though, don't you see? Not losin' sometimes is as good as winnin'. When they gonna run Rankin off? Lotsa talk over here says he's on shaky ground. 'Lumni ain't gonna put up with him long."

I grabbed one of Dexter's beers from his little icebox and drank it thirstily as Father rambled on and on.

Max Milligan took me aside before practice Monday. Before most of the team or any of the coaches had made it out onto the field.

"McKay, we stink like fresh-flopped cowshit. We are gonna be lucky to win five games this year, and them are just thanks to Vandy and a few other weak sisters." He looked around, making sure neither Coach Rankin nor any of the others were coming. "Son, I wasn't about to put you into that mess Saturday, no matter what Coach said. We didn't have a chance with our offense sucking wind so bad. There's no reason to waste a year of your eligibility on a lost cause. It ain't fair to you, son. Tack don't see it my way. He wanted to burn you Saturday. Stick you in there just enough that Frank could get taped and back in 'cause he knows Jesse ain't worth a tinker's damn. He's too stupid to get in outta the damn rain. I got my ass scalded about it. I just wanted you to know. Wasn't the smartest thing for me, but you got too good a future to waste a whole year like that."

I believed him. The man was on my side after all.

"You go on back to scout, now. I ain't tellin' you to dog it, but the less the old son of a bitch notices you the rest of the year, the better chance it's gonna be for you to be around for the next four. Trust me on this one, McKay. Trust me."

For some reason, I did.

"And for chrissakes don't mention this little conversation to no-body. Nobody. Coach would like to crucify me already. No need givin' him no more incentive. It may be that the old goat knows he ain't got much longer to go and he wants to cram it all into the next couple of years. Still ain't right to hurt somebody like you to do it. Now, git!"

Disappointed or not, I trotted on over to mimic an all-American from Alabama, our next opponent. For some reason, I felt much better about my not getting into the LSU game.

Wheeler's class that day was just like usual except, for some rea-son, Clifford now sat in the very back, almost as if he wanted to hide from Wheeler behind my broad shoulders. And even though the professor called on everyone else that day, as he usually did, Clifford was not part of the discussion. It was as if he did not exist anymore as long as he stayed back there in my shadow.

Maggie smiled at me when she rushed in, late, just ahead of Wheeler. We didn't talk. When class broke, she was gone. I hoped she had another class immediately, was just in a hurry to get there, and that she wasn't avoiding me after I had turned her down. I was watching her back as she fled and almost didn't hear Professor Wheeler call my name.

"Mr. McKay? A word, please."

My stomach fell. My last submission had gotten another D, and

I had been expecting him to call me up in front of the class, maybe to gloat. I had never gotten a D in my life, much less two consecutively in the same class.

"Yes?"

"I wonder if I could ask you to stop by and see me one evening this week. I'd like to discuss your work."

He sounded almost friendly. Not threatening at all.

"I think I have your office hours here somewhere. . . ."

"No, no. I can't get anything done in the office with all the interruptions. Here's my address. Maybe tomorrow night. Around eight."

He handed me a business card with a street address near the campus already scrawled in his familiar hand on the back. Surely if he was kicking me out of his class, he would have done it at his office or in the classroom. He would have been near help of some kind in case I went berserk, as all athletes are prone to do, of course, and resorted to animal instinct, or if I used my brawn to try to take him apart.

As soon as I burst into the dorm room after practice, Dexter offered me a joint as usual, but this time I took it. He was stunned. I didn't even know how to smoke it, but I tried to do it the way I had seen him do, holding it and sucking in the burning smoke, keeping it in my lungs as long as I could, then spewing it out. I was so confused anyway that I didn't even feel any unusual sensation from the grass. I was as tired as I had ever been in my life.

"All right! Mr. Linebacker's gettin' stoned!" He laughed crazily and rolled on the bed. "Call *High Times*! Get the Grateful Dead on the phone! Mr. Linebacker's gettin' stoned!"

But I was too depleted to yell at him. I must have dozed because he woke me up a while later.

"This came for you, Mr. Doobie Master." He was still laughing at me as he handed me a small envelope.

> *I hope Thursday evening at seven will be a good time for*
> *supper with Mrs. Claxton and me. West-side entrance.*
> *Ring the bell. Looking forward . . .*

> Dr. Grover Claxton

Well, that really cut it! Somehow, I had gotten dates with my writing teacher and the president of my university. But not with Maggie Vinyard. Where, exactly, had I screwed up?

SEVEN

How the hell can writers spend so much time talking about death? Not one of them has ever experienced it and come back to life to tell about it. That's like all the many writers and poets who poured out their souls through the ages, screaming about their love for women, when they were in reality gay, their sonnets and couplets intended more for George than Mary. Or writers dissecting the reality of life when they stayed too drunk or too stoned to ever really experience much of their time sober on this planet. Coleridge, Hemingway, Faulkner, Poe. What could they tell us besides what the world looked like through the bottom of a glass?

Just because I'm now the world's greatest authority on death, though, certainly makes me no expert on life. God knows, I didn't get to live very much of it, and just when I did, it got shut off so quickly I only got a bittersweet taste.

My short matriculation at Sparta University was a yo-yo, and Professor Langston Wheeler just the latest one to jerk me around. Tuesday practice was pure hell. We would run five plays, then do wind sprints in full pads until everyone was retching. Then we'd do five more of the plays that we planned to run against Alabama. Then more gassers until we dropped. If someone blew an assignment or fumbled the ball or muffed an easy pass, the coaches screamed like banshees and had us bear-walking until we fell over. And the hell included everybody. Starters, scrubs, scout team. The defense, at the far end of the practice field, was on the same death march as we were. Only the wounded were spared, and it looked like triage for medevac in Vietnam as the ranks of the injured grew alarmingly.

Tack Rankin stayed high atop his tower in the middle of the field, between offense and defense, glaring down like God from his throne. We knew if any of us let up, he'd be down on top of us in a second. And you didn't want to be the object of Coach's wrath if he climbed down just for you. Player or coach or trainer. It didn't matter. Legend had it, he had once fired a line coach on the spot after scurrying down from his perch and that he had punched a halfback right in the face.

It was gut-check time. When we ran plays it was full speed, full contact. And it was vicious. At least two starters went down early, one with an exploded knee, another with a broken leg. Most were bleeding. All of us were scraped, cut, bruised. Even with his starting center writhing on the ground clutching his fractured leg, Rankin just stared down from the tower, then motioned impatiently for the training staff to get the man out of the way so we could run our next set of wind sprints before catching our breath.

The hot shower set every scrape and gash I had on fire, but the water seemed to heal a bit. So did the knowledge that tomorrow would not be nearly so bad, until the assistant coaches moved through the dressing rooms with the news that tomorrow would be full pads, too, with more contact. Nobody said anything. Nobody complained or even groaned. Nobody knew who might be listening, making notes of who wasn't willing to do whatever was necessary for the team. Whatever it took to win.

I let the walk home dry my hair, and was glad Dexter was off at a party. I was in no mood to listen to his craziness or explain exactly where it was I was bound that night. I wouldn't have had time for much chatting, anyway. Practice had lasted until almost seven. I was due at Wheeler's at eight. Painfully, I put on a long-sleeve shirt, as much to hide the bruises and cuts on my forearms as to stay warm, and actually moaned aloud with pain when I bent my knotted legs to pull on a pair of jeans.

The fresh, cool-approaching-cold mountain air felt good as it settled into my lungs. The exertion of walking eased the ache in my legs. It was a brilliant night, the sky a field of winking stars, and just a hint of an icy wind promised cold weather soon. I suddenly felt strong. Almost invincible. Even my sore muscles were powerful and responded to my commands to move and flex and propel me. The air cleared my head and I felt I could flex even my brain, make it perform feats of strength, too.

I vowed not to let Rankin or Wheeler or anybody else sap my self-confidence. I was an athlete. I was a scholar. They couldn't take either away from me.

Langston Wheeler's house was a small bungalow across a short stretch of browning, weed-dotted lawn and behind huge, ragged boxwood bushes. The steps were almost hidden by the overgrown foliage, and even in the starlight, I could see moss clinging to the house's roof. A torn screen door led to an enclosed porch, its cement floor cracked, paint peeling from trim and walls as well as the front door. I checked the number again. Pulitzer Prize–winning college professors should be able to afford more than this.

When I pushed the doorbell, there was only silence. I could hear no ringing inside. So I knocked lightly on the door. Panes of glass rattled loosely. Finally there were the muffled sounds of footsteps approaching.

Professor Wheeler seemed genuinely glad to see me. He smiled, said, "Hello, Mr. McKay . . . please, please come in," shook my hand vigorously and ushered me past stacks of books and papers that lined the tiny foyer. He was dressed casually, T-shirt, madras Bermuda shorts, sandals. The man who wore coats and sweaters on the hottest late-summer days now was half-naked on the coolest night of the fall so far. I wondered in what other ways this man might be out of synch with everything and everyone else around him.

He motioned me to a chair, then moved more books from the corner of a coffee table to make room for a glass.

"What would you like, Mr. McKay? Scotch? It's my drink of choice."

"Sure. Scotch's fine." I had never tasted the stuff but was polite enough to give it a try.

Wheeler disappeared through a doorway to what was apparently a kitchen and there was the ringing of glasses and ice and the clinks of a bottleneck on rims. The small room was packed with books and papers and bound volumes that appeared to be thesis after thesis. Furniture was under it all somewhere, but I could see no TV. A living room with no television! Imagine that.

"May I call you by your first name?" he asked, setting the auburn liquid on the coffee table's edge. He sat in the only empty place on a couch across from me.

"Sure. That's fine."

He took a noisy, thirsty slurp of his drink. The rattling of the ice cubes was the only other sound in the room and even that was deadened by all the stacks of printed matter that seemed to wall us in. I tried a sip of my drink and immediately likened its taste to some of Maw's harsh cough syrup, but I smacked and tried to give an impression of approval.

"Uh, what is it? Your first name, I mean."

"Corinthians."

He looked at me blankly.

"My folks wanted a name out of the Bible. I guess Mark or John was too common. Corinthians Phillipians McKay. They were really into the New Testament. Saint Paul. His churches. Letters to the followers and all. I've read up on it, since it looks like I'll be blessed with the name the rest of my life."

He still seemed to be confused.

"But most people call me C.P."

"Fine. C.P. it is, then. Since I hope we are friends by now. Please call me Langston." He smiled slightly. I couldn't imagine calling him Langston. "I'm afraid I'm not much on religion. I have to research any references in my work, and frankly, it bores the hell out of me. It's all quite unbelievable, actually. Supreme being, quick to anger at the frailties of the very creatures he himself created. Hardly likely, I'd say."

"I'll admit to similar thoughts myself."

"Good! Keep an open mind!" Taking another surprisingly long swallow of his drink, he appeared to be just a little uncomfortable. He looked around and seemed to notice the scholarly clutter in the room for the first time. "Please excuse my mess, C.P. I have this place leased the rest of the school year, then who knows? I have had some inquiries from an Ivy League school and one on the West Coast. They'd give me more money, more time to work on the next project. Pulitzers have a knack for allowing advancement. And I confess I fully intend to capitalize on the notoriety."

"I hate for you to leave as soon as I get here," I said sincerely.

"Oh, I suppose I'll be here awhile. Things move slowly, indeed, behind the ivy-covered walls."

"Good. The letter you wrote me, your being here at all, that's the prime reason I came to Sparta."

"Letter?" He looked confused again. Even more so than he was by my silly name a few minutes before.

"The one you sent by Coach Rankin. When he recruited me."

"I've never spoken to Coach Rankin in my life!" He seemed genuinely angered. "And what did my eloquent letter say, may I ask?"

"Just that you were excited about someone of my ability possibly choosing to attend Sparta University. And to want to be a part of the writing program. That's all." My face was burning. I felt as if it were I who had forged the letter, simply because I had believed it.

He held the glass against his cheek and looked into space for a moment.

"I've heard rumors the bastard would stop at nothing to get the young studs he wants. Such deceit would be in character, I suppose. Well, I'm flattered I helped convince you to attend our fine university, however unbeknownst to me my efforts might have been." He chuckled, took another generous slug of the whiskey and visibly relaxed, shoulders slumping, sliding down amid the volumes that surrounded him.

"Did you read my book?"

"Yes. Yes, I did. Twice."

"Out of necessity or because you enjoyed it?"

"Oh, I truly enjoyed it. I identified with Charlie totally. He seemed to have my thoughts so often it was frightening."

Wheeler's prize-winning book, *Blue Day, Gray Night,* was the story of a young man from the North who went to a southern military school in the mid-1800s, simply because it offered him the best education available, and despite the fact that he despised anything military. But when the Civil War broke out, he was drafted into the Confederate army along with everyone else at the school. He found himself being asked to fight against his own former neighbors, even the brothers of his fiancée. I could feel the character's torment. Of course the novel impressed me. And it had obviously impressed the Pulitzer folks.

Langston Wheeler suddenly leaned forward, touched my knee quickly with his free hand.

"Yes. Of course there would be common ground. A man torn between perceived duty and desire for learning. For taking the offered education but being asked to kill in return."

"Well, nobody's asked me to kill anybody yet. . . ."

"Metaphorically speaking, of course," he chuckled again, and once more tapped me on the knee. "Here, let me get you another drink. Your ice has melted and ruined that one."

He swiped the glass and disappeared again. For some reason, I was growing uneasy. Something was poised to happen. The five-foot-high piles of manuscripts and books seemed to be leaning toward me, holding me captive, shutting out most of the room's oxygen and light.

"Let's talk about you, C.P.," he said, again setting the full glass on the dusty table. This time he sat on the end of the couch closest to me. "Let me apologize for being so rough on you at our first meeting. I had no idea we had corresponded already."

He laughed as if he had made a great joke, and punched my shoulder. I forced a small laugh myself, but his lick had been right on target, smack on a lingering bruise from that day's hellacious practice.

"Surely you must know it is the task of any academician to challenge his charges to excellence. If you had simply accepted my rebuff and fled, it would have been obvious you did not belong in my classroom in the first place. You weren't intimidated at all. I greatly admire the fire you demonstrated, if not the choice of 'bullshit' as the most appropriate description of my methods."

Again he laughed uproariously and punched, but I dodged, and the blow just glanced off an uninjured part of my shoulder. I took another sip of the bitter liquid while he got control.

"C.P., I'll be candid. You have shown me promise, great promise."

"Well, thank you very much. I value your opinion." And I did. His words, along with the scotch, made my emotions soar.

"Of course, it's hidden well and you will have to work hard to allow it to come to the forefront. In all modesty, I think if you will follow my lead, listen to me, do as I ask, you have a wonderful chance to do well in my class. And your entire academic career as well. You will have to humor me my idiosyncrasies, though. My peccadilloes. I'll help you accomplish great things if we can only work closely together. Go into this relationship working together from the beginning. You have an excellent mind. Anyone who enjoyed my book so much would naturally have an excellent mind."

He laughed softly, no punch this time, then turned up the big glass of scotch and drained it dry. I saw that it brought tears to his eyes.

"C.P., I greatly admire someone like you. Clear thinking is a gift. A rare gift. The ability to express and interpret those thoughts on the written page is a gift also. And to be blessed with athletic ability as you are is almost unfair. You are, indeed, quite a package. A truly beautiful package."

He had leaned toward me again, and now his hand rested on my knee. I didn't draw back. I didn't know what to do. He had just given me the highest praise I had ever received. And coming from someone of his stature, someone I had admired so much, I was stunned. Even if that someone was obviously more than a little drunk.

"C.P., you profess a great affection for the Romantic poets." He suddenly stood, walked around behind me, and put his hands on my shoulders. I held the whiskey glass in one hand, scratched a sudden itch on my jaw with the other. The few drops of whiskey I had sipped were now burning in my empty stomach like hot coals, acid rising almost to my throat. "Romantic poets. Love couplets for each other as much as for the women they pretended to desire. I share your admiration for the fluid, easy way they blended their passion and captured it in rhyme and meter. The way they transferred their obsessions to the page. Why do you think it is so difficult for a man to express his desires for another, C.P.?"

He was softly kneading the taut muscles along my shoulders and neck. I was too surprised to stop him. And, to be honest, his fingers were finding exactly the spots that most needed massaging.

"Why do we have to rely on the words of enlightened men who lived a hundred years ago to express the emotions and desires we find impossible to put into our own words? We who make our living and our life with words and ideas? Why do you think that is, C.P.?"

"I don't know." The burning acid in my throat made my words thick.

"Ironic, isn't it? We can interpret what others have written, dissect their symbolism and every nuance of their verse, write endlessly about them in our scholarly journals, but we go tongue-tied when we try to say the right thing. When we can't string together the words that would make our intentions clear to the ones who really matter to us."

His fingertips touched my cheek. I fought the immediate urge to cock a fist and throw it at his face. His lips were now near my left ear, and he was still spewing the nonsense that was beginning to run together like slurred poetry. His sour whiskey breath was hot on my neck.

Instead, I carefully leaned forward and set my glass back on the wet ring amid the dust of the coffee table. I slowly stood and turned to face him. His hands were still poised in midair where they had been before I pulled away from him. His body leaned slightly forward, head tilted to where my ear had been. Defenseless, he could have been clocked then and there and left bleeding, rebuked cruelly.

"I have curfew and probably need to get back to the dorm now."

The excuse sounded so lame I almost giggled. It was barely eight-thirty. He stood straight then, dropped his hands, slid them into the pockets of his shorts, hiding behind the high back of the chair I had just vacated.

"Yes. And no doubt you have classwork to complete."

"No doubt."

"Well. I . . . uh . . . appreciate your coming by tonight, C.P. I hope we have made some headway in our . . . uh . . . relationship." Man of letters, master of language, stammering like a high-school sophomore.

"I appreciate your comments."

"Please keep in mind what I said, C.P. Please. I think you will have a very successful academic career if you . . . apply yourself."

He smiled crookedly, idly took a hand from his pocket, scratched his stomach, and finally shifted his sharp eyes away from me.

"Okay." I was moving toward the foyer, trying not to obviously bolt.

"Let's get together again soon. Maybe I could fix a little pasta or something for us. You've got to be tired of dorm food."

"Well, actually . . . sure. Maybe so."

"Good night, then. . . ."

My indigestion was growing, pushing, burning. I left him standing in the foyer and accidentally slammed the screen door loudly behind me as I danced hastily across the porch and down the front steps. I didn't look back until I had cleared the end of the block. He was still standing there, outlined in the light coming from behind him. I dove between two bushes next to the Language Arts building and vomited thick, stinging bile against the wall until I had purged myself.

I was shaking with a chill by the time I trotted up the front steps of Champions' Hall. Then, as I forced one foot in front of the other up the stairs, I was surprised to see two offensive players I knew only by sight coming out of my room. One carried a small paper sack.

I spoke, and they returned nervous nods, looking up and down the hallway as if they had been caught in the act of doing something they should not have been doing. The one with the sack shoved it into his letterman jacket pocket. Music throbbed from the room as I opened the door. It was dark inside except for the eerie glow of Dexter's lava lamp, and he was dancing wildly, galloping, doing "the pony" in the middle of his bed. He had not even had a chance to put away the money. It lay, twisted into a rubber band–wrapped bundle like a coiled rattler in the middle of my own bed.

"Hey, C.P., my main man! I thought you had a date tonight," he screamed over the wailing blues guitar of Duane Allman. The darkness, the blaring music, my nausea . . . it all combined to make me dizzy and disoriented.

"Teacher conference. No date." I slammed the door behind me, slapped on the overhead-light switch, found the stereo volume knob and angrily twisted it down.

"Hey, man! That's a great riff! What you . . ."

"What the hell is going on here, Dexter?"

He collapsed on the bed, grabbed a pillow and stuffed it under his head. He knew I had seen the guys leaving, and that I saw the money on my bed.

"Good old American free enterprise, my man. I'm a marketing major, right. I'm conducting my own little laboratory. On-the-job training. I'm just the middle man and I'm supplying the goods to an eager marketplace."

"You're dealing drugs in the damned athletic dorm."

"Hmmm. Crass way of putting it, Mr. McKay. I'm just meeting a need. And making a hell of a lot of money doing it, I might add. If I don't, somebody else will. And don't tell me you didn't know what was going on. That basketball player kicked my ass because my customers kept him awake at night. And because I couldn't get the steroids he wanted from my supplier. And man, I've been doing some fine business since I moved in here, what with you at the library or practice or suckin' up to your teachers all the time."

"Correct me if I'm wrong," I said as I collapsed on my own bed, stomach still rolling, shaking with chills, feverish. "But couldn't you do jail time if you get caught? Did you ever think of that?"

"I won't get caught. And if I do, I'll have enough salted away that a few years' jail time will be more than worth it. Besides, I'm a lot of people's best friend right now. Lots of people. I'm a very popular man around here these days, Mr. Football."

Frankly, the fight had left me. I ached all over and felt like I was going to throw up again. Dexter rolled to an elbow.

"C.P., my man. You look like death warmed over. You sick?"

"As a dawg."

"Here, try a couple of these."

He reached under the bed, slid out his briefcase, pulled out a pill bottle and tossed it my way. I didn't even read the label. I just took two of the capsules and swallowed them dry. Soon I slept a hot, painful sleep. And all night I dreamed that Maggie Vinyard was calling my name, reaching out to me from behind a veil of sheer blonde silk. But every time I reached for her, it was Langston Wheeler who leaned to kiss me.

EIGHT

Was I reading too much into the way Professor Langston Wheeler looked at me in class that next day? Was it just my imagination or was he fastballing everybody else with his usual smoking questions, while lobbing up big, airy, softballs for me to hit out of the park when it was my turn at bat? I wondered all day why I had not shoved him away, popped him with a forearm, coldcocked him, told him in no uncertain terms to take his poetic interpretation of the Romantics and put it where the sun never shines.

On one level, I had convinced myself I was just protecting my own best interests. Frankly, I couldn't afford to fail this class. Or to mess in my nest. I was learning. I was finding the give and take in his class wonderful and enlightening. But on another level, I was scared to death that I had actually been flattered by his seduction, complimented by his awkward moves.

God! Don't let it be so! Hell, yes, I was sensitive to it. Damned sensitive. Others had subtly accused me of it since junior high because I was bookish and studious, preferred reading to deer hunting, the library to a pool hall.

One thing was for sure, though. The way I felt when Maggie Vinyard walked into the class that morning was definitely the reaction of a heterosexual male. She wore a plaid blouse, open at the neck, tight jeans, her hair pulled back from her ears but long and flowing down her back. The smile she threw me warmed the entire room.

"How ya doin', Mr. McKay?" she asked as she slid into the seat next to mine and opened her textbook.

"Fantastic!" Her smile and Dexter's mystery pills had helped divert the virus or whatever it was that had attacked me the night before. "Now, anyway."

"You been sick?"

"Nah. Just working hard at practice and all. Studying a lot, too."

"Yeah. I guess. Look, I was wondering. What we talked about? If we could get together this week, maybe. Talk about class, you know. Writing. I got an F on the last essay. And I can't afford to fail. If it's okay with you, that is?"

She had lowered her eyes, her voice too, as if she was reluctant to ask again. As if she was leaving herself dangerously vulnerable by doing so. That one little gesture pushed me right over the edge. I knew then that I was definitely falling for this woman I hardly knew.

"Actually, I would like that very much, Maggie." There. I didn't care if my eagerness showed.

"Great! How about tomorrow night, around suppertime . . . ?" She had looked up at me again, but the expression on my face must have stopped her cold and taken the legs right out from under her enthusiasm.

"Oh, damn. I have to go to dinner with President Claxton tomorrow night." I tried to make it sound like I had been drafted for combat duty in 'Nam.

She slammed the book so hard every head in the class turned

from their gossip and looked to see who had fired the shot in the back of the room. Clifford, eavesdropping from the seat in front of mine, giggled once and covered his mouth with a skinny hand.

"Look, Mr. McKay. If you don't want to leave your thick-necked football buddies or your cheerleaders or your fraternity parties long enough to help me, that's perfectly all right, but don't feel like you have to make up some ridiculous cock-and-bull excuse that insults my intelligence. . . ."

Langston Wheeler broke off her tirade when he entered the room. The other students had been enjoying her anger as I quickly suffered a relapse of my chills and fever from the night before.

Then it was second grade all over again. The girl I liked was mad at me. I had to sneak looks at the teacher while I scribbled her a note on lined notebook paper and waited to pass it over to her.

> *Maggie: It is true! I do have to meet with Claxton. We're locked in Friday night and the game Saturday is late for TV. Sunday? Will Sunday be okay?*

One of our classmates struggled through a winding interpretation of symbolism in Faulkner. While Wheeler was distracted, reveling in the poor guy's flailing, I reached quickly and slid the folded paper under her hand. She glared, but finally undid it, read it, and looked at me cautiously. I smiled.

She only half smiled but her lips formed a hesitant "okay." She didn't look at me again. Wheeler had just punched her with an impossible, convoluted question and she was staggered. Then, when class was over, she was up and out and gone so quickly I had to rush to try to catch her. I thought I felt Wheeler looking at my back. When I turned abruptly he was indeed watching me. He gave a quick nod of the head and a hint of a smile. I hoped to be the only person who had seen it.

"Maggie!"

She ran better than some halfbacks I had chased.

"I've got to hurry, Mr. McKay. Sunday is fine. How about Drake's? Seven o'clock?" Drake's was a restaurant, a block off campus. It was supposed to have great hamburgers.

"That's great. I'll see . . ."

She disappeared through the bushes as she had done before. I stood amid the leaves and darting students watching the spot where she had gone. Suddenly, she was back.

"What is your first name, anyway?"

"C.P. Call me C.P."

"C.P.? What does that stand . . ."

"Trust me. You don't have time right now."

She smiled and was off again at a trot.

The girl had a real knack for jumping out of my life in a big hurry. Oh well. Hell awaited me anyway. I couldn't remember the last time I dreaded practicing football. I loved the game, even the endless grueling practices, but another day like the one before left me paralyzed just thinking about it.

It was worse than I had feared. Full-speed. Uncontrolled mayhem. Running our guts out. A cold, steady rain began an hour into the practice, setting the mood for everyone. Even as hard as we were working, over the yelling of the coaches and the constant bleating of their whistles, we couldn't help but hear the ominous groans of the players and then the horrible screams of agony from someone who had obviously been hurt badly over on the defensive side of the field. I sneaked a look through the haze and fog and lumbering linemen, but I couldn't tell who was squirming in the mud. I knew it was bad, and I hoped it wasn't Elgie. He was about the only one over there I knew well enough to care for.

A buddy or two bent over the player and everybody else stood at a distance, as if the injury might jump over to them. Then the offense was back to the line of scrimmage, ready to run at us again and I wasn't able to watch anymore.

It was obvious who it was that was hurt, though, when Max Milligan trotted over between plays and screamed my name.

"McKay! Quit loafing over there and come help us out a minute. Anytime before dark's okay, so don't hurry or nothin'."

Trainers worked over Frank Short but they were having trouble keeping him on the ground. He kept reaching for his leg and I could see it was bent at an odd angle halfway between knee and ankle. Snapped almost in half like a rotten piece of wood. I felt sick. Milligan put his arm around me as we walked toward the defensive huddle and spoke softly into the earhole of my helmet.

"Well, you wanted your break, darlin', you got it. Dumb ol' bastard going full-speed this time of year is crazy as the dickens. We be lucky to have enough players to dress out a full squad against Alabama. Ain't no way I'm gonna be able to save your year now, son. Give it your best and don't waste it."

We only ran another half dozen plays. With me swapping out every other one with Jesse Franklin, it was over before I realized I was about to be thrown into the thick of the battle against Alabama in three days.

Those of us who could still stay on our feet ran wind sprints until dark caught us. Coach Rankin called us to a big huddle in the middle of the muddy, bloody practice field.

"I told you that I hate losing. I will not lose. I will not let you forsake yourselves and your school again. We will beat Georgia on Saturday."

One of the other coaches almost corrected him, told him it was Alabama we were playing Saturday, but then thought better of it. It had been a long-enough day already.

"If you need treatment, get to the training room. Get in early tomorrow. Sweats and helmets. It'll be a learning day. We'll be getting mentally ready from this point on. We're physically ready now."

I glanced at the thin ranks. At least five starters were hobbled; most everyone else was whipped and beaten. Then he led us in a team prayer and we were gone.

The drizzle continued so I was soaked by the time I got back to the dorm. Dexter was sound asleep, snoring loudly. He had ranted and raved and pranced all night the night before, but I had been so exhausted, sick and knocked wacky by his medicine that I had hardly been aware of him. I dried off again, put on my only dress shirt, tie, sport coat, and my only pair of khaki pants. They were all too big. I must have lost twenty pounds since I got to Sparta.

The president's mansion was an antebellum-style home that covered most of the block. Huge columns rose from freshly clipped foliage and a massive chandelier beamed from the foyer inside the front door. I took the brick path past banks of chrysanthemums to the side doorway. A doorbell button was practically hidden by climbing rosebushes. It rang softly inside when I touched it. A black woman in a maid's uniform opened the door a few inches.

"Mr. McKay. To see President Claxton. Invited, I was."

"Certainly, sir. Please come in."

She led me past rooms filled with what appeared to be antique furniture, up a small staircase and through a doorway into a parlor or sitting room. The couch was so plush I almost lost my balance when I settled into it.

"Would you like some tea or coffee, sir?"

"Tea would be fine. Thank you."

I sat in the quietness, listening to the big clock tick loudly on the fireplace mantel. The only other sound was a soft rush of air from floor vents as they warmed the room. The maid was back immediately, carrying a tray with a single cup on it. I took it, sure she had brought me coffee anyway. No. It was hot tea. I had assumed she meant iced tea. I was almost nineteen years old and had never tasted hot tea, but I slurped some from the cup, ignored it when the hot liquid scalded my tongue, and pretended to enjoy it as the maid retreated.

Two quiet minutes later, she was back.

"Sir, Mr. and Mrs. Claxton are waiting for you at the dinner table. Won't you follow me, please?"

We wound through a short maze of halls and small rooms and entered a massive dining room with a table at least twenty feet long in the middle. Dr. Claxton rose from his chair at one end, while an old withered woman kept her seat to his right, head down. I shook hands with him. The maid pulled out the chair to his left, indicating my seat. I had been afraid I was supposed to be at the far end of the table and I wasn't sure I had the strength to carry on a conversation from that distance after the day's practice.

"Mrs. Claxton and I are so glad you could join us, Mr. McKay," he said, smiling and pumping my hand. The older woman just sat, staring at her lap. "Yes, it is far too rare for us to have a chance to meet with our students on such a personal level. Isn't that right, dear?"

"Yes." She spoke, and finally moved, as if the question had shaken her from her reverie. She reached for a glass of red liquid and turned it up, drained it, then sharply struck the table with it twice. The maid instantly appeared and filled it to the brim. She turned it up and drank half in one gulp.

Grover Claxton was rambled on about students, school, how big the university had grown, how impersonal, how he wished he could still get into the classroom again. Botany. That had been his field. Botany. How much he missed the give-and-take with eager students. Even grading exams. Reading research papers. Many don't like that. He did. Missed it every day now that he was chained to administration. Dealing with the board of trustees. Begging for money from the legislature. From donors. Endowments. Underwriters. Estates. Staff. Budgets. Not what he had chosen an academic career to do at all. But it was a challenge. A real challenge.

"I envy you very much, son. Just beginning your journey of discovery." The maid had set flat dishes covered with lettuce and purple stuff in front of us. I watched his actions to see how to eat it and almost forgot to spread the thick cloth napkin in my lap first. Mrs. Claxton ignored the salad but took big, noisy swallows of her wine. "Oh, to be eighteen again with the whole world before me. What is your proposed field of study, young man?" He talked with his mouth full, food flying, but I was so busy trying to spear the limp lettuce that it didn't bother me.

"Creative writing. Literary criticism. Something in that area."

"Excellent! Fantastic!" He threw down his fork with a rattle and slapped me on the shoulder. His salad was gone. I had so far only managed to corner a cherry tomato and its juice had squirted all over my tie when I stuck it. "Absolutely perfect!"

"Thank you, sir." I didn't know what else to say. Mrs. Claxton was banging her glass on the table again and I noticed for the first time how yellow she was. Just plain yellow. The maid was taking my plate and Dr. Claxton pounded my shoulder again.

"Chauncey Forrest and I were just talking yesterday about young men like you, Mr. McKay. Do you know who Chauncey Forrest is?"

"I assume the man you were with at practice yesterday."

"Yes indeed. And one of the finest alumni of Sparta University, too. He was one of our two Rhodes Scholars, you know. Brought great honor and recognition to the school. And he has been one of our greatest benefactors down through the years. He's an heir to the Forrest paper-products fortune, you see."

"Yessir." The maid had set a huge plate in front of me. A tiny dot that looked like some kind of meat was encircled with what looked like slivers of raw squash and a few hairy bean sprouts. It all resembled a small lonely face, frowning in the middle of a giant china head. Again, I followed Dr. Claxton's lead, carefully trying to carve the meat with a big knife while I held it in place with my fork. I could have finished it in one bite. Carving was just being polite.

"He was responsible for the refurbishing we did on the Language Arts building, you know. Paid for the entire foreign-language lab himself and he's endowing the chair for translation studies. Yes, Chauncey Forrest is a great friend of Sparta University."

Try as I might, I couldn't get the tiny piece of rubber meat cut into pieces, so I spent time idly turning the squash slivers over and back, pretending to chew, sipping the now-lukewarm tea occasionally. Mrs. Claxton had gotten her drink refill and I noticed she had slipped lower in her chair and was in real danger of sliding under the table. I was not at all sure what reaction on my part to such an occurrence would be most polite. Oh well, I'd just follow old Grover Claxton's lead on that one, too.

"Tell Charles everything was absolutely delicious, as usual, Gloria," he was saying to the maid, who was snatching up our plates briskly. "Mr. McKay, what say you and I take our dessert in the parlor and talk a moment or two, then I'll allow you to return to your studies."

"Fine sir. Delicious meal. Really enjoyed it." I started to speak to Mrs. Claxton, but she was bent over, face almost touching the tablecloth.

We returned to the room in which I had waited earlier. Claxton motioned me to a chair and he took one near me. Close enough to cuff me on the shoulder again if he got carried away, I noticed.

"I'm going to be honest with you, Mr. McKay. I am very impressed with someone of your ability. It is very rare to find someone with your combination of scholarship and athleticism. Rare indeed." He loosened his tie, and the gesture struck me as being as out of character for him as a belch might have been. "Let's talk turkey. Son, I believe you have every potential to become our next Rhodes Scholar here at Sparta University."

"Why, thank you, sir. Thank you." Damn! I was flattered!

"And do you have any idea how important that would be to our school?" He hesitated. "Oh, and to you and your future, too, of course. You know what a great emphasis the selection places on well-rounded individuals. And I'm confident you offer them exactly what they look for."

He sat back as if he had finished whatever it was he had to say. I could only offer another thank you and wait for him to talk again. The clock was ticking loudly. Gloria appeared as if on cue with a tray containing two saucers which held minute slices of cake and two cups of black coffee.

"Jiminy, Gloria. All this food! I won't be able to eat for a week!" He immediately gobbled up the cake and took most of the coffee in one swallow. Suddenly he leaned forward and spoke again.

"Here's the bottom line, son. Chauncey Forrest has committed an amount of money to this university that absolutely staggers the mind. Millions of dollars. Millions. It would be enough to complete the Language Arts annex, endow several chairs, add our Chemistry building we have needed so long, establish research fellowships galore, build a library wing . . . well, we could get any number of ambitious projects off the drawing board and into fruition. And once other donors see what he has done, it will snowball. Snowball, son! To the point we will no longer be just a football factory. No longer be the whipping boy of those effete Ivy League snobs. We could be a shining jewel of southern higher education. Number one in something besides football and draft-dodgers!"

A cake crumb flew from his mouth and over my shoulder. I held my position, though, and didn't duck. He was wild-eyed in his enthusiasm, but suddenly sat back and seemed to relax.

"But here's the catch, son. And there is always a catch, it seems." He chuckled, and it was as false as the tie-loosening. "He is withholding the generous philanthropy until we once again have a Rhodes Scholar representing Sparta University. It's that simple. He told me again yesterday. The day the scholarship is awarded, he will deliver me the signed check."

Mrs. Claxton suddenly appeared at the parlor door, walking slowly, half staggering toward the stairs at the edge of the parlor.

"Good night, dear," her husband sang.

"Good night, Mrs. Claxton. Thank you for the hospitality," I said.

"Yes," she gurgled, and made a slow, hesitant climb up and away from us.

"Obviously, this is where you come in, Mr. McKay. You have an excellent academic record from secondary school. Your entrance scores are exemplary. You are clearly a superior athlete or Coach Rankin would not have you here. Do you have any idea how long we have waited for someone with your obvious proficiency in both areas to matriculate here at Sparta? My, how long!"

He paused again. Gloria had filled our cups again and he took another big drink of the coffee, as if steeling himself for some momentous task. My cup was empty, my saucer devoid of any more cake. I must have finished them already, although I had absolutely no memory of having done so.

"Now," he finally said. "As to the future. Please understand that I fully expect you to fulfill the scholarly promise you have shown. No doubt in my mind. And if you do, there is no way the Rhodes Scholarship will not be yours. And Mr. Forrest's bequest will be ours. But . . ."

He scratched at the backs of his hands. Rubbed his knees. Licked his lips. Took a sip from the empty cup of coffee and swallowed as if he had actually drunk something.

"I want you to fully understand what I am about to tell you, son. If you work hard, apply yourself, excel at your athletic career, develop academically . . ." He cleared his throat. ". . . we will make certain you will not fail."

"Exactly what are you saying, Dr. Claxton?" His tics and gestures made me nervous.

"Don't misunderstand. I am simply saying that each of your instructors will most definitely be expecting only your best work. But so much of your curriculum is graded so damned subjectively. Not like my beloved botany. Or mathematics or science. They are exact. Cut and dried. Black and white. But literature. So often it is merely the opinion of the individual instructor as to whether the student has accomplished his assignment correctly. So damned subjective!"

I couldn't believe what he was saying. At least what I thought he was saying.

"And all I am telling you is that your instructors will be aware of what you will be trying to achieve, and of its importance to the university."

"But are you telling me you will ask my teachers to . . . ?"

"Please! Don't misunderstand, Mr. McKay. I am only telling you that you must do your best. You must excel. We are only going to make sure that one or two professors don't get their noses out of joint or come to class someday in a bad mood or have some slight disagreement with you over some thesis you may be called upon to defend and ruin a good thing for everyone concerned. That's all I'm telling you. They will be utterly fair with you."

For some reason, for the second time that week I felt that someone was trying to rape me.

"I suppose I should get back, sir. I have an essay."

"Very good." He stood, shook my hand, followed me down the hallway pointing the way through the maze to the side door. "I'm glad we had this chance to talk. You are a very important student to Sparta University, Mr. McKay. I don't think you will let us down."

He shook my hand again and I trotted away into the cold fog. Halfway across the flower-dotted lawn of the beautiful mansion, I turned to look back. The president of Sparta University stood in the doorway, silhouetted by the light from inside, watching me disappear into the mist.

NINE

knew they'd come to their senses. I knew it! About time somebody up there showed the sense God gave a billy goat!"

"But Father. I don't think I'd be playing at all if Frank hadn't . . ."

"Hot damn! Tell your maw howdy real quick and let me get the bet down before everybody and his brother finds out about it and the line goes sky-high."

"Father. I think we have a chance to beat them."

"Y'all beat Alabama? Bear Bryant? Do you think so?"

"Yeah. I do."

I could hear him thinking, breathing hard into the telephone. I had really called to tell them they could finally come up to Sparta for the game, use the press-box seats Coach Rankin had promised. Not just sell the tickets I had been sending them for God knows how much money. I wanted them to know that I would get to play my first downs of defense for Sparta University against the Crimson Tide. No telling how much, but I would play. It seemed like decades since I had been in a real game, not just eleven months. And this would be big-time. Southeastern Conference. NCAA. Against one of the legendary teams in the college game. Alabama!

"Know what, boy? You may just be right. The line's at ten points their way already, and when everybody hears about all the players that's out of the game, it'll go to eighteen at least. And with you playing . . ."

Maw was less than happy about the whole turn of events. She didn't share my excitement at all.

"What did you say happened to the other boy, Corey Phil? The one you're gonna go in for? Broke his leg?"

"Yes ma'am."

"Oh, Jesus! I pray every night that you don't get hurt, darlin'. Pray to God that He'll keep you safe. Such a rough game."

"Aw, it's okay, Maw. I'm in the best shape I've ever been in. We've got good trainers. They take good care of us." I didn't tell her I'd lost over twenty pounds and my stomach hurt all the time.

"I'm dependin' on your guardian angel, Corey Phil. You're in the hands of the Lord, and His angel won't let nothin' bad happen. I gotta believe in that, at least."

I still got nervous every time she talked of guardian angels and such. If she started humming that damned lullaby, I was hanging up the phone immediately. Of course, I didn't tell them of my private audience with President Claxton that week. I doubted if they would know who he was anyway.

It was almost impossible to keep my mind on Western Civilization lectures that droned on and on while my fellow scholars snored all around me. The other classes were just a blur the rest of the week. Even Wheeler's usually stimulating give-and-take seemed halfhearted that Friday.

Maggie wasn't in class, either. I had wanted to tell her of my field promotion and see if she had any interest in using one of my tickets and maybe coming to the game. Even with her low opinion of athletes, who knows? But she was absent. I hoped our date was still on for Sunday night, because I was thinking about her almost as much as the upcoming game.

The team was to go through our usual pregame ritual on Friday night: hotel, movie, in bed by eleven. Dexter watched me pack my duffel bag while he smoked a joint and listened to The Who at full volume. He had become even more open with his drug dealing since I had walked in on him earlier that week. Other players, people I didn't even know, older people who didn't really look like students, all dropped by my room or talked with Dexter from their cars in the far edge of the dorm parking lot, under the canopy of big evergreens. It was my chore to try to ignore it all, to hope it would go away somehow if I did.

"Big man!" he said when the thumping music finally stopped. He rose, unsteady, and went to turn the disk on the turntable over to the other side. "Gonna start against 'Bama, huh? Like lambs to the slaughter, man. Lambs to the slaughter."

"Maybe not, Dexter. Maybe not. Where's your school spirit?"

I had touched a nerve.

"To hell with school spirit. You fags ain't got a chance, you know."

"What do you mean?"

"I know about Frank Short and all the others that got crippled up this week. Y'all will be lucky to have eleven chumps to start the game."

I reached and grabbed the tone arm before he could set it back onto the record and send the dizzyingly loud music spinning again.

"How the hell did you know about that, Dexter?" Coach Rankin had promised to castrate anybody who said a word about our injury situation to anyone outside the team. It couldn't be allowed to get to the papers or the opposition. Let Alabama prepare for a whole different Spartan team, not one that was crippled and maimed. Father and Maw were the only people I had mentioned the injuries to, and I felt a little guilt about that.

"Look, you redneck hillbilly, most of the team buys merchandise from me. Frank got enough weed from me last night he won't be needing anesthesia for that leg for a while. Don't much get past the Dex-man. These boys will tell me all the news when they are being customers, if you know what I mean. And that's real valuable information to some other folks I do business with, too. News like that is just another commodity, and I can make more money with that than selling a few kilos of smoke to bone-headed . . ."

Red. I saw red. Before I even knew what I was doing I had grabbed him by the collar of his frayed yellowed T-shirt and lifted him, slamming him brutally against the wall. The Who record went sailing across the room and his framed Grateful Dead poster crashed to the floor behind him. This freak was messing with my team! Telling stuff that could make it harder for us to win!

"Put me down, you jock asshole!" He fought for enough breath to curse me between clenched teeth. "It ain't like the whole damn world don't know it already anyway."

I let him slide down the wall but still held my fist and his shirt tightly bunched at his neck. The other fist was cocked, ready to let fly. I was about to hit him hard. Frighteningly close to it.

"You ain't seen the line? It's sixteen already. Sixteen damn points! Rankin's hair was black as jet and the damn team was lily-white the last time a Spartan team was a sixteen-point dog."

What was the use? I slung him across the bed. He just lay there and laughed sarcastically.

"You too damn serious, C.P. It's just a game. It's all just a silly game. Two years, three years from now, hell, by the time they tee it up and kick it next September, ain't many folks gonna care if you lost to Alabama by three or by seventeen. Just the ones who gave the points and the ones that took them. They'll be counting their money or kissing it bye-bye. They're the only ones who give a rat's ass."

He rolled to his elbow, found the still-smoking joint somewhere among his filthy covers, took a toke, and grinned at me. I was stuffing a change of clothes and a few books into my duffel bag viciously, imagining it to be Dexter, Wheeler, Claxton, that I was chunking away, out of sight, out of my suddenly complicated life.

"Hell, you're only acting like another gung-ho freshman, Mr. McKay. Look, man, you're gonna be a goddamn hero someday. You'll go play some pro ball and make yourself a million dollars or two. You'll marry the prettiest girl in town and screw most of the others. Then you'll get to where you can't get out of bed in the morning it hurts so bad, and you'll retire and open a chain of restaurants or put your name on a car dealership and you'll play lots of golf and buy drinks for everybody at the country club till you go broke a time or two. Then you'll sit around in bars telling everybody how goddamn great you were until you die. Man, I envy you your exciting career, C.P. I envy the hell out of you." He laughed again.

"You be gone when I get back here tomorrow night, Dexter. I don't care what you tell them, but you be gone. If you're not, I'll kill you." And at that very minute, I would have. He exhaled blue smoke at me as I threw the duffel over my shoulder, stomped out, and slammed the door as hard as I could behind me.

The movie that night was one of the James Bond films. I don't remember which one. The meal at the hotel and anticipation of the next day's game had left me just a step before nauseous. I envied the guys who actually dozed and snored as 007 gambled and killed and took beautiful women left and right up on the screen. Kids and their parents gawked at us as we filed in and out of the theater. A brave few tried to get to us for autographs, but the trainers shooed them away. Drivers blew their horns at the buses as the blue-lighted police cars escorted us back to the hotel. Students leaned precariously out their car windows to scream Spartan cheers at us, while some Alabama fans cursed and shot us one-fingered salutes.

The cool air after the show helped, but back in the hotel room, I couldn't find sleep, try as I might. I was rooming with Benjie Caruthers, one of the scout-team defensive backs, and I hated him for the ease with which he passed away, dead to the world the instant his head hit the pillowcase. I finally took out my Western Civ text and read. That usually put me out in a minute, but not that night. I made it all the way to the Enlightenment but the only thing that went to sleep was my whole left side. I gave up and stared at the circles of light on the ceiling from the lone lamp, listening to Benjie breathe, and moan for his mother a time or two. I almost got up once, with the intention of slipping out and running awhile, but I was afraid there would be a bed check and I'd be a dead duck.

For a while, I rehearsed what I would say to Maggie Vinyard when we met Sunday night. How I would be glib and charming like James Bond if I could just manage to find the words. I went over the game plan time after time in my head but I could already picture every single page in the playbook. There was no doubt what I was supposed to do in any situation during the game. If I could just make the plays when I got there.

If. That was the word that suddenly reared itself like a 250-pound blocking tight end. For the first time since I had pulled on my little Hutch helmet and kicked the pebble-grained football all over my front yard up on Signal Mountain, I let that tiny word dominate my thoughts. And it was powerful.

Sleep finally got me sometime before dawn, and I might have slept right through kickoff if the trainers had not banged on our door at seven, alerting us for breakfast. My eyes were swelled, my legs and arms stiff from lying awkwardly trying to read the history book before I fell asleep.

God, what a glorious day! When they make football movies, they look like that day did. Leaves golden and scarlet, air ripe with smoke and excitement, crowd pumped and frenzied as they milled through the streets around campus or ate picnic lunches off their tailgates or from the trunks of their cars. Vendors sold souvenirs, hot dogs, soft drinks, on practically every corner. Fraternities had their pledges rope off chunks of the student section for the upperclassmen, and they were there early with their dates, in suits and party dresses, already well-oiled and screaming when we first trotted onto the field and stiffly warmed up an hour and a half before kickoff.

We had just broken up into groups for drills when Max Milligan came up to me with a sardonic grin on his face. He just stood there watching me stretch. It was not like him to stay wordless for so long a time, so I knew something was up.

"You got the start, kid," he said finally. I had just been elected president, crowned king, named pope.

"What?"

"You got the goddamn start. Can you remember what color jersey to tackle and which color to leave the hell alone? Just try to go after whichever one of the sons of bitches has the ball, okay?"

"Sure, coach!" I was afraid I was going to hyperventilate so I reached for more air and concentrated on measuring my breathing. I tried to keep the drills half-speed, as they were supposed to be. I was just about under control, but almost lost it again when the public-address announcer said my name as he read in a metallic monotone the list of starters. Man, the way it sounded as the words echoed off the still-half-empty bleachers, the crescendo of cheers from those already there with each starter's name, including mine, as if they really knew and cared who C.P. McKay was.

Once, I looked to the far end of the press box that wrapped around the rim of the south side of Spartan Stadium like a broad, toothy grin. There, in a patch of golden sunshine, was Father in a bright white dress shirt, and, standing nervously next to him, in her pink-flowered print dress, was Maw. Even from way down there on the grassy green floor of the field, I could see her wringing her hands, and him smoking a cigar, its blue smoke like a halo around his head. He was pounding the arms of the wheelchair with his clublike hands on the proudest day of his life.

Then the band played the alma mater, and followed it with the national anthem, while I forced myself to resurrect quotes and passages from Chaucer and Beowulf and Milton and all my other least-favorite literary thoughts, to keep my breakfast on my stomach and my heart from jumping out of my mouth and embarrassing everybody. Television cameras were set up in each end zone under the scoreboards. Others gazed down from the press box at us, and a row of at least two dozen film cameras watched from the roof of the stadium. There was Bear Bryant, in his houndstooth hat, pacing across the way, and I recognized a half dozen of the players in their white jerseys and crimson numbers who were all-American or all-conference. God knows, I had no business on the same field with them! But in just a minute I would be.

Thank goodness, we kicked off. If I had had to stand on the sidelines and dance up and down while our offense tried to move the ball, I'm sure I would have wet my football pants. The ball was sailing, end over end toward a scat back who took it at the three-yard line, twisted, cut back, and finally went down on the thirty-eight in a twisting pile of red and white.

Great field position, Curt.

Yep, that's where you want to start from, for sure, Chris. And this fine Crimson Tide team needs no help at all.

Things were back to normal. I was into the game, doing play-by-play in my head. Describing to myself the first play as it unfolded right there in front of me. As the quarterback tossed the ball to a big, fast trailing back, scooting in my direction, just as the film I had studied for hours had shown they tended to do. As I played off the blocking back with a stiff left arm and a sharp shove downward with the right, moving him out of my way as I tensed for the fake I knew would come. As I watched the running back's belt buckle to ride out the feint and reached for his pumping legs. As someone from the blind side laid a malicious block on me that left me flat on my stomach, spitting grass and bits of tooth grit.

Somebody managed to trip up the runner somewhere behind me, but I knew from the groan from the stands that he had gained ten, maybe fifteen yards. The man in the white jersey who had just sliced me in half reached to help me to my feet.

"Hi, rookie," he said, grinning. "Nice try."

Then he trotted back to the huddle to get set to come after me again. I slapped my thigh pads so hard my hands stung, but they didn't hurt nearly as badly as my pride.

Okay, so I made the next play. Same thing. Toss sweep, my way. They knew the freshman linebacker was out there. Run it at him until he stops it or they pull the jerk and get somebody else in there. I stiff-armed the blocking back again, but this time, I was aware of where the tight end was as he bore down, faked him with a move like a running back might have used, felt the breeze from his bulk slide by just as I met the runner straight up and took him down hard. One side of my body went numb for an instant with the force of the impact, but I was back up quickly, not wanting to let anyone see how bad it hurt. How wonderful it felt. Just another play, made the way I was supposed to make them if I was going to be all-American someday. Two-yard loss. Runner trotting to the sideline, trying to not let anyone see that he was listing, a little gimpy. Crowd going wild. Public address calling my name. Second down and twelve yards to go.

"Tackle by McKay, number fifty-five. Loss of two."

By this time, Father would be almost coming out of his wheel-chair. Maw would be checking carefully for signs of a broken leg dangling from her baby boy, or staggers brought on by a concussion.

Second down. Tendency from the films was misdirection to the weak side. A cross-buck with the ball going to the halfback diving over the guard. But somehow, with the field position and long yardage, I felt they would try a pass. Something short, safe, sure, right at the rookie. And there it was, unfolding in front of me as if in slow motion. I ignored the fake to the running back, diving toward his guard's butt and away from me, hands clutching an imaginary football the quarterback had pretended to cram into his gut. That was supposed to suck the defensive end and me into the middle, blindly following the decoy. Man-cow Malone, our defensive end, bit big-time and swallowed the fake like a bass grabbing a careless June bug. Then, there was the ball in the air above me, tossed gently, floating like a big brown bird. Just me and the full-back, both drifting under it as relentless gravity pulled it back down from its arc. I got there an instant before he did and grabbed the ball just the way I had the afternoon Father tossed me the long-lost football as I waited on the front steps. Hanging on, clenching it tightly, even as the fullback climbed up my back and tried to knock it loose and take my head off with a vicious swat at the same time. Then it was just a matter of waiting for the pile to get off me, toss the ball to the official nonchalantly, as if I had done it a million times before, and trot without swaggering to the sideline. Ignore the crazed crowd that chanted my name. Never mind the slap of approval upside my helmet from Tack Rankin, even though I had completely played it wrong. Disregard the whacks on the shoulders and butt from the other players who had hardly known my name until this instant. Try to overlook the tears that spilled from my eyes as if I had absolutely no control over them.

The rest of the game is all fuzz to me now. I took some licks that left me woozy, but I made the plays, too. Everybody told me I did. The films that week showed I usually did. But so did the other players. I could see it in their eyes. Hear it in their voices as they talked quietly, assuredly, to each other during the game and on the sidelines. Even the coaches had the same look. The same assured strength in the way they talked, strutted, did their jobs.

We got three points after my interception on a long field goal. Led six to three at the half. Nine to six after three. Won the game nine to eight after an intentional safety in the last few seconds. Didn't allow them a touchdown. The offense was awful, unable to complete but a handful of passes and it seemed when Skip Gross changed plays at the line, he invariably switched to the exact wrong choice. But we held as a team and we won as a team.

The feeling was unbelievable. Something Dexter Flynt or Langston Wheeler could never understand. We had risen to the occasion, put together everything we had mentally and physically, played as a team, as one hungry animal, and defeated a superior opponent. I was too tired to take off my pads and just got under the hot water of the shower with them all still on. And I was one of the ones the reporters sought out. God help me, I had planned, scripted, the words I would say when the time came, but it was the same old clichés that spilled from my lips. I didn't care. Half sick from the victory cigar I had inhaled, bruised, sore, numb, bleeding, I was so high I didn't think I would ever come down.

Now it was time to find Maw and Father. The sun outside the locker-room door was even brighter and more glorious than before the game, the colors sharper, smells more sensual. A pack of rabid fans still stood in the west end zone, waving flags and cheering drunkenly. I looked their way and grinned and shot them a vee and they pumped their fists and screamed even louder back at me. How many people's lives had I made a little better today by making a tackle, picking off a pass?

Then, there he was, silhouetted darkly by the sun. Standing

along the chain-link fence near the goal line. Hands in his pockets. Hat tilted back on his shiny peak. Light glinting off the chains that squirmed on his chest.

"Damn fine game, boy. Damn fine game."

I ignored him, looked up to the press box for my parents.

"You're supposed to say, 'Thank you, Cooter.' I know your momma raised you more polite than that. Maybe not your old man, but your momma . . ."

But I was past him and scaling the stadium steps three at a time, leaving him behind me like a bad memory.

"Damn fine game anyway, boy," he called after me, but I still pretended not to hear.

Father waited in his wheelchair at the near end of the press box. Tears rolled down his cheeks. He was crying too hard to say anything to me, just raised his right hand as much as he could and grasped mine in a surprisingly strong grip.

"Corey Phil?" Maw came from the shadows. "Are you all right? Are you hurt?"

"Aw, I'm fine, Maw."

"Thank the Lord! Your father has been like this since the thing was halfway through. Him hysterical and if you had'a got broke up . . ." She clucked and shook her head.

I rolled him to the elevator and Maw followed, cautiously avoiding looking over the edge of the stadium behind the press box, over its thin railing, and at the ground two hundred feet below. On the way down, I noticed the rolled-up program Father held loosely in his nearly useless left hand. It was open to the page with my picture, the ink now nearly smeared away.

Maw and I were lifting him into the truck when he spoke for the first time.

"Won." His voice was coarse, grating. "Won, boy. Won!"

"Yeah, Father, we won. We beat them."

"No. I won. Took the Spartans and the points for a thousand dollars."

"Jesus."

The sun was low as they drove away, back toward Chattanooga, hurrying to get home before it got too late. Bedtime for them was nine o'clock at the latest, and the difference in time zones still baffled them. I watched the truck turn the corner, Maw cutting across the curb, bouncing wildly. Father's head swung out of control with the motion, and then they disappeared behind the far corner of Spartan Stadium.

Suddenly I felt alone, abandoned. A cool north breeze rattled leaves and the debris the fans left behind. The warm sun had dropped below the big oaks that kept guard over Stadium Street, now empty of people. Bits of music and loose laughter from distant fraternity parties drifted by on the wind. There was no one at all to share my high with. Slowly, painfully, tiredly, I began the walk back to Champions' Hall, struggling not to let the burning glow of the win seep out of me. Fighting to keep the melancholy wave from snatching it away until I could find someone who would care.

TEN

Sleep refused to come and take me away to someplace without aches and hurt. Even as totally drained as I was, rest was impossible to come by. Finally, exhausted, I gave in.

Dexter had obviously gone for good, just as I had dictated. Not a sign of him except a hole in the Sheetrock of a wall where one of his giant stereo speakers had toppled over one night, and an envelope he apparently had left behind for me in the middle of my study desk. There was a note scribbled on it in his almost illegible scrawl:

> *Peace offering for you, C.P. No hard feelings. I know how tight you get wound up sometime, bud. Use these if you ever need to mellow out. I got plenty more if you want some.*
>
> *Dexter.*

There were a couple of red-and-blue capsules inside. Would the idiot try to poison me? I didn't think so. That was just the only way he knew to get back on my good side. His idea of a bribe.

My wind-up Big Ben alarm clock showed almost six o'clock in the morning. There was the threat of a sunrise behind hanging gray clouds out the partially open window. Cars had swooshed past along the street to Fraternity Row all night long, no doubt from parties just winding down. Then, finally, rain peppered the pavement and splashed against the glass while I stared at the drops' patterns. My body pleaded for blessed rest but all I had been able to accomplish all night long was to shift my aching, throbbing body around until the sheets had been ripped loose from under the mattress and were sticky with sweat, the quilt Maw had made for me kicked off the foot of the bed and onto the floor. I had tried reading a time or two during the dead hours, but the words kept squirting away from my eyes and made no sense at all. I turned on the radio once, hoping the music would soothe me to sleep, but every station was playing dedications, special requests for lovers or for wild victory parties in progress.

Finally, I stood, almost cried out as my muscles knotted, crab-walked to the sink, and popped the pills from Dexter's envelope into my sticky-dry mouth. I ran a handful of water from the faucet and slurped it up to chase the drugs down. Two minutes after I fell back on the ragged bed, soft, dizzy warmth swept over me. The soft swish of rain outside and the metronome ticking of the alarm clock gently carried me deep into a pleasant gray fog. I caught a glimpse of Maggie Vinyard waving at me from the mist before everything faded to beautiful, empty blackness.

I thought it was thunder that woke me up. But as I tried to roll over, find a position that didn't hurt, shut out the rude rumbling with the pillow, I realized it was someone banging on my door. I almost fell when I jumped from the bed, stood too quickly, and staggered to the door.

"You C.P. McKay? This the right room?" The voice came from behind a duffel bag and a pile of clothes, boxes, sheets and blankets. "They ain't give me a key yet."

"Uh huh," I belched, and then crashed heavily back onto the bed before I toppled over onto my face on the floor like a common drunk. Out of a corner of my eye, I watched the pile of stuff make its way into the room. Then, when he dropped the whole mess in the middle of the floor, I could see my newest roommate, Chris Littlefeather.

Chris was full-blooded Cherokee or Chickasaw or something. I had heard he had been kicked out of the University of Oklahoma for some reason and had come to Sparta. He was a sophomore or junior running back, sitting out a year of eligibility because of the transfer. He ran scout-team offense and looked like a good, fast, shifty back.

He introduced himself, then looked at me hard.

"Tell you the truth, you don't look so wonderful, McKay. What truck hit you, man?"

"Just having a rough night sleeping. And I got pretty banged up in the game today."

"Yesterday. Game was yesterday. It's Sunday afternoon. And you better hurry or you're not gonna make conditioning drills."

Somehow, I managed to turn my head enough to see two-fifteen smirking at me from Big Ben's face. Damn! I had slept until the middle of the afternoon. I had never slept later than nine o'clock in my life!

We were required to gather on Sunday afternoons to run, stretch, do light calisthenics, all to work the kinks out of our bodies from the game the day before. For the first time in my college career, I actually had some kinks to exorcise. It was tough to go that day, though. The coaches were in a jovial mood because of our upset win and didn't seem to notice my rubber legs and red-rimmed eyes.

Rankin wasn't even at the practice. Someone said he was still taping his TV show. Even he had celebrated the upset too much and missed his usual six A.M. taping time that morning.

"You had a decent game, McKay," Max Milligan said the first time I jogged past him. "Next thing, you'll be thinking you can play on this level or some such shit. Be reading your clippings and starting yourself a scrapbook and naming yourself all-American before we know it."

"Aren't I?" My tunnel vision, bone-weariness, churning stomach, or something, made me uncharacteristically bold.

"See, Junie, he's a legend in his own mind already." He and the other coaches laughed. "Where we gonna clean off a place and make room for his Heisman trophy?"

For the first time, I felt myself to be a part of this team. I felt like a Spartan. Even if it took another man's impairment to get the chance, I had done the job when called upon. And that made it as good as if I had earned it all by myself with no help from the orthopedic gods.

Dexter's capsules had done their job well. By the time the exercise had chased the poison from my muscles and the dust from my head, I felt as rested, relaxed, and contented as I had since getting to Sparta University. In about an hour, I would be sitting across the table from the most attractive woman who had ever stooped so low as to give me the time of day. I raced to the dorm after the practice, showered, and put on clean jeans and my high-school letterman's jacket.

Drake's appeared to be packed with students who were avoiding dining-hall food in the dorms and fraternity and sorority houses. I tried to scan the rows of tables for Maggie, but didn't see her anywhere. I had beaten her there, I supposed, and hunger was suddenly a factor.

"Sit anywhere you can find a flat place," one of the waitresses yelled over the din. She wore a garish paisley blouse and tight bell-bottom jeans, like a hippie gypsy. It seemed to be the uniform for all the waitresses who scurried about through the loud crowd and carried trays full of food or dirty dishes.

"I'm waiting for . . ." But the waitress was gone, swallowed up by a set of swinging doors at the side of the big room. A couple of guys who had finished eating at a tiny table along one wall stood. I grabbed the spot before someone else could and sat over a quart jelly jar of sweet iced tea while keeping an eye on the restaurant's entrance for Maggie. A herd of loud students, apparently half drunk, were at the table across from me. They seemed to be laughing uproariously at their own jokes. They looked my way a time or two, pointed and snickered, but I ignored their whisperings of "jock animal" and "hairless ape." The letterman's jacket, my thick-muscled neck, and close-cropped hair were a dead giveaway. It wasn't the first time I had been the object of such stereotypical attention. It went with the territory and it certainly wasn't my job to set everyone straight. Let them think what they wanted. I was here to meet Maggie Vinyard for the closest thing to a date I had had since high school and I certainly didn't have the time or inclination to get into a tussle with such jerks.

It had never occurred to me she would stand me up. The thought had begun to occur to me by the time the sweet, cold tea had disappeared and I was in urgent need to find the men's room.

That's when I felt a warm hand on my shoulder.

"We're kinda busy right now, C.P. Can you give me a few minutes? I'm sorry."

There she was, face flushed with exertion, hair a little unkempt, trayful of dirty dishes balanced over a shoulder. Somehow, the paisley blouse and bell-bottoms didn't look quite so tawdry on Maggie Vinyard as they did on the other waitresses.

"Sure. No problem."

She smiled and I threw one right back at her.

"I'll get you a burger. On me. All the way?"

"Well, sure, but . . ."

And she was gone in a flash, just the way she disappeared from class every time I had watched her.

The hamburger was wonderful, especially considering I had not eaten since the pregame meal the day before. I guess I had just forgotten. Maggie came past my table several times, always on the run, smiled at me, and kept scooting among the other tables and booths while delivering platters of food. She winked at me when she dropped off fresh beers at the loud students' table next to mine, then danced away from their gropes. Meanwhile, I devoured the burger and home-cut fries and put away two more glasses of tea, then sopped up with bits of bun the drippings and ketchup on my platter. Even the rowdy group of students at the table next to mine couldn't distract me from the incredible meal. Even when they continued to point at me and whisper like kids at the gorilla cage at the zoo.

"I'm finally finished. Sorry to keep you waiting. How was the burger?" She had slid into the chair across the little table from me. Even with tired eyes and drawn face, she was staggeringly lovely.

"Beautiful. Uh, I mean, great. I was hungry as a wolf."

"I thought they fed you football animals better than that."

"Well, we get kinda tired of raw meat every night."

"Oh, I see." There was a hint of genuine amusement in her exhaustion.

"Hey, miss, how about some service over here!"

One of the students at the other table, mouth twisted, eyes glazed from drink, was leering at Maggie. She didn't even look at him.

"Sorry, I'm off work now. Someone else will . . ."

"Look, bitch! My buddies and I want some more beer and we want it right now or . . ."

Maybe it was him calling her a bitch, or his sneer, or the rich cashmere sweater with the Sigma Chi pin stuck to his chest, or even the way the bunch of them had been acting toward me and Maggie for the last twenty minutes, but something primal yanked me out of my chair and across the narrow aisle to where the bastard sat, giggling with his friends like a bunch of junior-high-school troublemakers. I heard Maggie say, "No, C.P.!" but her words weren't nearly strong enough to stop me. My hand closed on his button-down collar. I pulled him to his toes, his red, swollen face near mine. I loved the sudden look of sheer terror in his eyes. Dishes and half-eaten food scattered everywhere with a clatter as he struggled to get loose from my grip. His friends scattered, too, like roaches when the lights come on.

"You know what I'm going to do to you, you bastard? Do you have any idea what I am going to do to you?" I spoke through tightly clenched teeth, just loud enough for him to hear, so angry I could easily have broken the fool in half. My threat was empty because I didn't know what I was going to do with him, now that I had hold of his throat.

"No. No! Just don't hurt me. Don't hurt me." The creep was beginning to cry. Big tears dripped onto his chest. For an instant, I seriously considered slamming him against the wall with enough force to maybe crack some ribs, bruise him enough that he would feel my wrath every time he breathed for a while.

God help me! Right here in front of Maggie, I had been fulfilling every jock cliché she could have ever held. I was reacting physically to someone weaker, solving a simple problem with muscle instead of mind, being Father and slapping someone around if he or she crossed me in some way.

The restaurant was quiet now except for the peal of dishes banging together and some kitchen banter. Everyone in the packed dining room had stopped eating, some in mid-chew, and now watched me and the guy I held by the throat, waiting for the big tough football player to kill the skinny drunk frat rat. This kid who was so stupid as to poke at the ape with a sharp stick and to foolishly stick his hand through the bars of the animal's cage.

"Are you listening to me?" I asked him.

He blinked a yes, said nothing, suddenly sober, fear so strong it could be smelled on him as sourly as his beer breath. I took a breath, raised my voice loud enough to be heard back where the dishwashers laughed and splashed, and spoke slowly, enunciating the words perfectly:

" 'Why, what a wasp-stung and impatient fool art thou to break into this woman's mood, with thine tongue tied to no ear but thine own.' "

Oh, the fear was still in the jerk's eyes, but just a hint of puzzlement had crept into his expression.

"Shakespeare. *Henry IV.* You may have heard of it."

God knows where that all came from! My brain and mouth had acted of their own accord with no guidance from their boss. I had had every intention of drawing blood from the rich son of a bitch, but I quoted him Shakespeare instead. Now my hands got into the act, disobeying me boldly. The left one lowered him back to the floor and released the guy's throat completely. The right one wiped away a tear of fear that had dropped onto his gold Sigma Chi pin. Then, I reached back without even checking to see if Maggie was there, took her hand in mine, and led her to the door as the restaurant's customers, waitresses, the loudmouth's buddies, and the blue-haired lady behind the cash register quietly watched us go.

After the morning rain, the day had grown steadily cooler and foggier. I thought I noticed Maggie shiver as we passed under the bug light at the doorway. Without asking, I took off my letterman's jacket and slid it over her shoulders. It wasn't a shiver. She couldn't hold it any longer and burst into laughter as soon as the door slammed behind us. It was a laugh as sincere as a promise, as sweet as joy.

"Damn, Mr. McKay! You were great!"

We walked even though I had no idea where we were going. I only knew that I had taken her hand in mine once again after I gave her the jacket, and so far she had let me keep it.

"Thanks for seeing me tonight, C.P."

"No, I've been looking forward to it. Talking about your essays, that is."

"Sorry about working tonight. They called me in last minute and I had to go. Not everybody can get an athletic scholarship." She looked up at me, as if to check and see how I took her unintentional remark. I ignored it. "I work at Drake's four nights a week and a work-study job at the infirmary twelve hours a week. It doesn't leave much time for anything else like a social life or studying or breathing."

"I'd be right there, too, if it weren't for football." I hesitated. "Regardless of what you might think of football, it does pay the freight and keeps me here."

"You don't have to apologize to me, C.P. I just don't care much for the cretins I've seen . . ." Her voice trailed off. "I'm sorry. You seem different."

We ended up at the library. A dense fog veiled big oaks that lined up in a march away from the building's front steps. The few streetlamps we were able to see through the murkiness had gray halos encircling them. The cold dampness seemed to muffle all sound around us. We had found ourselves in a cocoon, sheltered from anyone else, invisible to all but each other.

The cement steps were wet and cold, but we sat down anyway. Without even meaning to, we drew close to each other for warmth.

"I love this building," she said, and she had to know from the way I looked at her quickly that I did, too. Maybe she knew I had been about to say the exact same words. "All I want to know is everything that is in there. Everything. That's why I came here in the first place. Why I'm studying literature. Why I wanted to be in Wheeler's class so bad. I want to learn how to read the thoughts of wise, articulate men and women. Study, interpret, understand what they have to tell us. Not just to get a grade or a degree or the approval of a teacher. Can you understand that, C.P.?"

Understand it? She was singing my song! And I tried to tell her, but I hardly knew how, sitting here so close to her that I could feel the warmth of her breath as she spoke, see my reflection in her glasses. I came down with a bad case of stumble-tongue. It took me a moment to realize something. This was the first time I had ever opened up and truly talked with another person about how I felt. And it was with a person I hardly knew, that I was quickly falling for.

Maybe if things had not fallen so perfectly into place that night on the steps, everything would have been different. If the fog had not been so protective, so shielding in its seclusion, or if just one late-studying student had hopped down the library steps near us, breaking the mood. Maybe if the cold clouds had suddenly decided to open up and rain on us as we sat huddled closely on the steps, chasing us to some less magical place. Or if Maggie had not spoken the exact thoughts I had kept so privately close to my own heart all my life. Maybe then I would not have revealed myself to her as I did. Or she might not have allowed me to see so deeply inside her. And maybe we would not have permitted ourselves to become so vulnerable to each other.

And we would not have fallen into desperate, dependent, stone-hard love within an hour. We kissed and held each other. There was passion but there was so much more. Our kisses and embraces were just more exploring of each other, learning each other.

Maggie was the stronger of us.

"C.P., I've got to go. I don't want to. I want to talk all night. I want to know you better. Find out everything there is about you. But I've got to go."

We stood.

"I don't know what to say, Maggie. I've never felt like this before. I want to see you again. Soon."

She smiled.

"Wheeler's class. Tomorrow."

"Not exactly what I had in mind."

"Me either. Here's my dorm phone. Just ask whoever answers to get me in 308." She scribbled the number on the back of a page of English Lit notes.

Then I held her awkwardly. She didn't seem to mind that I was almost a foot taller than she was or that my chest was too big for her to reach around. Her arms slipped around my neck as I bent to meet her lips, our bodies close. We learned a few more things about each other before we finally broke the clinch. She slipped off my jacket, handed it to me, smiled, not just with her lips but with her eyes, her whole face. Then she was gone, lost in the thick fog as it swirled in her wake.

I could smell her perfume on the jacket. Onions and french-fry grease, too. I wanted to cry with happiness and cry with sadness that she was gone when I was only beginning to get to know her, to let her get to know me. I was revealing myself to her, and she seemed to like what she was finding out about me. Not that I could tackle running backs and knock down passes in a football game, interpret a sonnet and divine symbolism from words on paper. No, it was the deeper things I wasn't even sure I knew about myself that she was uncovering and loving in me. And all that in an hour in the damp, cold fog on the colorless steps of the library.

I ran. I ran around the quadrangle, past the Theater building, the Union, and near the president's mansion where a lone dim light shone from what must have been Dr. Claxton's bedroom. The fog parted in my wake. The cold, drizzly air whistled past my ears and left them tingling in the chill. I ran around the stadium, tripping over the litter of the previous day's game, and up the hill past the beautiful, old solid-brick homes occupied by tenured faculty, all safely protected by massive willows that stood in front like immovable sentries. My tired legs warmed wonderfully as fresh-driven blood pumped through them. Back down the road I ran, along a street that bordered a tumbling stream that raced and roared with the morning's rainfall and behind the geometrically perfect engineering buildings, through the dense, dark cedar thicket, and across the athletic-dorm parking lot. Five miles and I wasn't even winded. My aches and pains were forgotten. My heart beat fast, partly from the running, but just as much from thinking of Maggie Vinyard.

My clothes were soaked, but I didn't care. The inside of the dorm seemed hot and stuffy as I took the steps three at a time to my room. The lights were out when I opened the door, but something flickered on Chris Littlefeather's side of the room. He sat cross-legged on a rug, encircled by two dozen small candles. His hands were spread outward, his face to the ceiling, eyes closed. He was chanting something.

The shaft of light I let spill in through the open door didn't seem to faze him. He kept singing, clenching and unclenching his fists, as I eased the door shut quietly and edged over to sit on my bed. He knew I was in the room but he didn't allow the interruption to stop whatever ceremony it was he was performing, whatever prayer it was he was sending up to whatever deity he worshiped.

Then I realized something. His song seemed familiar somehow. I had heard it somewhere before. It was eerie, discordant, more a hum than a lyric. I realized then that it was very much like the lullaby Maw used to sing for my brother. The one she sang the day she sent him to be with his guardian angel. The thought of it made me shiver and I suddenly felt feverish and weak. I slipped out of my wet clothes as easily and quietly as I could, lay back on the bed, pulled the quilt up around my neck, and let Chris finish his ceremony.

After ten or fifteen more minutes of the eerie singing, he stopped suddenly, as if someone had switched him off like a radio. He rose to turn on the lamp beside his bed, blew out the candles, gathered them all one at a time and deposited them in a suede or leather bag he slid back under his bed. Finally, without a word to me, he folded the brightly colored rug and almost reverently placed it in the bottom drawer of his chest. Then he sat on the bed, back against the headboard, and went limp all over, his strength apparently sapped.

"How you doing, McKay?" It was as if I had just that moment walked in.

"Fine, Chris. How are you doing?"

"Can't complain."

My Big Ben ticked so loudly it hurt my ears. Some of the other football players were having a loud, frisky game of two-hand touch football in the hall just outside our door.

"A religious thing?" I had to ask.

"Yeah."

"It's cool, man."

The clock was louder now than a church bell. A pile of the players crashed against a wall with a sound like thunder and I could hear the sound of splintering wood. Some laughed, others cussed profanely in anger.

"I was raised in Dallas," he finally said quietly, sliding down to lie flat on his back on the bed. His words seemed reluctant, as if he didn't really want to tell me what he was doing but knew he must. "Big-city kid. Never even saw an Indian reservation except on vacation one time when we drove up to Oklahoma. And at the movies. On TV. Cowboys and Injuns. My old man was ashamed to be an Indian so we had nothing to do with it in the house. Said it was next thing to being a nigger. Worse in a lot of ways because we had no Martin Luther King or anybody. He even changed our name. I was Chris Littleton until I came out here. I'm gonna change it back legally someday to Littlefeather."

The roughhousing in the hallway outside grew louder and more violent. Chris's voice stayed low, almost a whisper. I had to strain to hear him over the game and my clock's marking time.

"Then my grandma died and my grandfather came to live with us because he had nowhere else to go. He saw what my father was doing and it made him sick. He slipped around behind my old man's back and taught me a lot of stuff. Said it had to be handed down. If it died with him, it would be dead for good. I don't make a big deal out of it, man. I really don't. It just makes me feel better sometimes. Something to fall back on if things get rough. If it bothers you, let me know and I'll do it when you're not around. I don't want to spook you like I did my last roomie. He kept reading me the Bible and quoting me scripture and shit. But mainly I think he was afraid I'd scalp him or something while he slept."

"Hey, do what you have to do, Chris. It won't bother me. I'm like a sixteenth Cherokee myself. On my mother's side."

"Oh. But let me know if I bother you. It's pretty weird to some people. Really wigs them out. Me talking to spirits and stuff. Smoking the pipe. Just let me know."

The laughter and cursing and thrashing around outside our door had reached a crescendo, and only the yells of the dorm coach eventually put a stop to it as he chased the overgrown kids back to their rooms before they did some real damage. Finally, it was quiet. The big-faced alarm clock showed it was past midnight. I was almost asleep when Chris spoke again.

"Thanks, McKay. Something told me you'd be okay with it."

I grunted.

How could I be so tired? I had slept most of the day away. I had plenty of studying and writing to do, but I just let the warmth of

Maw's quilt take me under, and I was out like somebody had unplugged my lights.

Sometime later, my eyes opened suddenly, my heart racing. Something had lifted me out of the darkness of dead sleep in a hurry. The room was black, the window a gray glow. There was some kind of sound, continuous, melodic, almost inaudible. It was Chris's chanting, but this time higher in pitch, even closer to the way I remembered Maw's singing.

I made him out, sitting cross-legged on his bed. He hushed with the movement of my head as I turned toward him, then he spoke.

"I had a dream. You were in it, McKay."

I shivered.

"You were in a clearing, standing high on a bald rock, surrounded by animals that were snapping and snarling at you, trying to drag you down. Then an eagle flew down from out of nowhere and cut your head off with its talons."

"Chris, you must have had the dining-hall meat loaf too close to bedtime," I tried to joke, but my voice was weak, unsure.

"But you kept talking. Just your head, sitting there on the rock, talking."

"How am I going to start against Tech Saturday if my head gets cut off?"

He ignored me.

"There was a wolf, a bear, a lion, I think. All snapping and snarling and clawing. And the eagle. I think it was an eagle because she had big, wide wings, and it was so real I could feel the wind on my face when she flapped them."

"Man, everything I said a while ago . . . about you doing whatever you like and it wouldn't freak me out? Forget it and go to sleep." I buried my face in the pillow.

"If Grandfather was alive, he could tell us exactly what it meant.

Either the future or the past. He would know which one."

I heard him settle back down into his bed.

"Future or past. God, I wish I knew which one."

The incessant ticking of the Big Ben seemed to get louder and louder, but I was too tired to move, too weak to reach and try to sling it across the room or smother it with a pillow. Suddenly, though, it stopped cold. It had wound down completely. And I was certainly too weary to reach and wind it up again.

Finally, sleep pulled me under again, but words kept running through my mind as it did. Words from Kipling: "If you can keep your head when all about you are losing theirs and blaming it on you . . ."

ELEVEN

A dozen devils pitchforked me all night long. But each time my aching body woke me up, it was Maggie that I was thinking about. I called her early the next morning, keeping my voice low so I wouldn't wake Chris. I did anyway, though, as I drummed my fingers impatiently on the nightstand while the girl who had groggily answered the phone went to find her. He just grunted, turned over, and covered his head with his blanket.

"Did I dream what happened last night, Maggie?" The question was hard to ask. I was afraid it had been a fantasy and asking the question would make it all unreal.

"If you did, so did I, and that would be kinda freaky, wouldn't it?"

"Look, I've never . . ." Words failed me. Her too. There was only the drone of the phone line until we both broke into silly giggles. Chris covered his head with his pillow.

It was hard concentrating on Nathaniel Hawthorne that week

and hard thinking about Georgia Tech's offense. I read *The Scarlet Letter* twice and watched two hours of film after practice each day, but it was Maggie who had captured my mind.

Professor Wheeler stopped me after class on Wednesday to tell me with a smile how much he had enjoyed my most recent essay. So much so that he had shared his enthusiasm over my work with Dr. Claxton at that week's faculty luncheon. Coach Rankin climbed down from his tower that same day, trotted over to where the defense practiced, put his arm around me and screamed at the others: "This is the way I want my defense to play! The way this young man plays it!"

Father called me Thursday. I was looking at the words of Hawthorne but thinking of Maggie's face, voice, eyes. We had met briefly for lunch at Drake's, held hands like high-school sweethearts until she had to run to her job at the infirmary. Now the telephone sang until I answered it, hoping it was she.

"Boy? That you?" His voice was rough, gravelly. Neither he nor Maw had ever called me. I didn't think they even knew how to dial long distance.

"Father? Is Maw okay? You all right?"

"Aw, hell yeah. I'm just checking on Saturday. We gonna be down there watching you. How you think it'll go?"

"Father, Tech hasn't won a game all year. They even lost to Vanderbilt."

"Shoot, I know you'll beat 'em. But the line's twenty-eight. Twenty-eight damn points. I'd hate to give that many points if it was on the damn Green Bay Packers."

I didn't want to talk gambling with my old man. I wanted to read and think. But I guess I owed him that much.

"Listen, why don't you sit this one out this week? Rankin is not likely to run up the score or risk getting any of the starters hurt with Georgia coming up."

He was quiet. I could hear his phlegmy breathing.

"Boy, you are absolutely right. I got a little riding on Tennessee against Alabama anyway. . . ."

I let him rattle on until he ran out of breath, asked to speak with Maw, and found out she was gone, cleaning somebody's house, and wouldn't be back until after nine.

"Tell her I love her and . . ."

"Yeah, yeah. Hear anything on the Tennessee and Alabama game? Anything I could use . . ."

The team bus out to Sparta's tiny airport left before time for Wheeler's class on Friday, so I only got to talk with Maggie a few minutes early that morning. The ride down to Atlanta was bumpy and most of us were as sick as we had been on the bus ride to my first junior-high game. Then, on the way to our hotel, I was shocked to see familiar territory out the bus window. We rode right past the old apartment building where we had once lived on Ponce de Leon. It was still there, but seemed much smaller, more weather-beaten. The park where I had ridden the ride-with-no-name was gone. Row after row of brick government housing stood where the swings and monkey bars had been. And the stadium that Maw and I wandered into that evening was gone, too. In its place was a shopping center with a grocery, a beauty shop, and a liquor store where all the wonder and color and noise had been. The place where I saw my mother laugh and cry both in the same night.

Georgia Tech. That was the game in which Man-cow Malone and I collided head-on trying to mash the quarterback. It was mid–third quarter and we were up by fourteen then, although I'm not sure we deserved it. We were flat, emotionless, still drained, I suspect, from upsetting Alabama. Man-cow and I both were probably forcing the action a little bit, trying to make a big play that would bust the thing loose.

I woke up in a hospital emergency room. I was lying on a gurney with nothing on but the T-shirt I wore under my pads, sweat socks, and my jockstrap, and not even a sheet to cover me. My head felt heavy as a bowling ball, my vision was smeared, and my fingertips on both hands tingled with little jolts of electricity every time I tried to move them.

"Are we still winning?" I directed the question to a fuzzy form hovering a few feet away.

"Y'all won by twenty-one," the shadow answered. "You played a helluva game, boy."

"Thanks. Thanks a lot." The voice was familiar, but I couldn't pull a face from the murkiness that filled my head.

"Yep, you got a real knack for this game, son."

It wasn't the face that came clear to me. It was the glint of yellow light from the shadow's chest that stabbed me in the eyes and screamed at me who the man was.

"What the hell are you doing here?" I tried but couldn't muster much vehemence. My head throbbed, my voice was weak.

"Just checking on you for a friend, boy. That's all. Your poor old daddy can't hardly get up all the stairs in this place in that rolling chair, now can he? And your momma? Lord, she's about hysterical. Carrying on down in that waiting room about the angels taking you away and all."

Anger quickly chased away the tangle of spiderwebs in my head and I sat up suddenly, fighting vertigo and the sudden urge to retch. I shook my fist at the man.

"You get the hell out of here! And stay away from my folks. You hear me?"

"My, my. Boy has a couple of pretty good games and forgets his old friends real quick."

He turned to go, stopped, spun around and pointed his finger at me, wiggled it as if he was pulling a trigger.

"You and me, we gonna have to have a little heart-to-heart. You love your momma and daddy as much as you act like you do, we have the basis of a business relationship. C.P. and Cooter, Incorporated. I like the sound of that."

He vanished, quick as the devil.

Something was digging into my crotch. It was the folded love letter from a nurse who had helped work on me somewhere along the way. I wadded it up and flung it as hard as I could against the far wall of the hallway, almost hitting Maw as she raced around the corner where Cooter had disappeared. She kneaded her hands and rushed to grab me, almost knocking me back down flat on my back on the gurney.

"Oh Jesus, Corey Phil! I just knew the Lord had called you home! The way you run head-foremost into that nigger. The way they carried you off on that stretcher. That doctor working on you like he did."

It took some doing, but I was able to convince her I was perfectly okay. Despite the thunder in my skull that threatened to behead me.

"I'm just so afraid something is gonna happen to you, Corey Phil. Something's gonna hurt you. I even had a dream about it."

Oh, God! Not her, too. Chris Littlefeather and Maw were both dreaming about me. And the only one I wanted to dream about me was . . . Jesus. What was her name? I could see her face clearly but her name was lost somewhere. I sank back on the cot, let the fog take me back while Maw went on and on, while the team managers and a doctor tried to reassure her it was just a mild concussion. Nothing serious. Maybe a headache for a day or two. That I'd be fine.

I was on the plane, almost back to Sparta, before I could remember Maggie's name. And I'll admit that scared me.

Scared me so bad I practiced remembering everything I could, all the way back from the airport to the university on the bus. All the way as I trotted from the football complex to Champions' Hall. Multiplication tables. Treaties that ended wars. Vice presidents' names. How many acres in a square mile. I got most of them but my head still pounded, my stomach rolled, my fingers tingled.

Maggie had not heard about the injury because she was working and didn't even listen to the game. I didn't tell her. She just seemed so glad to see me and pretended not to notice my bloodshot eyes and the black bruise on the side of my head.

We played Vanderbilt next. A conference game, true, but the Commodores were anemic. You would never have known it from Rankin's demeanor all week in practice. We might as well have been playing Notre Dame or somebody for the national championship.

"We gotta get this one, men," he preached at the Monday team meeting. "If we want to be in the hunt for the championship, we gotta get this one. If we want to go to a bowl game, we gotta get this one. If we want to get into the Top Ten, we gotta get this one. If we want to be winners, we gotta win this one, too."

Of course we won easily, but it was another road game, all the way on the bus up to Nashville. Another night away from Maggie. Another Thursday telephone call from home. I could hear Maw pleading in the background for me to be careful until Father cursed at her, told her to shut the hell up and that she could talk with me when he finished and not a damn second before. I knew he would have hit her if he had been able.

Thursday also brought a note to my mailbox. I rarely got a letter from anyone, except for fan mail, and that went to the athletic office to be burned before we even looked at it. Coach didn't want us wasting game preparation time or getting big heads from fan mail. I rarely checked the little box behind the entryway desk downstairs at Champions' Hall. I didn't know anyone who would be writing me there. But for some reason, I did that night.

> *Congratulations on the fine game Saturday. I have been watching with great interest. Good luck this week and in your midterms also. We're counting on you!*
>
> —*Chauncey Forrest*

Well, I guess the pressure was on.

I had a good week's practice. They held me out Monday because of double vision. I still saw everything in a blur the rest of the week and during the game on Saturday, but I wasn't going to admit it. Then, with the game out of hand early, us firmly in charge, they pulled me and I only played a few minutes after halftime.

The locker room was jubilant. Cigars were passed around and I soon had triple vision from the stinking stogie I smoked. Sportswriters all wanted to know the source of our turnaround. Why was the team playing so much better now?

"We've always been a good team," I told them. "We just came together as one. Started playing team ball. Put ourselves in a position to win. Worked hard. Sacrificed. Got better as a team."

I was almost sick when I saw those quotes of mine in the Sunday paper the next day. How hackneyed could I be? Did I miss a single cliché?

Maggie was waiting under the shadows of the cedars when the bus got us back to the field house. She had to have been cold, standing there in the middle of a wet, sharp wind that promised cold rain or snow soon. I felt an elation I had never felt before when she met me, kissed me, took my arm in hers and strolled with me back toward the dorm.

"I listened to the game on the radio today."

"What did you think?"

"It didn't make any sense at all. I just listened for your name."

"Well, we won."

"Yeah, I got that much."

She was quiet. A whippoorwill's cry wavered in the wind, echoing in the cold air. I loved the feel of her next to me.

"C.P.?"

"Yeah?"

"Why didn't you tell me about getting hurt last week?"

"It was no big deal. Where did you hear about it?"

"The men on the radio. They said it was amazing that someone could come back from a concussion that quickly. And play so well, too. Why didn't you tell me?"

"Aw, it was nothing. Little bumps and bruises are a part of the game. . . ."

She stopped, looked up at me, the moon and a distant streetlight giving her face an angelic glow. But there was just a spark of anger in her eye, too. A sharp edge to her voice when she spoke.

"Let's get something clear, C.P. McKay. I love you. I've never loved anybody like I love you. I care what happens to you. And when you don't tell me something like that, it's the same as lying to me."

"But Maggie, there's nothing you could do. . . ."

"That's not the point! When I love somebody it means I want to share everything about them. The good, the bad, the wonderful, the painful. I don't care. Do you understand that?"

I kissed her then because there was nothing else to do. Save for Maw, nobody had cared for me, loved me. What are the odds that the one other person who did just happened to be the woman that I was coming to love more than life itself? What are the odds?

Somehow, we wandered from the path among the big, ancient trees. I spread my letterman jacket on the ground and we settled on the soft bed of cedar, locked together. The bite of the cold was no factor. The threat of someone else wandering through the grove was not even a consideration.

We could only lose ourselves in each other. And we did.

It wasn't the chill that left us trembling. Not the icy, damp wind that swept down the side of the nearby mountains that made us tingle. There was no other world but us. No football. No class. No hard work or crazy family. Just Maggie and me, merging, becoming one in the wintry blackness under the cedars.

Finally, breathless, I held her close to me, tasting her closeness, her warmth. Kissing her far more gently than I had just a few moments before. Searching for the words that could let her know how deeply I had fallen for her. But I couldn't find them at all and just let my caresses and kisses try to say it for me. Some writer! As I stammered, stuttered, tried to express myself, she put one finger on my lips, then shut me up with another kiss while she tried to draw closer.

No telling how long we would have lain there, wrapped in each other, had the breeze not brought a sudden peppering of sleet and cold rain. We didn't hurry, though. I helped her stand, almost too weak-kneed to pull her up, then we buttoned each other as best we could with cold, uncooperative fingers. We walked briskly through the stinging deluge, breath fogging, laughing as we slipped and slid on the instantly icy sidewalks. I kissed her again at the door to the dorm, refused to let her go, kissed her again, long and deeply, then finally let her slip away regretfully, already hating the distance that was growing between us as she slowly climbed the steps, up and away from me.

She spun at the door, turned to me and gave me a girlish wave and a smile. She was gone.

The sleet was mixed with heavy, wet snow as I walked the mile back to the athletic dorm. I could still smell her scent on my fingers, still feel the heat of her breath on my cheeks where the ice now bit like tiny bullets.

As soon as I got to my room, even before I got out of my wet, tangled clothes, I reached for the telephone to call her, but Chris was obviously struggling over books, slamming and cursing, and I didn't want to disturb him. I took a shower instead. The hot needles stung the bruises and scratches from the day's game. Aches and pains had been completely forgotten for the last few hours. Then I forced myself to study, write, fight my memories of the wonderful night under the cedars after the bus brought us back to Sparta just ahead of the ice storm.

Bone-weary, I finally gave up on getting any work done and dove into the warm bed.

TWELVE

How could I have been so damned stupid? How could someone who could pick up the change of pressure of a pulling guard's hand on the ground and use that knowledge to predict a pass play not have seen the signs? How could I be so adept at hearing a change in inflection in a screaming quarterback's voice that tipped a line-of-scrimmage play change and yet be so unaware of everything else going on around me in my life?

The surprise two inches of snow paralyzed the whole area. Classes were canceled Monday and Tuesday. We moved to the gym for drills, frantically getting ready for Georgia the best we could. With nothing else to do until practice at three-thirty, I tried to call Maggie and see if she wanted to meet somewhere, but she was out all day Monday and not in her room that night. Probably working. She may have gone home, the girl who answered the phone told me Tuesday morning. Home was Memphis. She had not told me anything about leaving. Not even a message. The roads were still treacherous until past Nashville and I was worried about her and afraid something bad had happened to call her back home so suddenly in such rotten weather and without telling me.

The girl at the dorm desk Tuesday night told me she had signed out Monday afternoon because she had to visit her sister in Nashville for a few days. The blue-haired woman at Drake's said she was not scheduled to work until Thursday. She was out of town and it was awful 'cause the snow had doubled her business but left her short-handed. The infirmary said she was supposed to work Friday and to please move along because every student at Sparta University had come down with the flu since the weekend and the cold snap had just made it worse.

I looked for Vinyards in the Nashville phone book at the library but there were none. I left messages at the dorm and stayed close to the phone in my room but there was no call.

Chris looked at me as if I was crazy.

"Man, you got it bad."

"I can't help it. I'm in love."

"Nothing wrong with that. She'll be back. Everything'll be okay."

Sometimes I thought Chris knew more about things than he let on, because there was no conviction in his voice.

We practiced indoors again Tuesday and the coaches were all surly because our preparation was hampered by the weather. Georgia was a must game, because it was a conference game and we could clinch at least a tie for the championship with Tennessee. Because it was "the next one," as they said. Max Milligan screamed at me when I blew two assignments in a row. Then exploded again when I went the wrong way on a new stunt we had put in that week. He was standing face–to–face mask, giving me and most of my relatives a good cussing when a shadow suddenly appeared next to us.

"Max! Lighten up!"

It was Tack Rankin, down from his balcony at the end of the

indoor practice facility. Max looked stunned.

"Jeez, Tack. This thick-headed bohunk has done blowed every play we've tried to run all day. . . ."

"I said lighten up. He'll get it down. C.P. will make the play. You can count on that. Okay, Max?"

His voice was calm. There was a warm smile on his face. He patted me on the helmet. Max Milligan looked as if he had just seen a Martian strut onto the field in full football gear.

"Max, take it easy and get on with practice. We got ten other men who need these drills a lot worse than C.P." And he turned and walked back toward the ladder to the balcony.

"Jesus, McKay," Max was sputtering. "I ain't never seen that old son of a bitch do that. You must have pictures of him naked with a donkey. That's all I can figure."

I called Maggie's dorm again as soon as I got back to Champions' Hall. The girl who answered the phone was irritated with me.

"Look, I've told you . . . Wait a minute. Yeah, she's in now but she's got a 'Do not disturb.' Probably studying. It is midterm, you know."

"Please connect me. I really need to talk with her."

"You got any idea how many men I get with that same story? Sorry. I could lose my job if I override a 'Do not disturb.' Why don't you take a cold shower. . . ."

I slammed the telephone down so hard Chris Littlefeather almost fell off his chair.

She certainly would be in Wheeler's class Wednesday. Then I could find out what was going on.

The snow was almost gone by Wednesday morning. A southern breeze boosted the temperature back into the sixties but threatened rain. It made quick work of removing the freak snow and ice from the streets and sidewalks. I sleepwalked through my morning classes and fought the urge to run to Wheeler's classroom in the Language Arts building after lunch.

Was that a smirk on his face when he spotted me at the door? He tossed a quick, nonchalant wave.

"Good morning, Mr. McKay. How are you this morning?"

"Fine. Fine, thank you."

I found my usual seat. Maggie was not there, and she didn't come in before class started. Wheeler was up and preaching, probing for some obscure answer from the usual victims of his vicious teaching methods. As was his custom nowadays, he left me alone. Maggie's desk seemed to take on a life of its own there next to me and I half expected it to move, shout, take a tumble. But it just sat there silently.

As if in a daze, I rose to leave when everybody else did. I gathered my notebooks and made ready to escape as quickly as I could. I aimed for the doorway, but something made me stop, turn, go back to where Wheeler was stuffing notes into his ragged briefcase.

"Excuse me, Dr. Wheeler?"

"Yes, Mr. McKay?"

"Could I ask you something?"

"If it's about the Emerson research paper, you have nothing to worry about. Very well done. Very well done, indeed."

"Well, no, not exactly, I . . ."

"In fact, with your permission, I would like to submit it to the *Sparta Critical Review* for possible publication. It is certainly worthy."

The Emerson paper was weak as water, a sloppy, poorly written, scantily researched piece of junk I had thrown together in fifteen minutes one night after practice. Wheeler was kissing my ass.

"Sure. Sure, that's fine. Thank you. But there is something else."

"Yes?" The bastard knew what I was going to ask about. He knew.

"I was concerned about Miss Vinyard. She and I have been working together on some of the projects, and I was concerned that she wasn't here this morning."

He made a big show of referring to his notes, his grade book, running his finger up and down rows of names and student numbers.

"Oh, yes. Miss Vinyard. She has dropped the course. Took an incomplete. For the best, too, I'm afraid. I appreciate your trying to assist her, Mr. McKay, but all for naught. . . ."

He was still talking as I turned dizzily and made for the door. I almost didn't hear him when he called my name.

"Mr. McKay! How does early next week sound for dinner? I owe you pasta."

"Fine. That's fine."

I didn't even realize what the question had been until I was half-way to the field house. Damn! Maggie wrote well. Loved Wheeler's class. Was smart enough to be there. Why had she dropped out? Was it me she was avoiding? It had to be! What had happened?

I tried to keep my mind on defensive reads and keys and drop-back pass coverage that afternoon. When I blew one play so badly I was all by myself, fifty yards from the play when the whistle blew, Max Milligan didn't say a word to me, but I could see him biting his lip, digging his nails into the palms of his hands hard enough to draw blood.

"Sorry, Max. Rough day at class."

"It's okay, sweetheart. Would you like to go lie down in the shade for a while? Maybe have one of the trainers bring you a glass of lemonade?"

I could only grin at him.

The girl at the desk at Maggie's dorm almost bit me when she looked up and saw me again.

"She's checked out. At work, it says here."

"Not tonight. She's not scheduled to work tonight."

"Well, excuse me! I only have six hundred women to keep track of. Says 'work' here. Drake's. That's all I know."

The lady at Drake's with the blue hair rolled her eyes at me when she heard my question.

"I done told you she don't work till Thursday. Now buy a burger or get along, please."

Maybe it was a mistake. Maybe she was at the infirmary instead.

They were no help. "Not on the schedule till Friday. Now, if you don't need penicillin then make way for somebody that does."

I left two more messages at the dorm that night, but there were no calls.

Chris was chanting in the corner, surrounded by the little candles. I fell back on my bed after leaving the final message, letting his song hypnotize me. I was almost asleep when he stopped.

"C.P., are you awake?"

"Yeah, Chris. Just barely."

"I had that dream again. The one I told you about? Something's up. Something no good."

"Look, I don't want to hurt your feelings, but I never put much stock in stuff like that. Religion. Dreams. Fortune telling."

"I didn't used to, either. But Grandfather told me too many stories. Too many times things in nature gave warnings that weren't heeded by thick-headed people. Dreams showed the way to something real and profound, but they were ignored. Look, my nightmares may not be anything at all. But they were so real, man, so damn real."

"Well, I appreciate it. Just try to dream about sex and stuff like everybody else from now on, okay?"

"I will." He grinned, then suddenly lost it. "But you tread lightly, C.P. Lots of mean, vicious critters clawing at you, it looks like. Don't let them take you off the rock. And keep an eye out for that eagle. She's the one that got you in the dream."

"Okay."

And I drifted off, assignments unfinished, thinking of Maggie under the cedars, warm, loving, all mine.

Thursday blurred. I didn't leave any more messages. She certainly knew by now that I wanted to hear from her. Maybe if I didn't call, she'd get worried and call me if she was just playing hard-to-get. Maybe I'd go by Drake's after practice.

Halfway through the light workout, I saw the assistant coaches' eyes suddenly swell. Tack Rankin was down off his tower again, heading for where the defense worked. Max Milligan winked at me.

"Here he comes again, McKay. Pucker up. He may kiss you on the lips this time," he whispered.

"Boys, you're looking good!" Rankin said. Everybody relaxed. "If you fellows show this kind of spirit and hustle against the Bulldogs, we will win the game."

We all cheered. He started to walk away, toward the offensive end of the field, but seemed to remember something. He turned, walked straight back to me, and pulled me down close to his face with a hand to the back of my helmet.

"McKay, if you can, please stop by my office tonight. Six-thirty?"

"Sure, Coach. Six-thirty."

"Don't say anything to the others . . . or to the coaches. Okay?"

"Sure."

God! Now what?

I skipped supper, spent a few wasted minutes on notes for a history midterm exam, and then trotted back toward the athletic office. The corner window on the top floor blinked at me with a flickering light, the only one I could see burning in the entire building.

I had been up the thick-carpeted steps to Rankin's office only once before, on my recruiting trip, and that seemed a century ago, but there was no trouble finding his side of the building. His was the biggest door at the end of the most opulent hallway. There was no one at the ornate receptionist's desk in the huge anteroom and the lights were dimmed to dusklike. Gold-framed pictures of professional football players, movie stars, and presidents of the United States covered the walls. Each famous person was shaking hands with or had arms thrown around Tack Rankin. The same light I had seen from outside flickered through a partially open set of double doors at the back of the room.

I knocked lightly. The thick carpet and lush fabric wallpaper seemed to soak up the noise completely, so I knocked again, harder.

"Yes?" It was Rankin's voice.

"C.P. McKay, Coach."

"Come on in, son. Come on in. Make yourself at home."

The room was dark except for the brilliant square of movie screen illuminated by a projector at the rear of the office. Players scampered around, jumped jerkily backward, then scampered forward again. My eyes adjusted and I could see Rankin's form next to the projector. He stopped the machine, the room fell totally dark, and then he flipped on a desk lamp.

"Get you something to drink? Maxi-Cola?"

He was already up and taking a step to a door in the wall. It was a refrigerator, full of the product he praised every Sunday on his television show. He didn't wait for an answer from me but pulled out a bottle, flipped off the cap with an opener, and handed the smoking soda to me. I turned it up and drank it as if I was starving.

"Good stuff, huh? They give more than a half million dollars a year to the athletic department here at Sparta University. Oh, they pay me a pretty penny, too, but I wouldn't be their spokesman unless the university benefited also."

He leaned toward me to emphasize his point. There was an odd smell in the room but I couldn't quite place it.

"Son, I wanted to show you something. And ask for your help, if I could."

What was the ominous feeling I was getting? The same one I had had when Wheeler made his pass and when Claxton placed the entire future of Sparta University on my broad shoulders.

"Do you have any idea what it costs to run an athletic program at a major school like Sparta?"

"No sir."

"Well, unfortunately, as athletic director as well as head football coach, I have to know. And the amount is staggering!"

He shouted the word and leaned toward me again for emphasis. The smell again. Sweet but sour at the same time. Whiskey. Coach Tack Rankin was about half lit!

"Jesus, there are a lot of small countries that don't have the budget we have here. Not just football. Yeah, football could pay for itself. But basketball? They get more people at their goddamn antiwar riots than we have at one of our basketball games. Never mind track and baseball and all that crap."

He leaned way back in his big chair, stretched mightily, and I was afraid he was going to tumble over backward.

"That's where Maxi-Cola and U-Build-'Em Homes and State Banking Company and Freedom Fidelity Insurance come in. I talk pretty about them on the air and our fans spend billions of dollars with them and they send money to the school by the bucketful. To me, too, but the school is what I'm looking out for. Sparta University."

He had named all the sponsors of his TV and radio shows. Why was he telling me this? He leaned forward again, grabbed a quart fruit jar from the corner of his desk and drained it of some kind of brown liquid.

" 'Mmm-mmm! Maxi-Cola means maxi-taste!' " Just like on TV. "But the money. It's still not enough. We can't build stadiums big enough to make money on gate admissions, even for football, I'm sorry to report. We build a hundred thousand seats, we can't sell season tickets 'cause everybody figures he can get a ticket the day of the game, without donating anything to anybody. Then, we have a bad year, lose the first couple of games, we play to a half-empty stadium. Alumni's all screaming about prices already, and how much money they have to contribute to the school to even get the right to buy tickets in the first place. We can't cut back on expenses. Hell, we have a tough enough time recruiting top athletes like you already. Tennessee builds a new weight room, we gotta build one with five more machines and another wall of mirrors and five hundred more square feet. Alabama gets a new whirlpool for the training room, we gotta go buy one that much bigger and better and more expensive."

He seemed to be talking to himself as much as me now, and he was slurring his words noticeably. I drank my Maxi-Cola and stared at more pictures of celebrities that covered the walls.

"More corporate involvement, Mr. McKay. That's the only answer. Let the artificial-turf people pay us to use their stuff in Spartan Stadium. We just cut the deal this week and they'll be laying the stuff in the off-season. Car dealers give us vehicles for the coaches and donate money for us to drive their cars so their salesmen can tell a customer that this car's the one Coach Rankin drives. I can endorse whatever I must to keep the coin coming in.

"Don't get me wrong, son," he said, apparently having a sudden thought. "We are not going to sell out. No sir! We are only going to do what's best for Sparta University and the football program. Oh, and the other sports, too, of course."

He had pulled something from his middle desk drawer which I imagined to be chock-full of whatever it took to establish common ground with whatever high-school kid he was trying to recruit at any given time. Now he was fumbling clandestinely with something behind the desk as I sat in my plush chair and finished up my Maxi-Cola. I could hear the liquid gurgling into his fruit jar. The aroma of Jack Daniel's perfumed the office. He was quiet until after he had sipped and swallowed and leaned back again in his chair.

"You want to know what the next big-money product is going to be?" He didn't wait for my guess. "Athletic shoes. Japanese are just getting going and there's several companies on the West Coast who are going to create a market for the things. Not just your old-fashioned tennis shoes. No sir. Running shoes. Basketball shoes. Exercise shoes. Men. Women. Kids. You name it. Everybody'll have to have two or three pairs. And you know the best way to create a market for the things? 'The shoes the Spartans wear.' They see us and Alabama and Southern Cal and Notre Dame and the Jets and the Vikings and the Rams wearing a particular kind of shoe, they'll knock down the walls trying to get a pair of the damn things for themselves."

He belched loudly but didn't seem to notice his bad manners. I still had no clue what he was getting at, but it was obvious he was getting drunker by the minute.

"All we gotta do is let them give us the shoes. Let me talk about them in some TV spots and on the radio show. We get free shoes. That saves us big money. They give big bucks to the athletic department. Yeah, me too! I'll admit it. I'll make a dollar or two. But, shit, McKay! I'm sixty-four years old. I don't have much longer to screw around in this young man's game. Another year or two at the most, that's all. They can't begrudge me making a dollar or two after all I've given to this school down through the years."

He paused, his face twisted in an angry grimace. Then he seemed to remember I was still there.

"Hey! Don't you go telling anybody Tack Rankin's gonna quit in a year. Don't you dare! That'd ruin recruiting in a damn minute! That goddamned Bear Bryant would be dancing on my grave."

After another belch, he leaned forward and continued talking.

"I've got a chance to land Jima. They're the biggest. I could tell you how much money it'd mean to me . . . the school, I mean. But we probably can't count that high, both of us put together. And if we get them, the jersey people and the helmet people and the weight-machine people and God knows who all else would be beating down our door, trying to throw money at us. Jima. Damn Japanese! I tried to shoot as many of them as I could once upon a time. Now look at me. Flying to Los Angeles and eating high on the hog with them. Put up in the fanciest hotel. Them offering me whiskey and prime rib and girls. . . ."

He stopped, again seemed to realize he was saying too much, then stood unsteadily and walked slowly around the big room.

"Look here. Picture of me with Eisenhower, playing golf in Palm Springs. Ronnie Reagan here in our dressing room after the bowl game in '61. That's Marilyn Monroe there. Didn't know a football from an anvil but she got into that picture with us when we won the national championship. Everybody wants to be identified with a winner, McKay. As long as you're winning, you got plenty of friends. Start off like we did this year and you start to feel like a whore in church."

He heavily sat back down and drained the jar.

"The Jima deal was ours. Contracts were being drawn. In the bag. Then we were a little shaky out of the gate this year. Damn! We were playing some tough teams, son. What the hell do they expect, anyway? Jima gets cold feet. Starts talking to Georgia when they are out of the chute with some big wins early on the television. Damn!"

He slammed his hand down so hard on the dark mahogany desk that the framed pictures of what were apparently his grandchildren flipped over onto their faces. I jumped as if I had been shot.

"But we work hard in practice, make some personnel adjustments, and turn it all around. Beat some people we are not supposed to beat. Get on a roll finally. Now, the bunch of slimy bastards come back, hat in hand, with their latest deal. Us or Georgia. Whichever of us wins the conference gets the deal. Saturday's the day. We win, we're set, no matter what comes down against Tennessee. I don't have much time left to get mine. Get the school theirs, I mean. Yeah, they name the stadium after me someday. Let me come back and watch practice with the other old-timers. Big deal. You can't eat that. You can't take that to the bank. It won't keep you warm when the snow flies."

He leaned forward, toward me, exactly the way he had on my front porch by the light of the moon that night nine months before.

"Son, you got a chance to help me make it work. Oh, I think we can beat the bastards on Saturday. We got a helluva game plan. Everybody's about healthy for once. But I gotta make sure. There's too much at stake to risk it. And you're gonna help me."

It was too dark and he was probably too drunk to see the quizzical look on my face. What the hell was he talking about? He reached and finally found the switch on the desk lamp, flipping it off. I could hear him noisily breathing through his nose in the dark as he fumbled around, feeling for something. He knocked over an object on the desk but somehow got the projector switch thrown. It flickered to life, blinding bright on the screen on the far office wall.

"Number twenty-two. Roosevelt McGee. Watch him."

I had watched him all week in the film room, trying to forget Maggie by studying the Bulldog running back. McGee led the nation in rushing. Heisman Trophy shoo-in, if nothing happened. He was eighty percent of Georgia's offense. And the rest came when they faked the ball to him. Fluid, strong, quick, he seemed able to find a hole before it even opened. Then, when someone did get a straight shot at him, he almost always wiggled free, or had the power to bounce off and get more yards after contact.

"He's a fine running back. Without him, Georgia's mediocre at best. Now, watch this play. Watch it close, son."

The Bulldog quarterback took two steps back, pretended to give the ball to McGee, then raised it high and tossed it backward to another circling running back. No one was within ten yards of him when he caught it and he juked for a long gain.

"No, son, watch McGee. After the fake."

He slapped switches on the side of the projector and the images danced backward until everyone was stooped over at the line of scrimmage again. Switches clicked. The quarterback spun toward McGee and kept the ball again. McGee took a step or two toward the riot breaking out in front of him, then trotted parallel to the line of scrimmage, stopped, stood straight up and turned his head to watch the play unfold behind him as if he were only an interested spectator.

"Watch this. Keep your eye on McGee."

Again the quarterback took the snap from center and twisted toward McGee, but once more he kept the ball and trotted away from his star back, looking downfield for someone to throw to. McGee took a couple of dance steps, then once again trotted to his left, stopped, stood up to his full height when it was obvious to everyone he didn't have the ball, then just rested, his head back, watching what was happening as if he had bought a ticket.

"You see that?"

"He doesn't do much after the fake, if that's what you mean."

"Bull's-eye!" Rankin's trademark expression, screamed full volume every time a good play unfolded on the screen during his television show. "That's where you get him, son. Right there."

I stared at him blankly.

"The dumbass is standing there, straight up, unprotected. They just faked the ball to him. He's fair game. Put a helmet right into the side of that knee and Mr. McGee's season comes to a screeching halt. And Jima is all ours."

I was stunned.

"But, Coach. I could never . . ."

"Just think, son. You can strike a mighty blow for Sparta University. In one play, you can go a long way toward assuring the football program remains the best in America. Oh, and basketball and track and the academic programs and all the other shit get their share, too. Don't worry about that. One play! Do you know how noble that is, boy? What a rare opportunity it is for you to contribute so mightily?"

"I'm sorry, Coach Rankin. I just don't think I can take a cheap shot like that."

"Cheap shot? Cheap shot? You're a Literature major, aren't you? Surely you can see the irony in that phrase. A cheap shot that means millions of dollars for Sparta University. Hell, that's no cheap shot!"

He laughed hysterically and clicked off the projector. Rising, he stumbled in the blackness to the wall and turned on the overhead lights. I was blinded for a moment, but when I could see again, he was back in his desk chair, sorting through notes on his desk.

"You simply have to do it for the school, Mr. McKay. You're the only one with the speed and smarts to do it so it looks natural. The only one on our fine Spartan team. And if anyone is suspicious about your motives, we just blame it on freshman eagerness and inexperience."

"No, sir. I can't do it."

"He's fair game, son! He faked. That's the way the play is designed. He is supposed to draw your attention. All you do is give it him, just like they want you to. One lick. Top of the helmet or a good shoulder pad while he's standing there admiring the play, and our worries are over. You said you'd do what it took to win when you came here. Here's one of the things you have to do."

He continued to sort through the papers as he talked, not looking at me at all.

"No, sir. I'm sorry. I'll play the game of my life. We'll do what we can to beat Georgia. But I won't deliberately do anything dirty like that. It's just not in me to do it. I'm sorry."

He still didn't look at me, but apparently found the paper he was looking for. He eyed it carefully. Slowly, he looked up at me as if seeing me for the first time.

"You roomed for a while with a young man named Dexter Flynt?"

"Yes, sir. For a while."

"Why did he decide to stop sharing a room with you?"

"I don't know." I lied clear-eyed, without blinking.

"He certainly does. He tells me he was greatly offended by your use of drugs on several occasions."

Someone had just put a hard helmet in my gut, driving the wind from me.

"No, Coach! No! I never . . ."

"You're telling me you never smoked marijuana since you've been here at Sparta? Or that you didn't take barbiturates at times to sleep? Both strictly against university and athletic policy. A clear violation of your grant-in-aid agreement. And Mr. Flynt is prepared to testify before the faculty senate if it should come to that. He has quite a willingness to cooperate with me these days if I should just give the word."

Without breath to push out the words, I couldn't say anything. The old gray-haired bastard laid aside the paper he was holding in his trembling hand, slid back in his chair and chuckled quietly to himself.

"And he was also very concerned that you may have communicated some information to gamblers. He said you had telephone conversations in his presence that he thinks he can quote letter and verse. You know our team policy on such activities, don't you, Mr. McKay?"

I, of course, couldn't answer. I was having a hard time breathing.

"Just like a good football game plan, C.P. Have your offensive and defensive game plans worked out to the letter. Rehearse them until you have them down pat, but be prepared for anything. Rain, a key injury, a funny bounce of the ball. Play fundamentally sound football, but always have a trick play ready for the fourth quarter, just in case you need it."

He motioned me up and out his door with a wave of his hand.

"Go on now, son. You probably have studying to do. I don't want to keep you late. Have a good game Saturday. A good game. And I truly appreciate what you are going to contribute to our great victory."

My stomach rolled and thundered and I felt unsteady, as if it were me who had been chugging the Jack Daniel's. Quickly I stepped to the door. The last thing I heard was his low chuckling and the clink of the whiskey bottle against the neck of his once-again-empty fruit jar.

THIRTEEN

T he disembodied voice from the darkness scared me so badly I went weak-kneed.

"Keeping late hours during midterms, aren't you?"

Since leaving the athletic office, I had walked several miles in the cool night, mostly around and around the quadrangle. I had tried to avoid a crowd milling near a bonfire in the middle of the quad. An ill-tempered, loud bunch cursed the war and shook their fists at the spot in the sky where the embers floating upward from the blaze disappeared into the darkness.

"I would think you would be studying somewhere, son."

It was Claxton. The president of a major seat of learning had nothing better to do than follow me around and criticize my study habits. He had fallen in step beside me, ignoring the profane crowd screaming and singing a hundred yards from us, threatening to get out of control.

"Sometimes I think better when I'm walking in the night air. Right now, I'm committing to memory all the kings and queens of England in the seventeenth through the twentieth centuries.

Wanna hear them, in order, with biographical notations?"

"No, no. Not necessary. I'm sure you'll do fine. Though Professor Wheeler reports you have gotten a little sloppy of late. Everything okay?"

"Just working hard at football. That's all."

"You sure? Everything all right at home? With your parents? No . . . distractions . . . here at the university?"

He said "distractions" as if he was spitting out something that tasted rank.

"No, no. Everything's fantastic."

"Well. I know it has been quite a while since I was an undergraduate, but I do remember the urges and diversions which can tempt a vigorous, healthy young man away from home for the first time. Just don't lose sight of the prize that can be yours, young man. We'll do all we can, the faculty and I, but you must give every appearance of excelling. Every appearance."

The protesters were now doing a frantic dance around the fire, whooping and waving smoking torches in the air. Claxton did a quick left turn and moved away from me and was immediately swallowed up in what darkness the roaring, crackling bonfire left for him to get lost in. I could hardly hear his voice over the chanting demonstrators when he spoke to me again from the shadows.

"Good night, Mr. McKay. Good luck on your exams."

Then I was at the well-worn path between the bushes next to the Language Arts building where Maggie had always disappeared. I couldn't help it. My feet took me toward Drake's. God knows, I needed at least one bright spot in my life just then. Maggie Vinyard was it.

"She left early," Blue-hair said. "Said she didn't feel well. Didn't look none too good, neither. Kinda peaked. She's comin' down with the grippe that's got us all under the weather, I reckon. Three girls come down with it yesterday. . . ."

The red-faced girl behind the desk at Maggie's dorm didn't even look up from her organic chemistry book.

"Got a 'Do not disturb' on. Can't bother her."

"Could I leave her a note?"

"I don't care."

I had the stub of a pencil and an index card with history notes on it in my jacket pocket. I scribbled the lines from Tennyson as nearly as I could remember them:

> Maggie,
> *"Dear as remembered kisses after death,*
> *And sweet as those by hopeless fancy feigned*
> *On lips that are for others; deep as love,*
> *Deep as first love, and wild with all regret;*
> *O Death in life, the days that are no more."*
>   *Please call me.*
>
> C.P.

The girl put it in Maggie's mailbox without looking. I almost went back and got it, to tear it up and maybe burn it in what was left of the war protesters' bonfire, but I didn't.

Father called right on schedule that night, about eight o'clock.

"Wadda you think, boy? Georgia's a five-point favorite. Y'all ain't gonna lose to them at home, are you?"

"Naw, Father. We'll beat them straight up. Take the points and run to the bank. And I have a good shot at making the President's List this semester . . . all A's."

"Yeah, but that McGee nigger's awful good, boy. Awful good!"

"Not after I hit him a time or two. They say I could be up for a Rhodes Scholarship, you know."

"Anybody hits the way you do, your quickness, you damn well oughta be! That's the attitude! Cut his damn legs off at the knees!

Yeah, you stand him up a time or two and he'll wish he was back in the quarters shining shoes and eating welfare cheese!"

He laughed uproariously. Maw kept asking him how I was. How my head was doing. I could hear her. He told her I was good enough "to knock the soot off that nigger back from Georgia . . . hit him so hard he'd be wearing his balls for ear bobs." He never did let her have the telephone. Just wanted to brag about being up several thousand on the season so far. How mad old Cooter Casteel was at him for taking so much of his money. That he believed he'd take the Spartans and the points on Saturday and swipe some more of the bald-headed bastard's blood money.

I cut all my Friday classes. It was just too much trouble getting up. I forced down a big breakfast, mainly because I had lost another ten pounds and was twenty pounds below where I needed to be. But the eggs and bacon and juice rode heavy on my stomach. Time dragged, too. Studying was no good. Reading was too much a chore. Chris's television showed nothing but insipid game shows and soap operas, and the radio played the same songs over and over.

Finally, about noon, I trotted over to the athletic building to look at some more Georgia film. Max Milligan was there already, head swimming in cigarette smoke in the dark room as he ran the same pass play over and over. He jumped when I spoke.

"They complete it every time, don't they?"

"Hell, McKay! You better get in the way of some of them passes tomorrow or they'll score a hundred points before the bands march at halftime."

"Watch the fullback's knees."

"What?"

"On a pass play, he hardly bends them at all, ready to step back into pass blocking. On a running play, his butt almost touches the ground. He has to get a good, low start or McGee will run up his back."

"Damn!"

He unspooled and watched several more plays as his cigarette burned almost to the vee of his fingers. He didn't even notice.

"Damn! You're right! How'd you notice that?"

"Saw it on the film the other day. I was going to mention it at the meeting this afternoon."

"You know what? You oughta look at our offense. Maybe tip Coach Tack on things we may be doing. The way our offense stinks, it needs all the help it can get."

I had a sudden thought.

"Max, I'd like to talk with you about something if you have time."

"Sure, kid. You keep making a dozen tackles a game and I'll come over and tuck you in and sing you to sleep at night."

"It's about Coach Rankin. And it's something pretty serious."

His expression in the shimmering projector light changed noticeably, the look of a man who might have just heard the flutter of vampire wings. He twisted out the cigarette in an overflowing ashtray, held up his watch to the screen for light and checked the time.

"Tell you what. Let's take a walk and get out of this smoke. We got a couple of hours before the meeting anyway." His voice broke just a bit. Then he was quiet until we were outside, out of sight of the football offices.

"I ain't totally paranoid, you see, but somehow the old man finds out everything that's said or goes on inside that building. He could probably tell you how many baloney sandwiches I got in my lunch sack if you was to ask him."

We were strolling slowly across campus, its population now thinned as students fled for home on Friday afternoon. I was following his lead with no idea where we were heading. He lit another cigarette.

"Okay, shoot. But don't tell me slow. I may not want to hear it."

"Well, I don't know how much to mention, Max. He told me not to tell anybody."

"Like that spy picture I saw on the TV the other night: 'Now you know too much. . . . I'm gonna have to kill you.' Look, kid. You don't know if you can trust me or not. But they's some things I need to tell you before you spill your guts."

He walked in silence awhile, took a big drag on his cigarette and then flipped the hardly-smoked butt into a bush.

"I don't know if you can actually trust me, McKay. If you tell me the old bastard grabbed your pecker under the table, it ain't no business of mine. But if you've gone and done something that could hurt this team, I gotta go to the man and tell him. See what I mean?"

We had left the campus behind and walked into a neighborhood I had not seen before. Tiny crackerbox houses were crowded together in claustrophobic rows along both sides of the street. Bare trees seemed to reach for any kind of light, and even the sunshine seemed somewhat dimmer here. Junk cars propped on concrete blocks filled many yards, leaves were unraked, paint on houses peeled and faded. The sidewalk played out and we continued on a well-worn but muddy path beside the cracked asphalt street.

"Well, it's neither one of those things. I just need some advice from somebody who knows Rankin better than I do."

He turned suddenly to the right, leading me past a long row of mailboxes, down a rutted gravel road and into a dingy trailer park. He stepped up onto the rickety wooden porch of the third trailer on the right and plopped down in a rusty metal lawn chair, motioning me to sit in a matching one next to it. The sun was warm, at least. The park was apparently deserted. He took the time to light another cigarette before he spoke again.

"Welcome to the mansion football has built for Max Milligan," he laughed, and motioned to the pitted, dirt-streaked mobile home behind him. "I've been an assistant coach here for six years and ain't got a pot to piss in. But, God, I love this game and most of the people in it. Especially you kids. Yeah, some of you are royal pains in the ass. But mostly I love you guys. I just feel lucky to still be coaching."

"Gee, Max, no offense, but I thought assistant coaches on this level did better than this." He winced. I bit my tongue, afraid I had hurt his feelings.

"Let me tell you a little story, McKay. Eight years ago, I was riding high and mighty. Defensive coordinator at Texas Tech. Had the number two defense in the country that year. I got interviewed for the head job at three Division One schools the same damn week. I was ready to take my pick of the litter, pack my grip, herd Missus Milligan and the children into the Caddy and turn the college football world on its smug ear."

He was quiet for a while, smoking, apparently thinking how he wanted to unreel his story from this point on. He lit another cigarette with the dying embers of his last one, sucking to pull it to life.

"Then they all three got wind of my little problem and pulled back like an old snapping turtle when it thunders. Wouldn't even return my calls, none of them. I just prayed it wouldn't get to my boss at Tech. But, of course it did. Reporters made sure of that when I didn't get any of the other jobs and they found out why I was being treated like a bad case of the clap."

He chuckled to himself and took a long drag.

"Hell, I was in the papers out there in West Texas more than Kennedy and Nixon and old Lyndon Johnson all put together for a while there. Shoot, you would have thought I'd took an ax to my wife and young 'uns and then barbecued them for Sunday dinner, the way they wrote about me. Every man's got a major strength and a major weakness, McKay. That's one of the meanest tricks God played on us, I figure. And usually, one or the other of them wins out in a man. Them that's supersuccessful in life, your presidents of the United States and millionaires and such, they figure out how to suppress their major weakness and capitalize on the major strengths. Then there's the bulk of folks that just lets the two tussle it out, along with the other things that are good and bad in their makeup, and they pretty much break even in life. And then, well, there's the rest of us. Life's colossal fuck-ups."

He waited while an old rattle-trap of a car chugged by. I stayed quiet as he waved and watched the car go by. If he wanted to tell me his major weakness, he would.

"I've loved football ever since I was old enough to tote a ball around. I was sorry as a player. Couldn't do squat. All I ever wanted to do was coach the game. And I craved being the head man. One who called the shots. I could have been a damn good one, too, McKay. I understand the game. I know what works and what doesn't. I don't mind the hours. The way the job can be a cancer on a man's life. But Missus Milligan never bargained for what it all involved. She was jealous of it all. Couldn't understand why I had to go back at night and look at film or work on a game plan all weekend when everybody else's husband was on the couch in front of the TV or mowing the lawn or whatever.

"I know some coaches' wives compensate with church or volunteer work or get all wrapped up in their kids. Lots of them screw around. Drink or take drugs. Missus Milligan spent money. God, she could go through a paycheck like Sherman went through Georgia. I was making good money. No lie. But I woke up one day broker than a hobo. Bill collectors calling me at the athletic department, ambushing me at my car after practice, threatening to take the house and attach our bank account and repossess Missus Milligan's fur coats and jewels and big Buick."

He was quiet for a while. I didn't know whether to say something or not. He was obviously dying to talk with somebody. Obviously I was it. He finally cleared his throat and went on.

"There was no prospect of getting more money at work. Then, I got a bright idea. Hell, nobody knew more about football than I did. Certainly not the bookies and gamblers. All I had to do was put that knowledge I had to work for me. Bet enough to get ahead again, then quit. But you know what? I found my major weakness. It was as bad as any drug could possibly be. If I won, I had to double it up and try to get more. If I lost, I had to get back even. And you know what else? The irony is, it don't matter how much you know about the game. The line's set by the bookies to get people to bet equal money on both sides. To make sure the bookies ultimately come out the winner. Don't matter what you know, in the long run you'll still lose more than you win. I lost, even when I bet on my own team. I never took the opposition. I didn't never sink that low. But God knows I lost. And before I knew it, I was beholden to them leeches, along with the bank and the IRS and everybody else and his brother. I had to tell them bastards things they wanted to know, just to keep them from cutting my nuts off. That's what got to the reporters and back to my boss. I lost my job, my family.

"It was Tack Rankin that saved my sorry ass. But he owns me now, too. I gotta work for what he pays me. Do what he tells me. He says, 'Jump,' I say, 'How high and how many times?' He says, 'Did that McKay kid say somethin' to you?' I gotta say yes and tell him exactly what, word for word like a goddamn tape recorder. You understand what I'm tellin' you, son?"

"Yeah, Max. I do. I'm sorry. I never meant to put that burden on you."

"Hell, I'm glad you got that kind of confidence in me. Listen. Whatever it is, you do the right thing in your own mind. Not what Rankin or me or anybody else says. You do what C.P. McKay knows is the right thing and you'll be okay. You're smart, boy. About as smart as anybody I've seen that was dumb enough to buckle on a football helmet, at least."

I stood and shook his hand.

"Thanks, Coach. See you at the meeting."

I looked back as I left the trailer park. He was still sitting in the rusty lawn chair on the rickety front porch in front of his rusted trailer. A shaft of gray cigarette smoke was rising straight up in the still air toward a warm sun.

FOURTEEN

I played the football game of my life that Saturday afternoon. If you don't believe me, you can look up what they wrote about me in the yearbook. Pull the newspaper clippings. It's all there. The television people named me Player of the Game and donated scholarship money in my name to Sparta University. The plaque is still right there, hanging on the wall in the wing of the athletic offices that they later named for me.

Lord knows, I didn't feel like it would be a great day when I first trotted out of the dark, cool tunnel into the unusually warm November sunshine. My stomach was twisted into knots and my legs felt weak and disobedient. Loosening up, I tried not to watch McGee in his white jersey and red helmet with the *G* on the side as he cut and spun and danced at the far end of the field. He looked even quicker and more special in person than on film. Even his teammates stopped their own drills to watch him do his tricks. A red cluster of Georgia fans in the end zone cheered his every practice catch and fake feint.

On the sidelines before we kicked off to them, Rankin gave me a look that could only be saying, "Do what I told you, or . . ." I tried to keep my expression noncommittal and my breakfast down. It wasn't that hard to avoid tipping what I planned to do, though. I still had not made up my mind. I had no idea what might happen. Rankin could ruin me. Or I could do something so alien to me I couldn't even picture it in my mind's eye. Sure, I played the game hard, rough, full-speed. But I had never taken a cheap shot or even thrown an angry punch in a game in my life. To end a man's season, and maybe his career, just because my coach told me to do so was hard to think about.

There was Maw and Father up in the pressbox. She was in the same dress she had worn to all the games so far. He seemed to be sitting even lower than usual in his wheelchair, slumped over, the twisted roll of the program blazing whitely in his hand in a maverick spot of sunlight. Keeping my father from getting seriously hurt at the hands of the bookies was another wild card in my trying to decide whether to do Rankin's bidding and cripple McGee that day. I knew he had bet more than he could afford to lose on the Spartans. And it was my fault he was in the wheelchair in the first place. I couldn't let him lose.

I was getting tired of the whole thing chewing on me. I just wanted the game to start, confident that once the heat of the war started, the right solution would present itself. And I could take it. After all, I felt most at home out there, between the chalk lines.

The first time McGee came my way in the game, I was so keyed up I almost missed him altogether, just grabbing a handful of jersey as he scooted by and then barely hanging on until somebody from the inside got out to help. Six yards. I reached to help him up after the whistle blew the play dead. He took my hand, let me pull him to his feet, patted me on the side of the helmet as if saying, "Good play," but his words were not toting the same sentiment.

"Hey, white boy. You better look at my face right now. It's the last time you gonna see anything but my ass the rest of the day."

I patted him on the rump, another signal of good sportsmanship to those watching from the stands and on television.

"And a nice ass it is, Roosevelt. Too bad it's going to belong to me all afternoon."

Jesus Christ almighty, I loved the game! Even the senseless juvenile jabbering we did at each other. Him against me. There might as well have been no one else on the field but us. The crowd could as easily have been mute, sitting on their hands. My teammates and the Georgia players were mere shadows on the periphery of my vision. I was so honed in on McGee that Maw could probably have taken the snap from center and hobbled a hundred yards for a score before I could have recovered and caught up to her.

I hated it when we stopped them short of a first down and I had to trot off to the opposite side of the field, away from McGee, so they could punt the ball back to us. I wanted to be back out there immediately, nose to nose, sparring, jawing, spitting, cussing, clawing, hitting.

"Good stop, McKay," Rankin said. "Stay sharp." And he winked. An evil, burning ember of a wink that only he and I knew said much more.

Our offense sucked wind, as usual. Skip Gross hit two of their defensive backs right in the hands with his first two passes. Lucky they were so surprised by his gifts that they didn't catch either one of them or they could have probably scored twice without breaking a sweat. Damn, I thought, it looks like he is throwing right to them! Luckily, we were able to run the ball some. But on a third and two at their twenty, Skip fumbled the snap from center and again we were lucky. Our fullback was alert and fell on the ball for a four-yard loss. The field goal sailed just inside the left upright. We led by three. Father was up by eight. Everybody was happy. Then disaster struck.

It was a blessing that Gross went down hard near the end of the half under a wave of red and white. He lay there for a while and one of the trainers reported back to Rankin on the sidelines that his quarterback had snapped his collarbone. He was gone for the day, of course, and most likely out for the Tennessee game and the bowl trip. Rankin turned white.

Lawton Gray, Gross's backup, was mostly ineffectual, but at least he didn't throw it to the other team, and he could take the center snap without dropping it. As long as he could make the handoff to our backs and get out of the way without stepping on somebody important, we had a chance to win the game.

When we went on defense after a second field goal, I had a strange premonition that something good was about to happen. The feeling was so strong it wiped out the uneasiness that had blanketed me all day, the quandary about what to do with Rankin's dictum. The Georgia quarterback was shouting an audible at the line of scrimmage already, his voice breaking in his eagerness to get the play under way. He had spotted something in our alignment he liked and was switching to another play from the one he had called in the huddle.

There was a slight, almost unnoticed movement in the backfield. The fullback's butt going straight up in the air a couple of inches. His knees unlocked, set to step back and block for his quarterback. Pass play. Pass play all the way. I would have to ignore the fake to McGee, hard as it would be. My first and strongest instinct would be to make a dive for him, but I knew he would only be an empty-handed decoy this time. There was no hesitation. Only a second or two to make sure my whole team knew what I now knew. I backpedaled into my zone, screaming, "Pass!" as loudly as I could. Elgie Munford believed me, even if I was only a freshman, joined my song, and slapped the linebacker nearest him on the butt as he shifted deeper, playing pass all the way. The quarterback's eyes looked to the other side, then back my way, too late to change the play again, with too little time to wonder how we knew. Then he called the correct number for the center snap.

The ball popped into his hands, the line collided with a chorus of grunts as he turned, pretended to give the ball to McGee but kept it instead, slipping down the line of scrimmage behind his blockers to my side of the field, then angling backward, backpedaling to set up to throw. Just in front and to the left of me, a white shadow with a red crown that was probably the tight end was sliding out, toward me, almost lost in the melee the snap of the ball had set loose.

Again, as it sometimes did when I played this game, everything seemed to slow down, to shift like a film into slow motion. The quarterback's arm was cocked back like a catapult. One of our defensive linemen, ignoring any chance of a running play since my cry of "Pass," materialized from nowhere, bearing down on him like a bull in full red-cape charge. Then, a half second before he really wanted to, the quarterback sent the football spiraling toward the white shadow that had drifted out in front of me. I ducked under the giant's outstretched right arm as he reached for the pass, felt the nose of the ball burrow into my belly like a bullet, and used both arms to cover it up, embrace it, not let it escape.

In the instant I realized I had it securely tucked away, I took as big a step forward as I could, knowing the victimized tight end was just behind me, ready to grab me, squeeze me, and try to shuck me of his football. I heard his futile groan, the roar of the crowd, the thud of somebody getting blocked hard to my left, and then I was running, screaming the code for an interception—"Bingo!"—so loudly my throat burned. Running as hard as I could, the wind whistling in my helmet earholes, pads popping and flapping with the motion. I could hear something halfway between a whine and a moan. It was coming from me! I just concentrated on not tripping over my own feet, keeping on my toes to try to accelerate, looking for an open field.

There he was. Roosevelt McGee, the best athlete on the field, was standing straight up and still, watching the play as he usually did when he wasn't involved, a look of shock on his face. He was the only one between me and the end zone that I could see. Him and me. The only two people in a suddenly silent, empty, slow-motion world.

Others might have desperately dived at me, or kept their feet and waited for me to pass by, get the angle on me and try to cut me off before I scored. But McGee was an instinctive athlete. He didn't let his surprise delay his reaction. He crouched, got into the perfect position to tackle me, watching my belt buckle so any evasive moves on my part wouldn't throw him off balance. I knew I should feint, fake, and try to go around him, but I couldn't. I would be no match for his quickness of movement. He could at least slow me long enough for someone else to catch up. And as fast as he was, he would run me down anyway if I managed to get past him somehow. I would be no match for his burning speed.

There's no way I had time to think of all the things I think I did in that split second. All the bastards who pushed and pulled at me, trying to yank me in their direction, shove me the way they wanted me to go for their own agenda, or simply left me twisting, dangling, loving but unloved. Claxton, Wheeler, Casteel, Rankin. Even Father and Maggie Vinyard. Whatever went through my mind convinced me the surest path to the end zone was straight through the Heisman Trophy favorite, waiting for me with a huge grin on his face.

I pulled as much explosive strength as I could muster, consciously concentrated it in my legs, instantly dipped my left shoulder, the one away from where the ball was nestled in the crook of my arm, and aimed all my frustration and disgust and anger and pain right at the midsection of Roosevelt McGee, whose misfortune it was to be at that very spot at that moment. The impact was so cruel, so vicious, my whole left side went numb. I heard the breath explode out of McGee's lungs like thunder and felt the spray of spit as the collision tore loose his mouthpiece. Somehow I kept most of my momentum and managed to lift my feet high enough to wade right through McGee as if he were merely tall grass. I kept on running without stumbling.

Then I was clear, pounding toward the end zone five miles and forty yards away. I felt as if I was carrying my stinging, tingling left arm like a dead tree limb, flapping at my side, unfeeling, useless. I tried to gobble up five yards with each step, but the goal posts and the frenzied, waving people in the end-zone seats seemed to blur and kept moving away from me in the distance, like I was running backward. I was amazed at the sudden quietness. I could hear only the wind whistling in my helmet, the clattering of my shoulder pads.

Then, I was startled to find I was almost there. Just short of the goal line, I could see someone's shadow overtaking me, hear pumping breath. He hit me hard from behind, but I used that boost of momentum from his lick to stretch out and hurl myself for the yellow-and-white stripe. The bomb-blast of noise from the crowd told me I had made it, but it was a while before half the Georgia team and most of mine got off the top of me and I could dance to my feet, jump up and down and spike the ball right in the middle of the giant lightning bolt painted on the sprayed-green grass of the end zone. Take that, Roosevelt McGee! Tack Rankin! All of you bastards!

Feeling had suddenly returned to my left side and my shoulder hurt like hell, but I didn't care. The shoulder wasn't dislocated because I was still able to lift that arm and the other one in my own exaggerated touchdown signal. And it seemed to work okay when I high-fived every player in sight.

It was only when I skipped toward the sideline that I noticed the activity out at the forty-yard line, the spot where I had collided with the great Georgia running back a year and thirty seconds ago. At least six people bent over Roosevelt McGee, who squirmed on the ground, holding his midsection. I could hear his groans above the still-buzzing crowd. Even the Georgia head coach was now trotting out to check on him. That meant the injury must be serious.

"Helluva play, C.P. baby!" Elgie Munford slapped me so hard on the butt it stung, but I didn't care. "You run through that son of a bitch like he was air, man. Like he was air!"

"I had to, man. I had to. Had to get the job done. It was the only way to the end zone. No detours. We don't take detours."

I told the reporters the same thing later in the dressing room. That's how the phrase "No detours" got on signs all over the locker room and became the Spartan slogan for years to come.

I was behind the bench and rotating my arm in the shoulder socket just to make sure it wouldn't fall off or stiffen up, preparing to go right back out on defense after we kicked off again. Rankin was standing there beside me before I even noticed him. Our eyes collided. He said nothing. Just a grim look on his face. Then, finally, he winked, smiled crookedly, and turned and walked back to his well-worn spot on the sideline. He knew I had found a way to do his bidding the right way. My way. Not his way.

Max Milligan was watching us from the other side of the bench.

"I told you the son of a bitch was going to kiss you on the lips someday. Hell, if he don't, I will." He shook my hand strenuously and hugged me hard. I didn't think he was going to let me go in time to get out and set for the next play, and I half dragged him with me.

I don't remember much more of the game. We beat them thirteen to nothing. They gained only fifty yards running the ball all day. McGee had every rib on his right side broken in our collision and missed the rest of the season. My shoulder was bruised so badly it turned black and purple from the nipple over the top to the shoulder blade. I never felt it when the pellets of hot water hit it in the shower, nor when the reporters and my teammates and the rest of the coaches in the dressing room and the mob just outside the door kept pounding it over and over, ecstatic with the win and the part I had played.

All I could think of was hurrying to the press-box elevator and getting up to see Maw and Father. They were still sitting at their usual spot on the end of press row when I got there. Father was crying, huge tears rolling down his gray cheeks. He was crying so hard he could hardly speak, and was shaking as if chilled.

"Boy! Damn! When you . . ." He gasped for breath, tried to raise his right hand, but it still gripped the ragged game program like a claw and resisted his will. "Stuck that nigger . . ."

"I know, Father," I said, looking around to make sure no black person was within earshot.

"Run over his ass. . . . Kept goin', runnin' like that. . . ." His voice was getting lower as if his batteries were running down. I could hardly hear him now, and bent close. ". . . got me up by eighteen over them goddamn bookies. . . . Big money . . . goddamn big money today, boy."

I felt a warm hand on my hurt shoulder.

"Corey Phil, are you all right?"

"Yeah, Maw. I'm just fine."

"I can't watch it no more. Can't stand to watch the way you run into them other players so hard, get knocked down and they all pile on top of you. I just can't watch it no more."

"It's really all right, Maw, we . . ."

"Your guardian angel saved you today. I know that. I just don't know how much longer she'll be able to, though. I got a bad feeling, darling. A bad feeling."

"Damn, Maw!" I was screaming at her. Two men sweeping up the press box looked our way. "We just won the biggest game of the year. I was Most Valuable Player. Seventy thousand people were screaming my name, and all you can do is carry on about guardian angels and bad feelings and such."

She looked so old. So lined and old. I instantly felt bad for screaming at her, so I took her close and held her like I had not done since I was a kid. She was trembling.

"I won't stand by and let nobody hurt you, Corey Phil. Nobody."

"I know you won't, Maw, but I'll be all right. It's the guys I'm tackling you better be worrying about."

She ignored my attempt at humor, finally pulled away, and reached to wipe a string of drool from Father's lip with a hot-dog napkin. He was trying to tell her something, but she ignored him.

"Lordy, we better be getting home. It'll be getting dark on us directly." She turned to me and I thought she was going to hug me again but she didn't. "Father wants to come down for the Tennessee game next week but he ain't doing too good, Corey Phil. He's suffering pretty bad. It just seems like he lives for these games. They're all that keeps him going. I don't know what he's a-gonna do when the season's over."

"There's next year, Maw, and lots more after that."

"Yeah, I reckon," she said with no conviction.

I helped roll Father to the elevator door while Maw held my arm and walked along with us. Her eyes were closed until we were past the railing, down to the ground and rolling out the door. Then they were gone, growing smaller until the stadium eclipsed them.

There again was that almost overpowering feeling of aloneness. Last hour's hero was now standing in the cold shadow of Spartan Stadium, all alone, unnoticed by a crew busily sweeping up all the garbage the fans had tossed aside. A couple of kids were chucking a football around on the beaten-down grass near the stadium, and one of them ran square into me as I reached up painfully and intercepted the other kid's pass.

"Hey, watch out, mister. Gimme my ball before I call a cop."

I flipped it to him and slowly started the walk toward the dorm. Two papers waited to be written and a book needed to be read. Just as I turned the corner, I heard the other kid yell to his friend:

"Try to run past me, Jimmy. I'll be C.P. McKay!"

Elgie Munford pulled up alongside me in his old rattle-trap Dodge. Its busted, chugging muffler made it hard to hear him when he yelled at me.

"Hey, man! Hop in! Party's just starting over at Man-cow's apartment."

"I may be along later. I want to get some ice on this shoulder."

"Come on over, man. We got women, beer, chips and dip . . . the four basic food groups!"

"Sure. I'll be over directly."

Blue oil-smoke obliterated the car as he clattered away.

I was in the dark, gloomy shadows of the tall cedars, almost to the dorm, when I felt someone following closely behind me. At first, I was afraid it might be Cooter, who always seemed to be lurking nearby on game days. Or Claxton, back to push some more. Maybe even Rankin, running me down to thank me for landing his goddamned shoe money.

But when I stopped suddenly and spun, it was Maggie. Neither of us spoke for a moment. Then she came to me, into my arms and we just held each other for a while. Finally, I spoke first.

"Maggie? What happened? What did I do?"

"Oh, C.P. I knew you would think you had done something. I knew you would blame yourself."

I held her back then, at arm's distance, and looked into her wonderful eyes, now wet, avoiding mine.

"But that night. It was so wonderful. . . ." I involuntarily glanced deep into the darkness of the evergreens where we had made love less than a week ago. "I thought we had something so special there would be no way it would end. Then you were gone. It had to be me. Something I did . . . we did."

"No. It's more complicated than that. And I'm not even sure I can tell you about it. For your own good, C.P. It's best you don't know. But it's not your fault." She finally let her eyes find mine. "I was quickly falling in deep love with you. And that would not be doing you any favors. I'm sorry. Just let me go." She had turned her face away and wouldn't even look at me. "This was a mistake, coming here tonight. Running you down like this. Look, it's best if I just go on now and leave you alone. Good-bye."

She slipped from my arms and began walking away quickly, escaping. That was it? Not my fault? In love but no favor to me? And then, just her back disappearing into the dusk.

"Maggie! Stop!"

And she did, but still faced the other way, ready to bolt on a whim.

"You can't just leave me like this. I told you that night. I've never loved anyone like you before. Hell, I've never loved anybody at all. You jumped on me for not sharing everything with you. Now you're doing the same thing. What's wrong? If you really love me, if you ever loved me at all, you have to tell me."

I had reached her by then, took my good arm and twisted her roughly to face me. Tears marked both cheeks. She slowly turned from me once again, began walking, not inviting me to follow, not forbidding me to, so I fell in beside her. We strolled a good hundred yards, a full three minutes, before she spoke to me again, softly, slowly, as if the effort of speaking the words pained her.

"That night . . . it was wonderful, C.P. Ever since I've known you, being with you has been nothing but wonderful. Falling so far in such a short time, though . . . It's not like me at all. I don't have much experience with such a thing, but I know that I fell in love with you. That was my first mistake. For the first time in my life, I let my guard down and sure enough, I fell hard. Maybe it's my totally screwed-up family. Maybe it's just my personality. But I've never let anyone get close until you. I knew it would be wrong. I knew there was no way I could ever deserve you."

She never glanced up, but kept her gaze on the sidewalk. I started to protest her words. Tell her no, it's me who let his guard down, fell harder than he ever wanted to, didn't deserve such love from anyone. But she kept talking.

"I expected you would dump me eventually. Or maybe someone else would come along who was prettier, richer, more appropriate for a football hero's girlfriend. That's what I fully expected. But I never anticipated . . ."

Her voice trailed off. I could feel the struggle she was fighting. I took her hand, we stopped walking, turned to each other again. We had made it to the walkway in front of the president's mansion. Only a dim light that spilled from the chandelier in its foyer and out the front windows of the beautiful building let me see the confusion that twisted her face as if she were in pain.

"Damn, Maggie! Tell me! If you ever cared for me at all, tell me the truth."

She sighed, a decision made, but still hesitant and unsure.

"It was Wheeler."

"Wheeler?"

"I worked early at the infirmary. The morning everything was closed by the snow? It was crazy there. All the flu and the weekend hangovers. I didn't get the word about classes being canceled. Or if somebody told me, it didn't register. I don't know. I was just anxious to see you. That's all I was thinking about. Wheeler's my first class on Monday. Nobody was there but him when I got there. He told me classes were called off, but that he was glad I came in anyway, that he wanted to talk with me. Privately. He told me I was failing and probably couldn't pull my grade up enough to pass his course. No way! C.P., I've never failed in my life! I was valedictorian. Scored a thirty-four on my ACT. I never got below a B in my life. I made the dean's list every quarter last year. Now I'm in danger of failing the most important class I've taken yet. Then it got real strange."

I glanced up and down the sidewalk, then pulled her to a wrought-iron bench at the edge of the mansion lawn, far enough away from a streetlight to give us some privacy, but in the clear so we could make sure no one else came close and overheard us. She took off her glasses, wiped her eyes with her sleeves, little girl–like, took a deep breath, and continued.

"Then he said he wanted to talk to me about you, C.P."

"Me? Wheeler wanted to talk to you about me?"

"He told me you had a wonderful opportunity to be considered for the Rhodes Scholarship. Your being an athlete, having such great academic credentials. I knew you were smart, but Jesus, the Rhodes? That's something, C.P. Then he said some problems had recently arisen. That you couldn't afford distractions at such a critical time. Anything that might take your mind off your football and classwork. At first, I didn't know what he was getting at. I didn't even know he knew about us. But he sat right there behind that dusty desk of his and did all but tell me to keep away from you or you wouldn't have a chance at the scholarship. Could even possibly lose your football scholarship if you didn't perform as well as you could on the field and in the classroom. I knew that would knock you out of school completely. And it would be my fault. I couldn't be responsible for that, C.P. I love you too much!"

The hair on the back of my neck stood up.

"Dammit, Maggie! That's all bullshit! You weren't . . ."

"C.P.! Calm down!" She had hold of my arm and I could see her jaw set firmly in the slight luminescence from Claxton's mansion. "Look, I shouldn't be telling you any of this. It's only going to make you so mad you might do something terrible and that would just make it worse. And that, too, would be my fault. See what I mean? About our going our separate ways being the best for you?"

"No. No. It's okay." I fought to keep my cool. Not to let a clip in the back force me into a slug that might cost a penalty. "Go ahead, Maggie. You can tell me everything."

"Promise you won't go off the deep end? If you do, it could hurt us both."

"All right." I smoothed her hair, nipped a tear from her cheek with a finger, and put my arm around her shoulders. She shivered. "It's just the redneck in me, Maggie. Sometimes it's hard to suppress wanting to beat the holy shit out of somebody when they do something like this. I'm sorry. Please. Go on. Tell me more."

"I told him our relationship didn't seem to be affecting your grades. And that you were helping me with my own work. That I thought I was doing much better since you had started tutoring me. He said yes, it was affecting you, and quite seriously at that. That your work had suffered noticeably in the last few weeks. That it could only be our 'little romance' that was keeping your mind occupied. That you were in danger of slipping, falling hard. He quoted some poetry I'd never heard, then told me it was his. Strutted around the empty room. Talked on and on about talents wasted, gifts squandered in the name of lust and love. Lecturing me as if the classroom was full. You should have seen him. Almost like a preacher really getting into a sermon.

"Then he stopped in mid-sentence. He seemed to realize it was just him and me again, and he got right down in my face. 'Miss Vinyard,' he said. 'I don't think you fully understand. Mr. McKay and I have a very special relationship. Something quite magical between us. Much more than student and teacher. I will not let you nor anyone else come between us. You must not be allowed to nullify his potential.' Those were his exact words, C.P. 'Special relationship.' I've heard things about him. But I never thought . . ."

She turned away from me then. Bile boiled into my throat and I thought I was going to vomit.

"Oh God, Maggie. That's . . . What he says . . . it's all . . ."

It seemed so ridiculous to have to try to deny what the bastard had implied that I couldn't even find the words. And it almost seemed a denial would give some kind of crazy credence to what he had told her.

Thankfully, she turned to me, smiled, touched my cheek.

217

"I never believed it. And I told him so. Real loud. Screaming like a madwoman. He waited until I was finished. I guess there was nobody else in the building or they would have called security. Then he told me he wanted to make me a deal. He admitted that he could make or break you, C.P. That one bad mark from him and you could kiss any hope of the Rhodes Scholarship good-bye. That he had enough pull to probably get your grades reduced in other courses, too. That President Claxton was in on the thing, too. I knew you had dinner with him one night, so I figured he knew what he was talking about."

God, I was so confused my head was spinning. My shoulder hurt like hell and my stomach was churning. I just sat there calmly, trying not to tense the arm that still circled Maggie's shoulders. I was fighting the urge to get up that instant and go murder Professor Langston Wheeler in cold blood.

"He told me, in no uncertain terms, to remove myself from the picture. That it was best for you. Not to tell you about our little meeting. Not to even talk with you again. Let you assume I had merely lost interest."

Her voice was shaking. A tear escaped each eye.

"He told me not to even come to class again. That he would make sure I received a B for the course and his glowing recommendation for 'all subsequent courses in the creative-writing curriculum.' He was bribing me, C.P.! Buying me off like a whore!"

Then she was sobbing as I pulled her to me, held her tight, said nonsensical stuff until she regained control.

"That's not why I stayed away, C.P." She pulled away so she could see my face. "Please believe me! He has the power to help you, but he could kill you, too. I had to do as he asked. Had to for your good. I think he's crazy enough to do something. You should have seen his face."

"I know, Maggie. I know." I wanted to soothe her, make her realize she had done right by telling me all this, but the urge to kill was so strong, I was afraid to say more. So I just turned her face up to mine, kissed her long and deeply, letting the feel of her lips calm my anger. The closeness of her body tempered my hatred. She finally pulled away enough to look into my eyes, and spoke.

"Come on. My car's over on a side street close to the dorm. I can't afford insurance for it so I can't get a student parking sticker."

She led me across the quad, past fraternity houses already in full party mode, to where the old Volkswagen bug waited. She drove somewhere out of town, up a patched asphalt highway that climbed above the valley, to a half-overgrown logging road, then pulled behind a stand of honeysuckle-draped trees.

"I found this place one day last year when I was looking for blackberries," she said, pulling the parking brake up and killing the ignition. Then, suddenly turning to me, her eyes wide, she said, "You do believe me? That I've never been parking here or . . ."

I shut her up with a kiss and pulled her as close as I could, ignoring the pounding pain in my shoulder and the gearshift lever in my side.

FIFTEEN

I was too tired and too happy and too angry to try much logical thinking on Maggie. She dropped me off in front of Champions' Hall well after midnight. She had to work the breakfast shift at Drake's and that meant getting up at five A.M. I kissed her one more time before letting her drive away, and made her promise we could get together and talk Sunday night. She was still reluctant and not sure she was doing what was best for me by continuing to see me. Not even the last few hours we had spent together were convincing.

I hopped up the steps, in the door, and then to one of the big ceiling-to-floor windows that peeked through white columns out onto the circular drive in front of the dorm. From behind a rich velvet curtain, I watched the tiny Volkswagen taillights get eaten up by the darkness and early-morning mist. Then, with Maggie safely gone, I trotted back down the steps and along the sidewalk.

Faster than a jog, but not quite a sprint, I covered the distance to Wheeler's house in five minutes. Neither the cold air, the ache in my shoulder, nor the lingering mellowness of my lovemaking with

Maggie could keep me from what I knew I had to do. There was no hesitation as I moved up the broken, chipped steps, through the ragged screen door onto the porch. I pounded on the moss-covered front door until I could hear someone stirring inside. The yellowed, dirty curtain beside the door moved slightly and I could see a hint of someone's shadow there. Then the handle turned, the door opened an inch, and Wheeler was peering warily out into the darkness.

"Yes?" He apparently couldn't see me in the shadows.

"I'd like a word with you, please." I was surprised how controlled and even my voice sounded.

"Who is . . . Mr. McKay? Is that you?" Now the door opened a little more. I could see he was in a ratty bathrobe, glasses on, as if he had been reading, hair uncombed and oily.

"Yes. Yes it is. A word, please?"

"Why of course. Come in. Come in. Please excuse the mess. . . . Been reading essays all day . . . doing some research." He was kicking books out of the path through the foyer and into the living room. He held a slender book in his hand, his place marked with one finger. "Please have a seat. Something to drink?"

I stood silently as he chattered.

". . . quite an unexpected visit. But totally welcomed. Totally welcomed." He was clearing a place on the couch, slinging magazines and papers to the floor. Suddenly, he seemed to realize how late it must be as he stood straight up and tried to make out the clock on the fireplace mantel across the room. His reading glasses made it impossible. "My, what time is it? It has to be quite late. I must have fallen asleep."

"I'm going to ask you one question and I expect you to answer honestly. Is that clear?"

He turned, dropped his book as well as his jaw, then slowly took off his glasses and absentmindedly combed his hair with his fingers. Wide-eyed, he quickly regained his composure.

"Then I may assume this is not a totally social visit?"

"No sir. It is not." Was it disappointment that instantly made his face a hard mask?

"Well, too bad. I had a fleeting hope you might have returned for . . ."

"Did you try to give Maggie Vinyard the impression you and I were anything else but teacher and student?" I chose my words carefully, afraid I might gag if I said what I really meant.

"But of course not. I was merely . . ."

"Listen to me. I want the truth," I said, teeth gritted now, and took a step toward him. He sat down hard on the couch, put his head in his hands. I waited a moment for an answer, and when it came, his voice was weak as he talked to the faded, dirty shag carpet.

"Perhaps there was a modicum of wishful thinking in what I told her. Perhaps I was acting out a dream at that moment." He raised his face and looked up at me and I was surprised to see tears there. "I'm sorry. I couldn't help myself. I fell in love with you the first day I saw you. Intelligence galore and in such a package! I had to have you! And just when I had deluded myself into thinking you might actually return my affections, there was that young woman getting in the way."

"But I never did anything. I never led you to believe . . ."

"Oh God, Mr. McKay! There is no way someone like you could understand the agony. The pain. You see someone you like, you make a pass. If she says yes, you are in. If not, it's okay. There are plenty more. Especially for someone like you. It's natural. But not for someone like me. Romance is quite simply hell. Hell on earth to be saddled with such a predilection. No, I guess there is no way possible for you to understand the desperation. The agony."

Somewhere along the way, without my even realizing it, my anger had turned to pity. I had been prepared to stomp this man a minute ago, had every intention of doing just that, and now I merely wanted to leave him here alone, crying and shaking in this sad, dusty, disheveled place. Instead, I eased my aching body down into the armchair across from him, suddenly overwhelmingly tired. My bruised shoulder throbbed. So did my head. So did my stomach.

"No matter—you can't mess with people's lives like this, Wheeler. You can't threaten people to get what you think you want. Ruin someone's academic standing for some childish crush you might have."

"I know that, of course. But you can't imagine the desperation that can drive one."

"Yes. Yes, I can. I was ready to come here and kill you tonight for what you did to Maggie. To us. Now, well . . . I just feel sorry for you. That's all."

He smiled slightly and wiped his face with the back of his hand.

"So, you've given me a reprieve. Perhaps there is an ounce of affection for me in there after all."

"No. No, I don't think so, Professor. Pity, yes, but affection, no. But you and I are going to cut a deal. And, if we aren't able to come to some kind of understanding, I will probably kill you."

I gave him my best running back–murdering grin, the one with the squinted eyes, clenched teeth, neck muscles flexed so it looked like my head sat directly on my broad shoulders, so often practiced across the line of scrimmage just before a play started.

He stared at me, a little fear still in his expression.

"First, you allow Maggie back into your class. You grade her honestly. She fails, it's her doing, not yours. She passes, it's her work that earns the grade. You have a conference with her anytime she needs it, at your convenience. You will make sure she gets her tuition's worth out of your class. Every penny."

He nodded.

"Next, you grade me as I deserve. If my work is not satisfactory, you tell me so. But if I do what you think I should, you award me accordingly. I'm in your class because I respect your work. You can be a great teacher if you don't think with your . . . Well, just allow me to take advantage of your ability."

He started to say something but hushed. My voice had grown deeper, almost raspy, unintentionally threatening. I knew it was fatigue taking over. He probably thought it was pure redneck jock testosterone.

"And you mention none of this to Claxton or anybody else. If he asks how I'm doing, you report honestly. The total truth as you see it. I don't want any favors from you or anybody else but I damn sure want what I earn. Do you understand that?"

He nodded again. I flexed my shoulder slightly to try to ease the ache that had spread over my whole left side, but he misinterpreted the move and jumped as if I had thrown a punch at him.

"Wheeler, you better be the best damned teacher since Socrates from now on. And you better do what I'm asking. If I even suspect you're not shooting straight with Maggie or me, I'll stop suppressing the latent white southern good ol' boy in me and revert to most of my kinfolks' way of handling stuff like this. And that usually involves spilled blood and broken bones. And then, I'll take the whole thing to the faculty senate. I'd say, between Maggie, Clifford, and all the other students you've hit on through the years, we could build a pretty strong case against you."

I was just guessing about "the others." There had to be more. His quick flinch, as if ducking another anticipated punch, told me I was dead right.

"Look. I don't care about your sexual preference. Who or what you date. I'm enlightened enough to accept things like that despite my upbringing. But you're no better than any other lecherous old professor hitting on sorority girls when you sink to stuff like you've tried here."

I tried to look as menacing as I could then as I reached down, pulled him to his feet by the frayed collar of his bathrobe, brought his face close to mine. He was trembling, avoiding eye contact, whimpering just a little.

"Please tell me we have an agreement, Professor Wheeler. Or I can start fulfilling my promise right here, right now."

"Yes. Please. I'm very sorry."

I was too keyed up to sleep when I got back to the dorm. I still had an image of Wheeler, once again standing in the dim light of his front door, behind the rusty screen, watching me as I left. I was sorry I had turned back to look. It only made me feel more sorry for the man.

Chris was tossing and turning most of the night, too, mumbling, involved in another one of his mystical Indian dreams, no doubt. Well before first light, I got up, pulled on my jacket and walked out of the athletic dorm, not really knowing where I was going. Somehow I landed at Drake's, and although I had almost no money, had a huge country breakfast: eggs, biscuits, sausage, gravy, grits, jelly, and Maggie's warm smile every time she ran past my table. She seemed glad to see me and that helped erase the ache in all my joints and the sandpaper in my eyes.

When she stopped for a minute, I blurted out that I had taken care of Wheeler. Her face went blank, eyes huge, as if she was afraid I had murdered the man. How could I blame her? I had gone to his house to do just that.

"Oh God, C.P.! You didn't . . ."

But she relaxed when I explained. We agreed to meet at the library after conditioning drills that afternoon, and we could get to work together on our next project for Wheeler's class. She understood I had brought us evenhandedness from the man and we would have to work harder than ever if we wanted to take advantage of it.

Sweet, deep, dreamless sleep finally came when I got back to the dorm and tried to read. Chris had to shake me awake in time to bolt to practice. The way I had played, being a few minutes late wouldn't have been a big deal, but it was not my way. I didn't want the rest of the team to even suspect I had let the success go to my head.

One of the trainers spotted my shoulder as I dressed and forced me to take therapy after practice. He threatened to go straight to Rankin if I didn't. It would be his ass, he said, if one of the coaches caught him looking the other way with such a shining injury.

We had run wind sprints and gassers for over an hour solid. Rankin was serious about beating Tennessee, even though we had clinched a share of the championship already with the victory the day before. He didn't speak directly to me during the practice. Only once during the brief meeting afterward did I see him glance my way, and it was almost too quick to notice.

I was not a good patient. The kneading of the trainer's massage and the hot water in the whirlpool only made the deep bruise ache to the bone, got it so irritated and riled it wouldn't quit throbbing, no matter what evil-smelling compound was rubbed on the purple-and-black-bruised skin. The liniment took my breath away and made my eyes sting and tear, and the pain pills instantly sent my stomach into spasms. I knew, too, that Maggie would soon be at the library waiting for me, so I hurried the guy mercilessly.

Finally, he gave in and let me go. I trotted out of the training room, down the drive to the football building, and along Spartan Drive. Just as I cut through the cedar grove to take the shortcut to the quad and across to the library, something brown and snakelike jumped from the bushes to my right and landed wetly directly in my path. I stopped to keep from running right into it before it splattered to the ground at my feet. It was seething, black, slippery. A long stream of fresh tobacco juice.

"How you doing, Mr. C.P. McKay?"

I didn't say a word, not even when Cooter Casteel stepped out from the dark shadows and stood next to me, his gold chains and jewelry clanking like rattling sabers. My first impulse was to hit him in the face with a quick jab and then run as fast as I could, but he had his hands thrust deeply into the pockets of his black suit pants. I couldn't hit someone so defenseless, could I? Only his venom-yellow eyes and crooked grin looked threatening as he answered his own question for me.

" 'Oh, I'm fine, Mr. Cooter. And how are you?' Just great, C.P., and thanks for asking so polite and all. Great, that is, except for that damn gimpy poppa of yours that keeps taking food out of the mouths of my babies. That's all. Thanks to all the inside dope you been feeding him about the team. I never had no trouble taking his money before, until his boy got up here and started tipping the old man off on every little bitty bit of news they was. Shit, you ain't been doing me no favors at all, Mr. C.P. McKay."

I still didn't say anything. I just took a short step sideways, making a move to get around him and be gone away from him, to the library and Maggie.

"Hold on, before you run off to that heifer you been seeing."

There was suddenly no air to breathe.

"I expect she'll wait on you a few minutes, a big old football hero like yourself. Me and you need to talk some business, sonny boy."

I struggled and finally found enough air to speak a short sentence.

"Cooter, we don't have a damn thing to talk about."

"Oh, *au contraire,* smart boy. We got lots to discuss. Right here in front of God and everybody, or over yonder in my car. Your choice."

The trees offered some cover, but teammates could pass by any minute. A coach, even. And I did not want to be seen talking to this viper. He seemed to read my mind and led me back to the street and his black Lincoln. He opened the door for me and I felt like I was entering the gates of hell when I stepped in and sat down in its deep, plush, bloodred seat. Thankfully, he drove quickly away from campus, leaving its ornate buildings, the huge library, Maggie Vinyard, all behind. He wound along, at least five miles, down narrow country roads, past dark farmhouses, bare, cold fields, almost-hidden side roads that seemed to lead to nowhere. He wouldn't shut up, just kept talking as he steered the big car easily through the hairpin curves and through four-way stop signs.

"Here's my proposition, Mr. C.P. McKay. Y'all are playing Tennessee next week if I'm not mistaken. And the damn game don't mean shit to nobody but me and a few good old boys who like to put down a dime or two. If Alabama beats Auburn, which they are gonna do with their eyes closed, then y'all win the championship outright. Don't say you heard it from me, but y'all are going to the Orange Bowl and play Notre Dame."

"But the bowl bids aren't even coming out until . . ."

"Done deal, baby. And that's the way it will be, even if Tennessee beats your ass seven ways from Sunday. Claxton's done shook on the deal and the rooms have done been reserved in Miami. Now, here's my point. And here's where you come in, mister."

He pulled abruptly into a roadside park, with picnic tables scattered under towering pines, trash barrels overflowing and a dusting of refuse littering the ground from the day's visitors. It was near dark, so the area was empty. He rolled down his window and spat another long stream of juice in the general direction of one of the barrels, then wiped the dribble from his mouth with his coat sleeve. I lowered the window on my side, just in case my nausea got any stronger.

"Since it don't matter squat who wins this damn Tennessee game, I want you to help me. I need to get back some of what your ol' man took from me this season." He ignored my sharp glance, busying himself with getting another fresh plug of Red Man chewing tobacco from his side coat pocket. "Here's the scoop, darlin'.

The betting line's gonna be eight points, y'all's way. I figure that's pretty much on the money, too, playing at home and all, even without your quarterback. All I gotta do is make sure y'all beat them by seven or less, or even lose the damn thing, and I come out way to the good. And I do mean *way* to the good. I'll get well in one fell swoop."

I was staring out the window, watching a squirrel chewing on an abandoned piece of bread atop one of the picnic tables. I was amazed at the audacity of this man and afraid of exactly what he was about to ask me to do.

"See, boy, I had it covered. Everything taken care of. My inside man understood just exactly what he had to do to make sure I come up a winner this time. And then he had to go and get his damn shoulder broke! Damn it to hell!"

Oh God. Skip Gross. No wonder he had such trouble telling their defensive backs from our own receivers sometimes. He was Cooter's man.

"So that leaves too much to chance, see. Way too much money at stake. Even your damn daddy, who use to couldn't pick a winner in a one-man race. He could have lucked up and hit on me again. Naw, I gotta have some surefire, can't-miss help. And you, Mr. C.P., are the very buck that's gonna assure old Cooter comes out of this screwed-up season smelling like a rose."

I wanted to stay quiet. Just keep staring out the window, watching the squirrel eating his newfound lunch. Ignore what the bookie was saying. But I couldn't anymore.

"No way, you bastard. No way. I'm not throwing any game for the likes . . ."

He held up his hand and gave me a look that froze me through and through. I hoped the gathering darkness would hurry and take those slitted eyes, that evil grin, from my sight.

"You don't understand, son. I wasn't asking you if you would. I was telling you that you will. There ain't gonna be no debate about it. All you gotta do is miss a tackle here and there. Knock down a pass that you might have picked off normally. Maybe be just a step or two out of place on a key play or two. That's all. You're good enough to pull it off and nobody will be none the wiser except you and me. Win the damn game by three or four or five. I don't give a damn. Just make sure it ain't eight or more. That's all you gotta do and everybody's happy as larks."

I started to say more, but he slapped the dashboard hard. The squirrel on the cement table outside stopped eating, looked around for the source of the noise, then resumed chewing, chattering between bites, upset with the interruption.

"Let me play my whole hand, Mr. C.P. McKay, before you go and say something that'll be hard to retract in a minute. It'd be a real shame if your poor ol' paralyzed daddy had some kind of horrible wheelchair accident and rolled off that mountain, now wouldn't it?"

He leaned toward me a little and I could smell his sour tobacco breath, feel the heat of his words.

"God help us if your sweet momma accidentally lost the brakes on that old pickup and run off the side of Signal Mountain one night or something."

Closer still, his eyes bored into mine, his brown-stained lips trembled with the sinister intensity of what he was threatening.

"Or if that sweet little coed you been screwing was to meet with some kind of tragedy while she was walking around campus, coming back from one of them jobs of hers."

Rage roared inside me. I half heard the chattering of the squirrel outside the car, as if it was urging me to say something, not sit there and take threats from this devil.

"You goddamn bastard! I'll . . ."

Sunk so low in the deep car seat, it took all the effort I could manage to try to turn and reach for his throat, now only inches away. But before I could get there, he slapped my hands away and, in one amazingly quick move, snaked a black, heavy, deadly object from his inside jacket pocket.

The explosion deafened me, the smoke blinded me for a moment, and I couldn't breathe. Jesus! The son of a bitch had shot me!

But no. There was no pain except for my ringing ears and stinging eyes. And when the smoke cleared, I could see his wicked face and his outrageous grin, still there, inches from my own face. The gun was still there, too, beside my right ear, pointed out the open car window on my side. Bits of gray squirrel fur and guts and red blood littered the picnic table.

"I hate it when somebody interrupts me while I'm talking." And he laughed. At least what must have passed for a laugh from someone like Cooter Casteel. "See, way I figure it, Mr. Football Hero, is that you ain't got a bit of choice in this thing. You gonna miss a tackle or two for your ol' paralyzed daddy. Drop a pass for momma. Stumble and fall on your handsome young face for that sweet little piece of tail you been tapping. Then go on ahead with your life. It'll all be over and you won't have lost nothing."

The urge to throw up was strong again, almost overpowering.

"Tell you what else, boy. I feel generous. Tell your ol' man to load up on Tennessee. Bet the house. Take the damn points. He'll go out a winner. Maybe even give you some of the haul so you can buy yourself a good set of wheels or something. Maybe buy Suzy Coed some nice perfume."

He laughed again, a deep belly laugh that seemed to come from his deepest gut and ended up in a phlegmy cough.

"All right, get out."

I finally looked back at him.

"Get out. Run on back to campus. Stay in shape. Think about what I told you. And remember. If anybody else hears about our little business arrangement, they gonna be some awful things happen. 'Bye, now. Take care."

He reached across, pulled the door handle, and used his foot to shove me roughly out, stumbling to stay upright.

"Real pleasure doing business with you, Mr. C.P. McKay."

Then he cranked the big car's engine and peppered me with gravel as he spun off and onto the blacktop.

Crickets were starting to sing. The air was cool and almost dark. I did exactly what Cooter had told me. I ran all the way back to Sparta.

S I X T E E N

I stared into Maggie's eyes and lied my ass off. She believed me when I told her practice ran extra long and the therapy on my shoulder even longer and that's why I was late and panting. I told her nothing about Cooter Casteel and our chat in the roadside park and my run back to campus. She had still been sitting there patiently, waiting alone at a huge table in the far back of the reference room, her beauty shining like a warm lamp's glow when I raced breathless and sweating through the doorway. No, I couldn't burden her with what I had had draped on my shoulders that afternoon.

For her sake, I forced myself to think of scholarly journals and critical essays for a couple of hours. It wasn't easy. Even the words of one of my favorites, Dylan Thomas, seemed to mock me from the pages of the book we were analyzing. My rage wasn't against any dying light, though.

Maggie looked at me funny, as if she was not sure who I was.

"Are you okay, C.P.?"

"Yeah, I didn't sleep much. Littlefeather had a bad night."

"You do look tired. Maybe we should wrap it up and try again tomorrow night."

"Naw, let's get this part finished. See, the poet's voice here is saying . . ."

Chris was sitting inside his circle of candles when I got back from walking Maggie to her dorm. Sitting there chanting his eerie song again. I collapsed on my bed and was almost asleep when he spoke to me. Why did he always wait until I was almost asleep to spring some mystical bit of news on me?

"Man, I don't know what it is, but something heavy is coming down."

"Hummm?"

"I know you don't believe any of this mumbo jumbo, C.P., but I feel like something is coming down and real soon. And you are in the middle of it. Watch your step. I saw the animals clawing at you again. And they were vicious, man. Vicious. Out for blood."

I lay there, quiet, still, trying to let the ache subside, his warning die, Cooter's grating voice fade from memory. Chris waited several minutes for me to respond, then, when I didn't say anything, he slowly stood and reached for a small leather bag that rested on the floor near where he had been sitting. He walked slowly, softly over to my bed, stuck a finger and thumb inside the pouch and pulled out a pinch of some kind of fine brown powder. He must have assumed I was asleep. Without saying a word, without asking me or explaining what he was doing, he began sprinkling the dust on my head, down my face, on my neck.

Honestly, I didn't mean to hit him. I was just so keyed up, so damned frustrated, I couldn't help myself. I had to lash out at someone and when the mess he was dumping on me tickled my face and sifted into my mostly closed eyes, I couldn't help it. With one quick unexpected slap, I sent his hand flying, spinning his whole body around, the dust still between his finger and thumb falling straight into my eyes and mouth, the rest of the stuff in the leather bag spewing out all over the carpet in a dim, brown arc.

"No! God, no, C.P.!" Chris screamed as if I had shot him. "There's no other potion this side of the reservation! No other way to protect you!"

I was coughing from the dust I had breathed, crying from what had landed in my eyes.

"Jesus, Chris! What the hell are you doing?"

"I told you. It's coming down soon. And you are in the middle of it. The powder is the only thing that could help you."

"Look, I'm sorry. I appreciate the thought, but . . ."

"My people always used it before battle. Sprinkle it on your hair and the enemy could never get your scalp. On your chest and no arrow could pierce your heart. All over and you are immune to most everything. But it's precious. I don't even know what's in it, but only a little could be made at one time. It could only be used on our most important warriors. I've been saving it for years. Grandfather kept it years before that."

He was on his hands and knees, trying to pinch some of the dust from the deep pile carpet, but he was obviously having no luck. I was sitting up in my bed, in the middle of a violent sneezing fit.

"Look, I'm sorry . . . ah-chooo! . . . Chris. I really am, but you sneaked up . . . choooo! . . . sneaked up on me while I was sleeping and I . . . uhh-shewww! . . . I didn't know. Anyway, my sinuses . . . ahhh-chooo! . . . are pretty well protected right now."

He wasn't laughing, just sitting on the floor now, staring at the carpet.

"At least your head is protected. But that's all. Please be careful, C.P. You're a good man. Be careful."

The day finally overwhelmed me. I fell back, dead asleep in minutes, sweat-stained clothes, liniment-reeking muscles, watering dust-filled eyes, tortured soul, and all.

Langston Wheeler hardly looked at me or Maggie that week, but when he hit us with discussion questions in class, or for comment on the day's reading, it was always stinging-tough. It was not the marshmallows I had become accustomed to recently. It was a pleasure being wrong sometimes, having to defend a weak premise or argue a shaky point with him. Maggie looked at the point of pain sometimes, but I knew she was really glad to be back, happy to be challenged.

Practice was hell. Rankin was a driven man, determined to finish the season without another loss. Tennessee, on film, looked a lot like us. Good but injured. Latrelle Warwick was their star running back. Good moves, strong, extra quick. He seemed to have his lapses at times, prone to fumbles at inopportune times during games, but a real threat anytime he touched the football. Chris played his part on the scout team and I hit him hard a few times, even when we were only in shoulder pads and helmets on Tuesday.

"Damn, C.P. You ain't still mad about the dust are you?" he asked, holding his ribs.

"No, buddy. Just trying to get the feel for Warwick. I'm sorry. I'll ease up."

"Maybe I ought to have sprinkled a dab of it on my rib cage." He dodged me the next time or two he came my way.

I didn't make love to Maggie again. She was extra busy at both jobs, and her other classes were piling it on for the rest of the semester. She was determined to make up the missed work in Wheeler's class, too, and we spent most of our time together in the library, hovering over huge open volumes, stealing a kiss when we were sure the work-study student behind the desk wasn't looking.

I only fell deeper in love with her, though. I loved the way she looked at me when I lectured her and the absentminded way her hand would come to my cheek as if she wasn't even aware of the caress she was delivering. I loved the way her body felt when I held her close and kissed her good night in the shadows just outside her dorm.

She had taken to writing me long letters when we were apart, while there were a few minutes of slow time at the infirmary or during endless, boring English Lit lectures. Then she'd slip them into my pocket, tell me not to read it until I was in my bed, ready for sleep. They would have invariably brought tears to my eyes when I read them if I ever allowed myself to cry. I had never experienced such a thing before, with such love for a person returned so freely.

I even caught myself a time or two wishing for the end of football season and classes. I could spend more time with her. Get to know her better. Learn even more about her.

"I want to meet your father and mother sometime," she said out of the blue, on Thursday night the week before the Tennessee game. We had almost finished our papers for Wheeler, and I was already dreading leaving her at the dorm, trying to prolong the study session as long as I could.

"Sure. I'd love for you to." Did she notice my hesitation? I had never been ashamed of my parents nor thought about what others might think of them. But Maggie mattered. Oh, Maw would be okay. They'd get along fine. But Father. . . . Well, I didn't know.

She knew that he was in a wheelchair, but she didn't really know how he had come to be there. I didn't want to tell her it was my fault.

"Will they be over for the game Saturday?"

I didn't even know Maggie knew there was to be a game. She still didn't keep up with football that much.

"Uh huh. I'm sure they will."

"Great! I can meet them there."

I was trying to interpret a passage from *The Scarlet Letter* and almost missed something important. I looked up at her quickly.

"Wait a minute. You're going to the game?"

"You're playing in it, aren't you?"

"But . . ."

"I want to see how the five-four defense works against Tennessee's I-back attack."

She was so serious, so sincere, I couldn't help it. I burst out laughing, cackling, drawing a funny, hurt look from Maggie, a mean glance from the work-study librarian, and shush or two from other students at nearby tables.

"Maggie Vinyard! Where in the world did you come up with that?"

She pulled a copy of the morning paper from her book bag. It was creased open to the sports page.

"I've been studying the game some. I still don't have any idea what is going on, but I think I'll be able to tell when you are supposed to be on the field. Offense from defense, at least."

Observers or not, I couldn't help myself. I wrapped her up like I planned to do Latrelle Warwick on Saturday, except I kissed her. Long, deep, trying to convey how much I loved her for trying to understand football, just for me.

Several of our fellow scholars at nearby tables cheered.

Twenty minutes later, I kissed her again on the front steps of Rachel Jackson Hall. A good-night kiss that lasted five minutes. She finally pulled away, smiled, said, "I love you," and was gone. For some reason, I felt the same melancholy loneliness I always had when Maw and Father left for home after my games. Total aloneness. A cold emptiness. Almost a feeling of abandonment.

There were two bonfires on the quad that night. A loud, boisterous crowd cheered for victory over Tennessee as they danced around one huge blaze. Another chanted and begged for the end of war as they sang and marched around another fire a hundred yards away.

Coach Rankin, President Claxton, our team captains, and others were on the trailer-bed stage, while cheerleaders jumped and twirled and the pep band played by the light of the roaring, smokey blaze. Near the other fire, students dragged dummies dressed like dead soldiers around the hot orange flames, while a trio played guitars and sang protest songs.

People on the edge of each crowd were jeering at those on the other side, and several fistfights were already breaking out. I merely walked on. I was too much in love to watch such carryings-on.

Not five minutes after I got back to my room, the phone rang. Father, of course. Voice so weak and distant I almost didn't recognize him.

"Boy? That . . . you?"

"Yes, Father. You okay?"

"Yeah, yeah. Doing okay, I reckon. Touch of the flu, maybe." He sounded awful.

"Where's Maw? She there with you?"

"Gone on up to Miss Ledford's. Cleaning or washing or ironing or something. She'll be back directly."

He paused to cough hard, then spat.

"But listen, boy. I need some help on Saturday." He coughed and spat again.

"Line's eight, Father."

"But they say your quarterback's out. Them Vols ain't bad, neither."

"Look, Father. Why don't you sit this one out? Who knows how it will go?"

There was silence on the other end of the line. I thought he might have fallen asleep. There was only his heavy breathing, a cough, a wheeze, then his voice, even weaker.

"I can't. I got to put something down. Give me something to go on, boy. Please give me something to go on."

"I don't know. Something doesn't feel right about this one. Save your money for the bowl game. . . ."

"Goddammit! Goddammit to hell!" He was suddenly screaming into the telephone. "I raise you. Feed you. Give you a good place to live, and what the hell do you do when I need you? Clam up! Get tight-assed on me! Too damn good for your old man! Keep your goddamn mouth . . ."

He might have gone on longer, but the coughing fit overcame him and he dropped the phone with a clatter on the floor. I didn't know what to do. I was afraid he was going to bust something, the hacking was so intense.

"Father! Father!" I called his name as loudly as I could. Chris Littlefeather looked up from his study desk.

Father was still cursing between the explosions of coughs. Somehow, he managed to pick up the phone and hang it up hard.

An hour passed. Then another. Eventually I dialed the number, hoping it would be Maw who would answer.

"Hello?" Thank goodness it was her voice.

"Maw, it's Corey Phil."

"Darlin'? Thank God you called! I've been so worried!"

"It's Father? Is he okay?"

"Father? Aw, he's as well as he can be, I reckon. I just got him to bed. He was so worked up over something that he was all tired out and having trouble getting his breath. Probably thinking about the game Saturday. He's okay. It's you, Corey Phil. I'm scared to death about you."

"Maw, I'm just fine. The best I've ever been. My shoulder is just about . . ."

"I've got this god-awful feeling, darlin'. It's been eating at me for weeks now. Something awful is going to happen. And I can't let it. I gotta make sure it don't."

Her voice sounded shrill, almost on the verge of hysteria.

"No, Maw, everything is all right. I promise. I'm going to introduce you and Father to Maggie Saturday after the game. I really want you to meet her."

"I been praying to God and to Jesus and to your guardian angel every night." She hadn't heard a word about Maggie. "I been begging them to keep watch over you. Something dark is hovering around you, Corey Phil. Please be careful till I can get there. Please." It was as if she was losing control.

"Maw, you gotta get a grip on yourself. It sounds like Father really needs you right now. Stay strong so you can take care of him."

"Just be careful until I can get there and take care of you. Let Maw take care of little Corey Phil so nobody will hurt him."

Chris was watching me when I hung up the telephone. The look on my face must have spoken plenty. He just shook his head. Dread washed over me. Oh Lord, how could I let Maggie meet my loony parents? I found myself worrying more about that than Cooter's threats. The night stretched on and on with no hope of sleep, no chance for rest.

Sometime before dawn, I rolled off the sweaty bed and quietly walked to my desk. I opened a fresh notebook and filled five pages with a letter to Maggie. Then, still not at all sleepy, I loaded up a half dozen more pages with a detailed account of my encounter with Cooter and what he had threatened. Of Claxton and what he had told me. Of Tack Rankin's attempt to get me to commit mayhem for money. And I even rehashed Wheeler's fumbling seduction attempt. I just laid it all out, and felt better for the bloodletting, as if I had lanced a nasty boil and purged my system of impurities.

Right on cue, Chris's alarm clock sounded as I finished the last page.

"Chris?"

"Hmmmm?"

"I need to ask you a favor. A helluva big favor."

"Long as it ain't anything kinky or costly."

"I'm going to leave some papers in an envelope in this desk drawer. If anything happens to me, take the envelope to Coach Milligan."

"What is it?" He was suddenly awake, curious. "What's gonna happen?"

"Never mind. And it's something you don't want to know. Trust me. You don't want to know."

"Okay. You got it." He was sitting up, still sleepy-eyed, but obviously serious. "You in trouble, roomie?"

"Nothing I can't handle. But just in case . . ."

I remember exactly what Maggie was wearing that Friday morning in class. The white blouse, dark jeans, a heart locket around her neck. Her perfume like fresh, warm honeysuckle. Her hair pulled back behind her ears. She smiled and slipped me another multi-page letter just before Wheeler stomped in and started the class. We talked for only a moment afterward. She was headed for the next class, then work. I was on the way to catch the bus to the team hotel and our usual pregame imprisonment.

"Look for me if you get a chance. I'll be somewhere in the student section. I don't know where."

"I will. And after the game, you wait for me at the press-box elevator. I'll bring Maw and Father down to meet you."

She smiled. I kissed her quickly, ignoring the throng of students milling around us.

She disappeared.

SEVENTEEN

I never lost that primal feeling I first had the night Maw and I had wandered into the stadium on Ponce de Leon in Atlanta. We had been amazed by the swirling colors, aromas, sounds. The electric tension seemed to crackle and snap as the teams got ready for war. The indescribable sensation swept us along on the emotional crest of a giant wave together with thousands of others of a like mind. The barrage of sensations made my mother laugh and cry, both in the same night.

That Saturday afternoon, I felt it all again, but it was magnified innumerable times by my being an active participant. Emotions were blown up to white-hot. My every move and action down there on the grass rectangle effected what those in the stands, those watching on television at home, those following the game through radio play-by-play were all collectively feeling. It was the communal oneness of thousands of people, bordering on barely controlled mass hysteria as they threatened to go over the raw edge.

I loved it. I breathed it in like cool, fresh, electric air. I felt alive.

Tennessee did their drills on the other side of the fifty-yard line. Their bright orange jerseys glared in brilliant sunshine spilling from a cloudless sky. The dim white numbers were hard to make out, but I finally found Warwick and watched him from the corner of my eye. I'd always found it a good idea to personify the other team in a star player or two. If I shut down their big gun, I knew I could stop the whole team.

For the second week in a row, though, I was entering a game in a quandary. Did I even have it in me to play less than my best? I'd never tried. There was a splotch of pink there at the end of the press box. I knew it was Maw in her regular flowered-print dress. I could see the spot of hair that was apparently Father, slumped so low in his chair that no more of him was visible over the rim of the press box. Maw would have to keep pulling him out of his slouch so he could see what was happening down on the field. Soon he would be cussing his inability to even sit up straight and watch the game.

And as I jogged toward the end zone, working the kinks out of my legs, I saw Maggie. Out of twenty thousand wriggling, screaming, mostly drunk students, I found her, framed perfectly by the goalposts. She was watching me intently, sitting still and quiet among all the turmoil and clamor, but she couldn't tell I was watching her as well, my eyes hidden by the helmet and face mask. I almost waved, then didn't. I was supposed to be concentrating on Tennessee and getting my "game face" on.

By the time the officials blew their whistles and motioned the captains to midfield for the toss of the coin, I had made up my mind. For the first time in my life, I was going to dog it. If I could figure out how, that is.

And for the first time in my career, I was glad we won the toss and elected to receive. Offense on the field first. Delay the betrayal. That's how I saw it. Betrayal of my teammates, my school, myself. But God knows, I had no choice. I could not take the chance

Cooter was bluffing. Something in his eyes told me he was deadly serious.

It was not long before I had to perform my act. Lawton Gray, our fill-in quarterback, was supposed to pitch the ball back to the trailing halfback on our third play from scrimmage. In his nervousness, he turned totally the wrong way and tossed the football to empty space. At least five Tennessee defenders pounced on the ball so quick and fast, two of them were shaken up on the play. Gray was crying pitifully when he trotted off the field.

"Shake it off, Lawton," I called, slapping him on the shoulder pad. "It's a long game. We'll hold them!"

He just sobbed and trotted on to his inevitable meeting with Tack Rankin on the sideline, ignoring me, not noticing the lack of certainty in my promise.

Latrelle Warwick was lined up deep in the Tennessee I-formation, at least fifteen yards behind his linemen. That was designed to give him a chance to build up momentum as he approached the line with the football, as well as an opportunity to look for exactly where the holes his blockers were punching out developed. I knew with certainty he would get the ball on their first play. Tendencies told me that. On something like seventy percent of first-down plays, the ball was fed to Warwick. The miles of film I had watched that week confirmed it.

I ignored the tendencies and pretended to follow the fake to the fullback, coming at me from where he lined up just in front of Warwick. I made it look for all the world like I had gobbled up the fake to him like a gullible goldfish, just the way the play was designed to make me do. I met the 220-pound fullback square-up in the hole that had opened in the line. Our head-on collision was colossal, the impact so solid we both crumpled to the ground at the very point of the impact. Neither of us had given an inch.

The crowd roared like an unleashed cyclone. I figured Warwick had gotten the ball, had tried an end run, and someone had made a good play on him. Then I realized it was I who had made the good play, that I was lying on top of the fullback as he struggled to get his breath back. He cradled something brown and dimpled in his arms.

The goddamned football! I had tried to blow the play and ended up making a big one instead! And, forgive me, but it felt wonderful.

I jumped to my feet and danced, high-fived my teammates, shouted a shrill string of patent nonsense, then watched with glee as the training staff rushed onto the field from the Tennessee sideline to get their man breathing again. Standing there, the crowd's acclaim not showing any sign of diminishing, I almost had a change of heart.

Then I saw Maggie, now standing, waving a Spartan pom-pom like any other crazy student fan, a smile on her face visible even to me, fifty yards away. I had to keep her safe. I had to keep her safe.

Warwick got the ball on the next play. A simple toss sweep, coming right at me. I saw it all the way. Even saw the substitute fullback who was supposed to be leading the blocking for him stumble over his own feet and go down like a felled tree. My worst fear. Just Latrelle Warwick and me, all alone, in the open field, with no one even attempting to block me. No excuses. No way to hide it if I deliberately blew the tackle.

I had no choice. I couldn't make the play and take any risks. I set up as if I was going to wait for him to get close, avoid the fake, and pounce on him. Then, when the fake did come, exactly when and how I instinctively knew it would, I dived in his general direction, but a little to his right, into what I assumed would be empty space that he had just vacated. I landed hard on my nose in the thick brown grass, burrowing into moist dirt with the forehead of my headgear, the perfect picture of a faked-out linebacker. But I was surprised when I felt my hand slap his thigh pad. Not enough to do any damage to a back as good as Warwick. But his move should have left me completely free of any chance of touching the man. Just snatching air.

Well, all the better. I had made a little contact as I sprawled on my face, grabbing at him. It would look better on the film Monday.

But the crowd roared again like a massive explosion detonated without warning. I pulled my head out of the turf just in time to see Warwick tumbling over and over as if he had been hit head-on by a semi. As I lay there and pulled mud and grass out of my face mask, I watched him drop the ball wearily, slowly climb to a knee as if addled and dizzy, and finally stretch groggily to his feet, favoring a suddenly gimpy leg.

I looked all around us to see who had passed the blow. Nobody within ten yards but him and me. He had been sent cleat-over-ass by the weakest of touches from me as I tried to avoid him altogether! Then Elgie Munford was tugging me to my feet and slapping me on the back so hard it started my bruised shoulder to smarting again.

Warwick edged over close to me on his way back to the huddle, his face mask almost touching mine as he gave the appearance to the crowd that he was jawing with me about the hit.

"Come on, you bastard. Give me a good try. Don't make me have to take a dive like that."

I lost my breath. Lord help me! The fix was on from the other side! Somebody had gotten to Latrelle Warwick, too.

Warwick just shook his fist at me as the referee jumped between us and limped on back to his huddle, looking for all the world to the fans like he was mad at me for knocking him down so rudely. I was still standing there, mouth open, when they lined up for the third-down play.

"C.P. Flex yellow! Get out there!" Elgie was screaming the pass defense and I dropped back in the general area of where I was supposed to be, still trying to figure what this new development meant to me and my assigned task. I had prepared myself to outperform the other athlete, and he was supposed to work just as hard to beat me. How in hell could I underplay an opponent who was trying to outdog me?

The Tennessee quarterback took the snap, dropped straight back behind his blockers and looped a perfect pass right into the hands of Warwick, flaring out to his left. I once again acted on pure instinct and left my coverage, shooting for where the running back and the flight of the ball would coincide. I consciously held back a step, though, fully intending to flag at him and hit the ground again with some semblance of having tried to tackle him.

Warwick dropped the football as if it weighed five hundred pounds. Then just stopped and looked at his hands in a way that implied the damned appendages had betrayed him. He slapped his thigh pads, avoided looking at me when I pulled up to a stop next to him, and then, a picture of frustration, trotted to his sideline to make room for the punting team.

I was so confused I almost followed him to his side of the stadium.

"Way to be in the right spot, baby!" Max Milligan screamed over the roar of the crowd for the defense. He was all grins as he followed me to the water bucket. He just kept hovering near me, as if he wanted to tell me something else but couldn't quite find the words.

"Look, this is the worst time in the world for something like this," he finally said. "Right in the middle of a blessed game and all. But I wanted you to know before the news whores start asking about it. Mainly because you helped me make it happen, McKay."

"What is it, Max?"

"Defense has done so good this year, somebody noticed and decided to give me another chance. Miller State over in Arkansas. Not a big school, but I'll be the head coach. I appreciate what you done, son. I just wanted you to know that."

"Congratulations, Max. You deserve it. Just don't schedule Sparta, you hear?"

"Hell, we could beat this bunch of pussies with our scrubs in wheelchairs!" He caught himself, remembered Father. "Sorry, McKay, I didn't . . ."

"No problem, Coach. I'm proud of you."

"Aw, shut up and get out there and kick some Big Orange ass!"

I just grinned. For a minute, I had almost forgotten my latest dilemma. Here I was subtly trying to hold the score down as much as I could, while the key player for the other guys was doing his best to accomplish the same thing. And right now, our raucous fans were beside themselves, as our quarterback had shaken off his nerves and was leading the Spartans to a touchdown. I jumped and hollered right along with them when halfback Clyde Groves spun off two tackles and plowed in for the score.

Maw was a distant blur in the press box when I looked up there. I still couldn't see Father. Maggie was lost somewhere in the writhing frenzy of the end zone.

I played the rest of the half straight up, making the plays I was supposed to make and getting to the others a second after they were over. Warwick had fifty yards, but most of it came in two- and three-yard blips. Nothing long. He seemed to be playing it straight most of the time, too. A time or two, though, it wasn't much of a lick that took him down. It seemed as if anybody could have seen that. What would he blame it on? Injury? Off day? If mine became so obvious someone would ask, what would I say?

We held them scoreless. Seven to nothing as we trotted off to make way for the bands and majorettes, so I guess I had done my job in a backward sort of way. The point spread was still under eight and yet we were still winning the game.

"Defense?" Tack Rankin yelled for us as soon as everyone had gotten water and a few players had gotten ankles and elbows re-taped and -wrapped. "Good job, men. Don't let them get so much on the look-in next time. Elgie, cheat up on the tight end anytime he does that little split. Man-cow, bump him hard every time. Make him work to get out there so he'll get lost in the crowd.

"McKay. Damn fine game so far. Don't slack up on twenty-one, though. He hasn't shown much, yet. He's saving it for the second half, I think."

Well, that was good. He hadn't noticed what I was trying to do at all, and if anyone could, it would have been him. But why did I feel so damned guilty? I didn't owe this crooked old son of a bitch anything. I didn't look at him as he spoke to me. I just nodded my head, let the sweat drip off my nose, and kept studying the chips and scratches on the top of my helmet as it rested on the floor between my cleats.

Twenty-one was Warwick. I knew he wasn't saving up for anything except maybe a car or some sharp clothes, but I didn't say a word, just nodded. Then Rankin yelled at the offense for a while and we broke up into position groups for second-half fine tuning.

I was standing at the urinal, doing my own final second-half preparation when it hit me square in the face like a double-team block. Like a forearm shiver to the face mask.

I had to play a great game! That's the only way to show Cooter Casteel that he didn't have me in his grip. I couldn't do what the scaly bastard had ordered me to do. There was simply no way.

My hands trembled as I relaced the front of my pants and cinched the elastic of my shoulder pads tighter. If I played his game, he had control over me forever. I would have helped him fix the point spread of a game. He could use that against me from now on, college or pro. Or all he had to do was threaten to hurt someone else I loved again. Allow him to use me this time, and I belonged to him for sure and from now on. I would belong to him as sure as the horde of habitual losers who placed bets with him, bringing him more money each week in a constant, hopeless struggle to get back even.

No, the only way to hurt him, to shake him free forever, was to go play this half of football the best I had played in my life and show him his intimidation was for naught. I'd do anything I could to make sure we won by eight or more. He wouldn't hurt anybody. He couldn't afford to. Hell, he was a gambler, not a murderer. He'd get his nut back. Gamblers always do. He was only looking for any angle he could find. I would have to bank on his threats being idle ones.

I could smell the popcorn, hot dogs, even a little whiskey, and the sun-warmed grass before we galloped out of the tunnel. The band played our fight song, cheerleaders squealed and the crowd roared as we emerged from the darkness. I imagined I could hear Maggie up above and behind me as we came out.

Some athletes call it "being in a zone," "on fire." Whatever it was, that day I saw plays develop before the ball was even snapped. I knew which way the ball was coming before it was even handed off. I felt blockers as they bore down on me from behind and shoved them aside like they were only angry bumblebees. I had no trouble reaching and beheading Latrelle Warwick, maybe because he was still lying down for whoever he had sold out to, maybe because I wanted so badly to cut him down for what he was doing. They weren't simple takedowns, either. Full body slams left him gasping for breath. The collisions probably should have hurt me, too, but I was feeling no pain. Tomorrow it would hurt. Today, no pain at all.

Finally, after an especially vicious tackle on the first play of the fourth quarter, he jumped back to his feet, slammed me with the ball and kicked me hard in the side of my helmet. I just laughed as at least five yellow penalty flags floated down around us. Warwick was gone for the day, glaring back at me with a venomous look as one of the officials escorted him to a screaming head coach waiting on the sideline.

"Wanna lay down anymore, Latrelle?" I screamed, not caring who heard or what they thought.

A couple of times, my defensive teammates had to drag me off the field after we held on third down. I didn't want to leave, but stay out there on the battlefield and hit somebody even harder.

It was mid–fourth quarter before the offense clicked enough to get into field-goal range. Tracy McGinnis kicked it through and we led ten to nothing.

I searched the crowd for Cooter, hoping against hope that I'd see his bald dome, the look on his face, the sun colliding with his neck chains. He was nowhere to be seen. I'd lost Maggie in the wild party that had once been the student section in the end zone. Try as I might, I couldn't make out Maw or Father in the dark shadows of the press box. There was a moment's question in my mind. But no, Cooter couldn't do anything here, even if he had any intention of fulfilling his threats.

It wasn't until I stretched, leaped as high as I could, and knocked down a desperation pass in the last seconds of the game that I knew for certain that it was over. We had won. I had won. Cooter had lost. I didn't care that I landed on the sore shoulder on the play. I hardly felt the tingling pain that shot all through my body. I didn't care. It was over.

Sure, a bowl game lay ahead, but we wouldn't be practicing seriously until before the holidays. Strength training went on all year and spring practice was only three months away. I only knew I now had time to be with Maggie. I could throw myself into my studies without the pain and fatigue of football to distract me. And right then, I felt no pain at all.

Our locker room was a mess of wet towels, naked men, cigar smoke, eye-burning liniment, hot steam, sweating reporters, feet-tangling discarded ankle-wrap, flying ice bags, and bloody bandages. The reporters followed me into the shower and back to my locker. It seemed to take forever to get them out of my way so I could start getting myself dressed. Even then, I paused for a few puffs on a victory cigar as I lay back in the locker and enjoyed the glow only a hard-won victory can bring. It felt so good I had to fight myself to get up and start pulling on my clothes, hampered by my now almost-useless arm.

It was a special occasion. I had carefully brought and hung up my best dress shirt as well as the tie I'd worn to my high-school graduation. I'd paid a buck and a half to have my dress slacks dry-cleaned and pressed. They were still wrapped in a plastic bag. I had painstakingly polished and buffed my scuffed shoes so they looked as good as possible. I took extra time in front of the big mirror at the end of the locker room, making sure my stubble of hair was at least all pointed in the same direction and slicked down. I left all my other stuff in the locker. I'd get it later. It wasn't going anywhere. I just wanted to get to Maggie and tell her how much I loved her, how wonderful it was going to be from now on for us.

The locker room was almost deserted by the time I finished getting ready. The equipment managers were piling up all the pads and uniforms to wash and sweeping up the flotsam of war. I took the shortcut I usually did after home games, out the tunnel, toward the field and the stadium steps that climbed up to the press box. A victory fireworks display rattled and popped outside the deserted stadium. Everyone had cleared out for the parties and celebrating that would rage on into the night. The sun was surprisingly low now, the shadows of the goalposts stretching almost to the fifty-yard line, and the air was cool and crisp.

A movement to my right stopped me. I had an instinct, I guess, from half seeing approaching blockers out of the corner of my eye and reacting to them even before they were close enough to do me any harm. And that's exactly how I reacted this time as I stopped, crouched, and turned to fend off my attacker.

But it was only Cooter Casteel and he obviously wasn't attacking me. He was only sauntering toward me, slowly, dejectedly, obviously whipped, taking a consolation bite from a plug of Red Man chewing tobacco.

"You got me, all right. Really showed old Cooter up." The grin on his face wasn't so much angry as it was subdued. "Really got me a good one, Mr. Goddamn Football."

"You hurt me or anybody close to me and our little conversation the other day will be in every newspaper in the Southeast. I've taken care of that already!"

"Hey, hey! Whoa, mule! Don't get your panties in a wad. You got me all wrong. I ain't gonna hurt nobody. Not you or anybody else. I took a long shot with you, boy. That's all. And I lost this bet. But, hey, I'll find me another pigeon on another day. I always do."

"You know somebody had a pigeon on the other side today, too, don't you?"

"Warwick? Yeah, it took me about two plays to know that nigger was selling it out to somebody. Even got himself kicked out of the damn game. But he come through when all's said and done. Made somebody a good payday today. Probably a dollar or two for himself, too. But I'll get it back. I always do."

"Yeah, that's sorta the way I figured it, too, Cooter. Now, if you'll excuse me, I need to get on up and see my folks."

"Yep, I expect you do. Have a good bowl game, there, Mr. McKay."

I didn't thank him for his kind wishes, but just turned and started across the field. He had turned, too, and was walking toward the shadows. He stopped and called back to me.

"Tell your old man hi for me, son. And that he can deliver the deed anytime he wants to. No big hurry."

"What . . . ?"

But he had vanished. Gone like a snake down a black hole.

There was more on my mind now than whatever he was talking about anyhow. I was about to introduce the woman I loved to my crazy folks, and I was already sending up prayers that they would behave themselves. I prayed that she wouldn't hold them against me or stop loving me once she saw where I came from. Please, Lord, let it go smoothly, let them get back into their rusty old truck and back to Signal Mountain without too much damage.

The press box was empty except for one old black janitor sweeping up the discarded paper, beer cups, and chicken bones the reporters had left behind. I nodded to him. He waved back. A cold wind hit me in the back of the neck, sending a quick shiver down my spine, and I was struck by the silence in a place so rocked by happy noise not too long ago. Maw and Father were not in their usual place at the end of press row. Maybe they got tired of waiting since I had taken so long in the dressing room, then got held up by Cooter. Maybe Maw had rolled Father out of the suddenly-cold wind that whistled around the corner of the press box.

But I couldn't imagine Maw pushing Father's wheelchair out to the elevator all by herself. She was too frail to tug the old man around much. And besides, she was terrified of the height and the way the stadium's floor dropped away to nothing beyond a pair of thin pipe railings next to the elevator doors.

Then I heard a darkly familiar sound. My skin erupted in chills. My hair was instantly on end. My stomach plunged as if it had been dropped off Signal Mountain. The sound drifted in the back door of the press box, borne on the breeze like the fragrance of funeral flowers.

It was the familiar, eerie keening of Maw's deadly lullaby.

EIGHTEEN

I knew at once something was terribly, desperately wrong. Maw was standing there on the deserted stadium concourse, facing me, her back to the closed elevator doors, hands busy at her waist as if she was trying to wring the blood from them. Her pink-flowered dress was wrinkled, her old gray purse she had had since I was a kid hung from the elbow of her skinny, brown-spotted arm. Tears rolled down her cheeks, but she had a strange smile on her face. She looked at me and kept singing her sad song with the words more a hum than a lyric, looking at me as if she didn't even know who I was.

"Maw? Where's . . ."

But there he was. I could see him for myself, his chair turned away from me, as if he had only been staring off into open space, maybe watching the just-finished fireworks. The air was still smokey and smelled of powder and fire, an occasional stray firecracker reverberating through the caverns of the stadium. Hesitantly, I walked sideways toward him, keeping my eye on Maw, afraid of what she might do.

"Father?"

He didn't answer.

"Father? Are you okay?"

Still no answer.

Then I could see his head, pitched forward, resting on his chest. I could see his ash-gray face, his blue still lips, his eyes open and staring but not seeing. Two small spots of dark blood seeped from his chest where his heart would be, staining his every-Saturday white dress shirt.

"Maw? Who . . . ?" Did Cooter . . . ?"

She finally seemed to see me, standing there next to Father. My mouth still moved but no sound came out. The band had struck up the Spartan fight song somewhere outside the stadium and a crowd cheered and clapped along, making it hard to hear her when she finally spoke again.

"Corey Phil? Ain't it wonderful what happened? He was hurting so bad. And today? Lord, he was so tore up about the game. Kept saying he had put the whole house up or something like that. And it was going right down the drain, he said. Kept saying that over and over."

"Maw? He's dead. What are you saying? What happened?"

"All gone down the drain. All gone. After the game was over. Him hurting so bad and crying and carrying on so it near about broke my heart. And the way all them people looked at him like he was crazy and kept their distance from us. That's when I got that nigger to help me and roll him out here into the fresh air and out of the cold wind. He always loved the fresh air, you know, sitting out on the front porch and watching the cars go by and the airplanes."

"Maw, please. He's been shot. We need to get somebody. The police, an ambulance . . ."

"Then I knew for sure that it was time."

It sounded like the crowd outside the stadium was cheering for what she had just said, but no. Someone was talking. Coach Rankin on a scratchy, distorted bullhorn, and the cheerleaders were chanting their nonsense, the crowd clapping along.

". . . thank you all for your support this year . . ."

Then Maw started singing her lullaby from hell again. It was mostly a lilting hum, but its repetitive, nonsensical words cut right through me like a knife.

". . . one of the happiest, most glorious days in Spartan football history . . ."

I knelt in front of Father, frantically feeling for some sign of life. But it was clear he was dead. Still warm, but dead.

". . . nothing can stop us now in our quest for immortality in the world of college football . . ."

"Maw!" I screamed her name desperately, heard my cry echo off the ironwork and cement walls of the stadium concourse, mix with the delighted screams and yells of the assembled fans at the postgame rally outside and below us. All entwined with the delirium the crazed fans exhibited as Rankin announced our bowl bid to take on Notre Dame.

Maw jerked, hushed her singing and looked at me as if she had forgotten I was even there.

"He was hurting so, Corey Phil. I couldn't stand it. I prayed. Asked God to send his guardian angel. And he did. I saw her, hovering right out yonder over that building just as big as a helicopter and bright as the star of Bethlehem."

"What happened, Maw?" I begged, voice almost stolen by grief. "Tell me now!"

Then she walked over to the wheelchair, and with her hand, felt Father's forehead as if searching for signs of fever.

"I just helped send him over."

"Oh God, Maw. What did you do? What . . ."

"Remember when Ricky Joe was hurting so bad and that beautiful angel swooped down and took him away to be with Jesus? Now your father is gone on, too. Gone on to where he can walk and feed himself. Run and play with Ricky Joe. Drive his truck and work again."

She was fiddling with something in her purse as she rambled on and on about angels and heaven and Jesus. Stunned, I walked to the railing and pounded the cold metal with the heels of my hands until they were numb. I leaned over the edge and watched my tears fall all the way down to the happy mob that milled below, bouncing their banners, singing the fight song at full volume as the band roared and pranced.

I almost didn't notice Maggie standing off to one side, near the elevator. She was smiling, clapping along, finally caught up in the Spartan spirit. As I watched her, my vision blurred by still more tears, she looked over to the elevator doors for a moment, watching, waiting for us to come out. I loved her so much.

The band finished, the crowd cheered, and then quickly broke up, heading for dinner and parties before it got darker and colder. It was quiet then, or I would not have heard Maw behind me, nor heard the strange, tuneless, slurred words of her lullaby again. I would not have heard her stop and speak to me in an otherworldly voice.

"Now it's you who's hurting, my darling Corey Phil. I can see the pain on your sweet face. I see how all them people down on the field keep running into you and knocking you down and jumping on top of you and hurting you so bad. They won't be hurting my darlin' Corey Phil no more."

I turned and faced her, but I could hardly see her now in the black darkness that had suddenly settled on us.

"Maw, it's just football. A game. Nobody's hurting me."

"And I seen the demons, too, nipping at you in my dreams. Them others that want to slice you up with their flashing claws and wound you and use your precious soul for their own evil purposes. I seen it all, Corey Phil."

Then she stepped toward me and I could see Father's big blue pistol that she held with both her hands. Its barrel was pointed shakily right toward me. And I could see her eyes and she was looking past me now, to something over my shoulder, out over the disappearing crowd and campus and streets below.

"There she is! Coming for you! And she's even more beautiful than the others. I knew she would be! A special guardian angel for my precious Corey Phil! Look at her, Corey Phil! She's gonna take you in her loving wings and carry you to the Lord. Carry you to where nobody won't ever hurt you again."

It was Maw and, crazy or not, she never lied to me. I listened to what she was saying and turned to see if I could see my guardian angel, flying out there above the quad, circling the clock tower at the Language Arts building. But, of course, there was nobody there. Nobody at all. Just an airplane off in the distance pulling a banner that said, EAT AT DRAKE'S . . . $1.95 SPECIAL.

Then she pulled the trigger. Quickly, without hesitation. Once, twice, three times.

I know you won't believe this. Even through my horror and pain and even with all my gyrations trying to dodge Maw's mercy, I clearly heard the thinning crowd down below us cheer each one of the gun blasts. I know now they just thought it was the lingering remnants of the victory fireworks, but at the time, in a flash, I thought they must be seeing my efforts to avoid the shots, cheering me on as if I was making one more tackle, one more interception.

But these, the most important set of downs I would ever play, did not leave me a winner. The bullets were tearing me apart, jerking me in all directions like a pack of vicious animals or a flock of starved buzzards.

The last thing I remember, my last living thought, was Maw standing over me, then kneeling, stroking my cheek, feeling my forehead as if for fever, kissing me gently on the lips, but all the while still humming and mouthing those same impossible-to-de-cipher words. But as deathly blackness compassionately took me away, I could finally make out the slurred words to her strange, repetitive lullaby:

"Two bits, four bits, six bits, a dollar . . ."

NINETEEN

Her bloody footprints led directly, deliberately, to the concourse railing. She had dropped the pistol and stepped over me, sure I was dead, set free, floating to heaven with my guardian angel. I can't imagine Maw doing what she did next, it was so against her nature: climbing up and using the wall of the elevator shaft for balance, standing on the top rail. I know how terrified she had always been of heights—how crazy she must have been to have done that.

But Maggie saw her from below, so I know that's exactly how it happened. She had been waiting at the base of the elevator, but had started to get worried about us. Maybe my parents had changed their mind and didn't want to meet her after all. Maybe I had been hurt during the game and didn't collapse until afterward, wracked by some kind of seizure there in the locker room. Or maybe my father had been taken ill suddenly. She knew he was frail, weakening in the last few weeks.

When the postgame celebration broke up and we still had not come down the elevator, she was really getting concerned. Then she heard the three quick blasts from Father's big blue pistol and knew they didn't sound at all like the firecrackers. She moved out of the chill shadows of the stadium and looked up, saw the blue smoke from the gun drift out from the concourse. Her stomach sank. Her imagination was unleashed.

Then, there was Maw, an old woman in a pink-flowered dress, climbing determinedly up onto the top rail. She climbed without hesitation, holding on to the wall next to her for balance.

"No! No, Mrs. McKay! No!" I had laughingly told her about the pink-flowered dress. She knew at once who it was up on the railing, two hundred feet above the pavement.

She was raising her arms to the deep blue sky. Raising them as if reaching out for someone to embrace her. Like a child reaching up for her mother, begging to be taken and held safely and securely.

"Please! Dear Lord, someone . . ." But there was no one. The happy crowd had wandered away, wrapped up in their own victorious ecstasy.

The old woman was leaning forward, seeming to hang in midair for a moment. Then she was floating free, almost, for an instant, as if she was flying. But then, falling. Falling.

"No! Please . . ."

She landed with a wet, sick clunk, not ten feet from Maggie who was by that time turning, running blindly, falling to the rough pavement, ignoring the pain of her skinned knees, bawling hysterically into her hands.

She recovered enough to ride to the hospital in the ambulance with me. I remember her talking to me. Telling me everything would be all right. That everyone would be all right. That's the only time I've ever known her to lie to me.

And me? I just lay there and watched the movie of my life unspool over and over, in remarkable fidelity and detail. The good, the bad, the indifferent. I got to make love to Maggie again in that replay, but I also had to watch Maw throw my little brother to the angels. I could smell the wonderful fresh-cut grass and hear the bluebirds out my bedroom window, but I also had to endure Father's whiskey breath and angry curses.

Anywhere else but a college town with a medical school, and I would have died right then and there. But they were developing all kinds of experimental things behind those austere brick walls. Maggie knew one of the doctors from the infirmary and begged him to do whatever he could. And he was a football fan, too.

"We'll need his family to sign, Maggie. It's experimental."

"He has no family anymore, Dr. Bryant. None. Please. Please do whatever you can."

"Well, to be honest, he won't last the night if we don't try something."

I heard it all, of course. It's one of the advantages of being a corpse. People don't think the dead can hear what is being said all around them. All the snide, sneering comments as they line up past the coffin. Things they would never have said to the person's face if the rose in his cheeks had been real and not smudged rouge.

"Don't he look natural?" they say. "Better than when he was alive, if you ask me."

"Hell, I never liked the bastard nohow. I'm just here 'cause the wife . . ."

Dr. Bryant did some kind of heroic thing to keep me breathing. I'm still not sure what all the bullets did, but there was something about nerves that had been severed, my spinal cord was swelling, blood had contaminated the spinal fluid, and there was brain damage. The first forty-eight hours were critical, he had said. But it seemed like I spent most of that in surgery. In recovery, choking, strangling on something rammed down my throat, but, amazingly, with no pain whatsoever. No pain.

Now, that did strike me as odd. Oh, there had been a moment's agony when the bullets first struck. It was so intense it seemed to take the air right out of my lungs. Lying there on the cement floor of the concourse, jostling around in the ambulance with Maggie holding my unfeeling hand, and through all the haze and hustle of surgery, I didn't hurt at all.

Later the headaches came. Even dead asleep, my head seemed poised to explode, a constant throb like someone was kicking me in the temple over and over. I tried to tell a nurse hovering nearby to get me some kind of relief, but she didn't hear me. No, I never spoke. My lids were not really open enough for her to see my wildly moving eyes. And I couldn't move my hand to get her attention. It seemed to be tied down.

Some kind of whooshing, clicking sound made the headaches worse. I don't know how long it was before I realized the sound was in synch with my breathing. I deduced a machine was breathing for me. If it stopped, if it gave me any relief for my throbbing head, I probably would no longer be breathing. I wished for it to stop and prayed for the goddamn electricity to go off, the machine to stop its never-ending whoosh and click. Just let me fade away, free of the booming starbursts that were detonated inside my skull every time the infernal machine whooshed and clicked.

Sometimes I was aware of Maggie, a shadow above me, her voice sweet and warm.

"You are going to be all right, C.P. I'm here. You will be all right. I've got so much to tell you. Open your eyes, darling. Open your eyes so I can tell you. Please let me tell you."

And I would try. Like lifting more weight than I had ever seen in the Spartan workout room. More weight than I could possibly lift. But I tried.

Tell me, my dear Maggie! Please talk with me! I can hear you, darling. I can hear you.

"It's such a beautiful day today. It snowed yesterday and the sun is out and the sky is so blue and the air is clean and cold. Just move your hand if you can hear me. Blink your eyes a time or two. I love you, C.P. I love you."

I wiggled my hand. Flipped it all around the hospital bed. Waved it at her. Tried to reach out to her and feel the smoothness of her cheek, to grab a handful of her wonderful hair and pull her down to my lips and kiss her. But the damned frozen hand never seemed to move at all. Not a twitch.

"If I only knew that you could hear what I'm saying, C.P. If I only knew."

Maggie! I can hear you! Talk to me! Tell me more about the sky and the cold air and that you love me. Whoosh. Click.

"I have so much to tell you that I'm afraid I'm going to explode if I don't. I need you more than ever, C.P. God, I need you. Please come back. Please come back to me."

I'm right here, Maggie. Help me to move. To talk. I've got a bowl game to get ready for. Is it Notre Dame? Orange Bowl? Like Cooter said? I've got film to watch. Drills to run. Conditioning. God, I will have lost my wind for sure, lying here like this and getting lazy.

"A bird is building a nest on the sill outside my apartment window. It reminded me of that poem by Frost you used to like so much. About the bird, singing in its sleep. It reminds me of you, C.P. I wrote the words on this note. I'm going to put it in your hand."

Thank you, dear Maggie. Thank you for the thought. But I can't unfold it and read it. For some reason, I can't even feel it there in my hand. And even if I could, this headache is blinding me, driving me crazy. Making me long for total death instead of this netherworld I occupy these days. If I can't talk with you, make love to you, then I have no reason to go on, dear Maggie. No reason to go on.

"Our baby kicked today."

Oh God. Oh, dear God. Please let me see her. Talk to her. Ask her the million questions that just materialized through the fog of pain.

"I was sick at work today. My legs swell so much and it gets so hot. I don't know how much longer I can work. Then, Lord knows what I'll do. My folks . . . well, at least I have my sister. She'll help as much as she can."

"Why don't you come home and eat supper with me and my husband, honey? We got plenty and . . ."

"No thank you, Nancy. All you nurses have been so nice. Thank you very much, but I'll just stay here. Just in case he wakes up."

Maggie, I'll pull out of this. After the bowl game, I'll quit school for a while. Get a job. Everything will be all right. I'll make everything all right.

"Maggie, I hope you understand this fully."

"I think I do, Dr. Bryant."

"This procedure is about the only hope we have of getting him out of the coma. It's new. Takes pressure off the brain. We just don't know if he has the strength to survive the operation. Or what effect it might have on his mental faculties. He could die. He could still be left . . . well, like this. Or he could eventually wake up someday. We don't know."

"I know it's what he would want. That it would have a chance to unlock his mind. That's what C.P. would want. Especially with him not ever being able to move again and lying here like this. At least we'd have a chance of giving him his mind back."

"I think you are right. From what you've told me about him, that is. Maggie, how are you holding up?"

"Fine. Fine."

"It can't be easy. Working, spending so much time here. You know nobody would blame you if you just let us pull the . . ."

"No! Don't ever say that! I'm fine. Just take care of C.P."

"Tomorrow morning, then. Pray, Maggie. Pray, if you're so inclined."

"I am. I will."

Robert Frost keeps coming to mind. What was that poem? The one about bumping his head and having his "native simile jarred"? Frost was okay when I was living, just seemed in a bad mood all the time, like he didn't have enough roughage in his diet or something. Funny how he seemed to fit so well with me in death.

When my eyes suddenly opened and I woke up that day, there you were, sitting right there. Right there in the same chair you're in right now. I'll admit, you scared the shit out of me.

See, I thought you were me sitting there looking back at me.

What an odd mirror that showed me myself as I might look sitting in a little room watching myself mouth-breathe and drool. But I jumped from the chair immediately when I tried to speak to myself, eyes big in amazement, obviously shocked to see the mushroom in the bed blinking and trying to speak at last.

"Your eyes moved! You grunted!" I said to myself, and bolted for the door. "Maw! I gotta get Maw! Don't go back . . . don't sleep! Stay awake now!"

And I was gone through the somehow-familiar door in the middle of a somehow-familiar wall.

The room was small. Exactly the size of the one I had in the little house on the breast of Signal Mountain when I was a boy. A square window in exactly the same place as the one in my old room, looking out on green and sunshine and a sky so blue it hurt my eyes. A television set blinked at me from a table across the room. A well-worn easy chair still rocked from where my twin had left it in such a hurry only a second ago.

Someone had placed a series of various-sized picture frames on a table next to the bed so it was easy for me to see them, even though I apparently couldn't move my head at all. A kid was captured in each one of the frames. They were succeedingly older kids: a tiny, swelled-face, dark-haired infant; a blond-haired toddler propped on a pillow with a wet thumb crammed into his face; a screaming four-year-old, not totally happy with being on Santa's lap; a smiling kid with a missing front tooth and a mask of freckles holding a bat and glove and dressed in a baseball uniform.

Each kid looked so familiar. Like me, I realized. But I had never had baby pictures made. Father never saw the need for spending money on such things. Never went to see Santa Claus. Never wore a baseball uniform. But there I was in another photograph, in a tuxedo, my arm around a redheaded girl in a prom dress. A cute girl but one who I had never seen before that I could remember. Me kneeling with a football under my arm. It was my number on the uniform all right, but not the jersey of any team I'd ever played for.

Then, I heard the hurried clicking of shoes on a hardwood floor. Wait a minute! My double had said he was going to get "Maw." Oh Lord. Maybe she was coming to finish the job. Go on and dispatch me to heaven since she had apparently failed the first time. Then a middle-aged woman crashed through the door at full speed, hand to mouth, eyes running a steady stream of tears.

"C.P.? Dear God, C.P. Can you hear me?"

It had to be Maggie's mother or an older sister. She had the same eyes for certain, the same high cheekbones, same mouth. But there were hard wrinkles there on her face where Maggie's was smooth, a streak of gray in her dishwater hair, a fuller body lost in a worn, threadbare housedress. My twin waited in the background, hiding behind the woman, apparently not sure what to do next or what to say. It was as if the play he had rehearsed for had started and he had forgotten his lines.

I tried to speak to them out of politeness. To ask where Maggie was. What day it was. Where I was. But I could only make what sounded to me like choking noises.

"Wait, darling. Please, just take it easy. Don't try . . ." And Maggie's mother was kissing me, hugging me, telling me how much she loved me, how much she had missed me. I was hopelessly confused.

Of course, it was Maggie trapped in that middle-aged body. And it was now about twenty years after Maw had tried to give me over to my guardian angel.

And the young man with my looks? That was you, our son, of course. She had named you Corinthians Philippians Vinyard. Much later, I mastered the art of typing on this computer keyboard you suspended over my face, using my Popsicle stick between my lips to tap out the words a letter and a space at a time. That's when I managed to fuss at her for hanging that god-awful name on you, too. Almost blew a fuse in the word processor I got so explicit. I'm sorry you had to be saddled with that bitch of a name, son. Sorry. But I guess you had a lot more baggage to tote around than that.

A vegetable for a daddy and a bitch of a name to boot! That's a hell of a cross to bear, son. But what was worse? Sitting there in that chair all those years, rocking gently, studying the great poets and writers, occasionally rising to suck the phlegm out of my breathing tube with a syringe? Watching me fight to live, if that's what you would call this hopeless existence? Was that the worst?

Or is it worse now? Sitting there in the otherwise quietness, hearing the click of the stick on the keys, my grunting as I strain to get the words entered before I tire and drop the thing, or half swallow it and choke and gag until you have to get up and come over and rescue me from the vigor of my own writing? The buzzing of the computer speaker when I hit the right keys to get your attention and order you over with the screams of my blinking eyelids? Force you, with the commands of my rolling eyes, to read the latest wisdom and truth I've committed to bits and bytes in the word processor?

But you are so faithful, my son. Doing your studying right in here with me. Reading to me. Discussing what you have read and written. Putting up with the slowness of my arguments as I peck them out a letter at a time. And me so stubborn that I won't use abbreviations or shortcuts. Yet you are invariably patient with me. Not patronizing, though. I especially love that about you, son. If you disagree, you stick to your guns. Even when I get red-faced in frustration, losing my whole train of thought when I try to get it on the screen.

And Maggie. Dear, wonderful Maggie. Always watching out for me. There for me. How many slop jars has she emptied in the last twenty years? How many times has she irrigated my feeding tube? Touched me gently on the cheek and asked me to wake up and been brazenly disobeyed? And then, when she finally gets her wish, it is a surly, desiccated dead man with only a smidgen of a brain and no body at all who awakens to be an even greater albatross for her to so nobly bear.

But she tries so hard to bring some semblance of life to this dead pile of bones and skin she has so cruelly inherited. Even after she has emptied bedpans all day at the hospital, she is never too tired to see to me. She dutifully rolls my bed to the window on bright, sunny days so I can see the bluebirds play around the little house someone has hung on a pine tree out near where the bluff drops off. Never mind that I'd prefer being back in my regular place against the wall with the stick in my mouth, typing another chapter, or silently, laughlessly watching the comedies and game shows that dot daytime television nowadays. That's all I watch, now that the bowl games have been played and the Super Bowl is history and it's a million years before they kick off another season.

And her voice keeps me breathing. She tells me the same stories over and over, but I always peck and click for them again and again. How it all happened that day after the Tennessee game, no matter how bad it hurts. How Chris Littlefeather did just what I asked him to do and took my long letter to Max Milligan. And good old Max! Took it straight to the newspapers in Nashville and they broke it all wide open. Rankin retired. Wheeler went to some small college up north. Claxon was busted to botany teacher again. Cooter Casteel was called up before the grand jury but managed to slither out of it all until he got murdered years later by somebody so desperately down to him that he could find no other way to cancel the debt.

And while she talks to me, your mother will sit on the edge of my bed for hours, trying to exercise my amazingly wasted legs and arms, as if there was ever any hope of them living and working again. I would prefer she just leave them alone, spare me the sight of the dead limbs, leave them buried under the homemade blanket. She should save herself the trouble and put the strength to some better use for her or you, but when I try to tell her that, she just clears the screen with a well-practiced set of keystrokes and ignores me. If I persist, she flips the switch on the computer's face and I am basically back in my coma, unable to fuss except with my eyes and a few grunts.

And there, C.P., is the ultimate irony. Pushed and pulled in all directions all my life, I now find myself totally at the mercy of you and your maw. To be pushed and pulled and kneaded at your pleasure. Never mind your honorable intentions. I can't do anything at all without you or her.

Until now.

Maggie was so happy to find the wheelchair and to have Father's old Eagles lodge raise the money to buy it for me. Between the two of you, you were able to drag my dead weight into the thing and strap me into what would pass for some kind of sitting position. And you were so patient, teaching me how to blow on the tiny switches strapped to my jaws that controlled direction and stopping and starting for the contraption. You were so good as I kept

272

running into walls and furniture and broke a brittle leg bone when I smacked into the dining-room table full-speed. Don't worry. I didn't feel a thing.

I'll admit, the first few trips around the house were a thrill. Exploring Maw's old room, the living room where *The Book of Knowledge* still rests in its cheap bookcase against the wall. And finally venturing onto the cement front porch where I could sit out on nice days and watch the clouds, the traffic going by, and the airplanes circling overhead for a landing at the airport.

I finally appreciated all the trouble your mother had gone through to get my old house. How hard she must have worked and saved to make the last of the payments to the bank. How brave she had to be to keep it from Cooter when he came to threaten her and try to take it. It was exactly the dose of familiarity I needed to avoid simply dying of frustration after the football season on the television was over.

But now, this is what I want you to understand. Both of you. It won't be easy, but hear me out.

I see what I am doing to you. I see the hurt in your eyes, Maggie, every time you look at me, no matter how hard you try to shield it from me. The dresser mirror lines up with the one in the hall just right so I can see you at the dining-room table, the same one Father threw my brother on the night he tried to kill him. But you are struggling with what could only be bills. The stack is massive. And I see your frustration in the way you stab the checks with your pencil, pound the table with your fists. I see how it is making you so much older so much sooner than you should be. A beautiful, intelligent woman like you deserves so much more than what life has dealt you.

And C.P.—I've asked but you've never answered. Why someone so obviously intelligent, so intuitive in your grasp of literature, is wasting your time with junior college. Why you didn't play football after your sophomore year when it was obvious you had talent, had inherited intuition for the game from me. Yeah, I know the answer. It was me, of course. Me getting in the way, robbing you of your childhood, your promise, your hope.

Well, now at last I have found the way to lift your burden. By the time you read this file on the computer, I will have set you both free. It will be easy and you will have lost nothing but a sac of guts and gases, weak bones and rebelling membranes. Even my mind is not what it used to be, and the dispiriting way I have to express myself often leaves me forgetting my original point by the time I get the first part typed out on the screen.

It's just a matter of time before it all goes. Before some sneaky infection steals my kidneys or a heavy sac of fluid grows inside my lungs and claims any breath I might suck in. And, with my past history, I'm sure I would linger and fight and claw for life until it robbed you of everything you had, money and strength, heart and soul.

I won't let that happen.

I am going to do what *I* want to do for once. I will not allow anyone else to deter me.

Here's probably how it will happen. I'll be enjoying the warmth of the spot of sun on the front porch one day very soon. C.P., maybe you will have gone off to class or to that junior college's poor excuse for a library, putting the finishing touches on your D. H. Lawrence research paper. Or working at your job in the bookstore. Maggie, my love. You are so tired these days, from work and crawling from your bed to check on me and my stupid needs all night long. It's not unusual on these still, warm spring days, for you to make sure I'm okay on the porch, then go lie down for a moment, confident I won't drown on my own snot while I'm sitting upright. You'll try to steal a nap before having to lug me back to my bed and put me down again. Please don't feel guilty about that! Certainly you deserve a few minutes of rest. And it will be the best thing you ever did for me anyway.

When I think the time is right, I can blow gently on the little switch at my lips and roll over to your bedroom window. When I see that exhaustion has finally won and you have found blessed sleep, and after I've selfishly observed your beauty for just a while longer, I'll blow again. I'll probably wince at the noisy whine of the electric motor of the wheelchair as it drags my worthless skeleton along the porch. Then I'll guide it to the ramp that gently falls into the yard. The one we built the summer before I left for Sparta to make it easier to roll Father's chair out to the truck so Maw could get him to the ball games. I'll slowly, patiently, ease down into the new, fresh-cut grass. I can't smell anything anymore, just another sense stolen by the bullets, but the aroma will be there all the same, even if I have to imagine it. Then I'll guide the chair with quick puffs from each side of my mouth, past Maw's Old Country rosebushes, already blooming a lively pink. It'll probably hurt my back some as the chair bounces over rough ground. That and the tickle of late-night tears on my cheeks are about all I ever feel nowadays. I'll blow some more to steer around rocks and blackberry bushes and big pines that were saplings when this yard was our football field. Maybe I'll take the time to watch the crows playing among the cedars or maybe a hawk standing on a wing out over the valley. Or maybe not. Maybe I'll just keep rolling down the gently sloping yard to make sure I don't lose my nerve and give in to what I know you would want me to do. Then, I'll be at the edge of the bluff. I won't hesitate now. Not after coming this far. I'm doing this for you. Both of you. So my course will be straight and true. Maybe I'll recite some Dylan Thomas or Longfellow to myself as the ground drops away from under my wheels, as the wind suddenly rushes up under me, making the chair's spokes sing an eerie song, its breeze on the little switches at my mouth confusing the electric motor, now not sure which way to steer or how fast to make the motor whir. The inspired words of one of the great poets will be my last as I close my eyes and wait to be plucked up by my guardian angel. Wait to feel the warm embrace of her enveloping wings. Wait to be carried to Jesus and Maw.

You see, Maw told me my angel was out there. And Maw never lied.